First published in Great Britain in 2009 by Comma Press
www.commapress.co.uk

'Beginning' was first published in *Decapolis: Tales from Ten Cities* edited by Maria
Crossan (Comma, 2006). 'The Shieling' was first published in *The Liberal*. 'Phantom
Pain', 'Witness', 'Regrets' and 'Wishing Well' were first published in *The Reader*.
'Living On' was first published in *Prospect* magazine.

The opening lines of 'Wishing Well' are from the author's own translation of
Friedrich Hölderlin's translation of Pindar's 8th Pythian Ode. Lines quoted in
'Living On' (p168) are taken from the author's own translation of 'Helena' by
Heinrich Heine, first published in NINE FATHOM DEEP (Bloodaxe, 2009).
Reprinted by permission. Lines taken from William Wordsworth's 'The Prelude'
Book IX, 308-17, 510-33 and 290-02, from THE PRELUDE: FOUR TEXTS
published by Penguin Classics, are reprinted by permission. 'March' from the
EDWARD THOMAS COLLECTED POEMS edited by George Thomas,
published by Faber and Faber, is reprinted by permission. Lines on pp179-180 are
from the author's own translation of Pablo Neruda's 'I'm Explaining a Few Things'.

A CIP catalogue record of this book is available from the British Library.

ISBN  1905583214
ISBN-13   978 1905583218

The publisher gratefully acknowledges assistance from the Arts Council England
North West, and also the support of Literature Northwest.

**literaturenorthwest** ◎

Set in Bembo 11/13 by David Eckersall
Printed and bound in England by SRP Ltd, Exeter

# THE SHIELING

by
David Constantine

# Contents

# Beginning

Coming home from visiting my mother, distressed that she no longer knows who I am and cannot make any sounds that I recognise as words, I set down the odd fact that on this day forty-five years ago, 31 May 1961, coming home from school under blue skies, I saw my first dead fellow human being. He was in the river under Victoria Bridge where I caught my second bus, the 64 or the 66. I was seventeen. I've seen few dead since then, far fewer than the averagely unlucky seven-year-old in Gaza or Baghdad has already seen. I had a good look at him. Scores of people were leaning over the parapet and doing the same. I looked and looked. And when I got home I wrote him up in my notebook, that drowned man.

On the first bus, the 42 from Birchfields Road to Albert Square, I sometimes met a girl and we sat together, if we could. Our meetings weren't arranged but they weren't entirely accidental either. I worked out what buses were most likely on what days, and went for those. But once, on a bus I had no hope about, nearly an hour later than our usual times, there she was. So really I never knew. We sat upstairs, if there was room, with the smokers. Often it was sunny and the curls, the ringlets, the spiralling, floating, unravelling tresses of bluish smoke in the beams of sun made a pretty effect. I say often, but I don't suppose I saw her more than a dozen times. I never even knew her name. All I know is it began with 'M'. She'd be there already, if it was a lucky day, sitting upstairs in the sunny smoke and saving me a place next to her on the front seat, if we were especially lucky. All we talked about was books, and I never touched her except in the way you are

1

bound to if you sit next to somebody on a bus and you turn and forget yourself in conversation. I remember her eyes, the soul staring out of them, eager and scared, and I remember her lips and tongue but not any single sentence that she said, only the tone, the rhythms, the feel of her speech, so close, the aura of her. She got off a couple of stops before me, near Central Station, and of course I don't know where she went from there. A couple of days before I saw the man in the river she gave me a present, as she was getting off. She took it out of her satchel as she stood up, thrust it at my heart, and was gone. I never saw her again.

I didn't open the girl's present until I was upstairs on the 64 on Victoria Bridge. The buses started from there and you might have to wait a while before they were due to leave. All the years I was going to school, and for many before that, so I am told, there was a madman on Victoria Bridge, called Charlie. He wore the cap and jacket of a sort of uniform and he believed himself to be in charge of the comings and goings of the buses on Victoria Bridge. He had a pocket watch, that he consulted frequently, and a notebook, and one of those pencils you have to keep licking to get it to write. The soldiers had them in the First World War. So Charlie, who might have been in his sixties at that time, stood all day and every day, rain or shine, on Victoria Bridge, waving the big green buses in and out, consulting his watch, shaking his head, and very frequently licking his bit of pencil. Everyone was nice to him. All the drivers and conductors acted along, pretending he was in charge, and even the real supervisor, who had a little office on the bridge, took it in good part and you might see the pair of them, the real one and the mad one, in a slack time sharing tea from a thermos. But that day I didn't look at Charlie, though I normally did, looked and looked, I sat on the front seat, from where you had a view, if you wanted it, of Telephone House on your right, Exchange Station and the cathedral on your left, the dirty river under you, and I undid the girl's present which she had wrapped very carefully and tied up with a red ribbon. I believe I was alone on the upper deck. I believe all behind me was empty space.

It was a Wilfred Owen she had given me, and on a scrap of paper, that looked torn out of a Woolworth's notebook, she had written: Here are his poems for you. With love from M. That was when I learned her name began with 'M'. First I looked to see how long the poet had lived. I had taken to doing that. I saw that if I were him I'd be two thirds through my allotted time already. Then I opened his book, nowhere particular, as I thought, and the space behind my back filled up with cold, it felt like a finger tracing my spine and inserting a tip of cold into the back of my head so that the hairs stood up there, I had ice around the heart and I lost the sight of his lines in a rush of tears. Then Charlie consulted his pocket watch, waved us away, licked his blue copy-pencil and made a note in his notebook of the exact time of day that particular 64 left Victoria Bridge for Peel Green.

The Irwell is the boundary between Manchester and Salford. The buses leaving Victoria Bridge cross it, back into Manchester, bear left along it past the cathedral and the station, and, turning sharp left, cross it again, back into Salford, and away. The man had been in the water for some time when I joined the others watching, and a couple of frogmen were in there with him, trying to push his head and shoulders through a life-belt, to haul him up. They had a hard task, he was so sodden and unhelpful. One took his head by the hair and tugged. The face was blue-grey. I realised that must be one of the colours of death, nothing that colour could be alive, or not in any way friendly to human beings at least. Though I didn't know I would never see M. again – it was only a couple of days since she had given me the poems and we often went that long or longer without meeting – I was already beginning to be anxious. I had to talk to her about Wilfred Owen; and while I was watching the men in the water under Victoria Bridge I was wondering whether I should tell her about this event, and how I would say it if I decided to.

High above the river, just below street level, on a rather ramshackle platform affixed to the bridge, two policemen were watching their colleagues in the water and handling the ropes by which the drowned man was to be hauled up. I thought you might get to the platform through the supervisor's little office on the street side of the parapet. Had the river been a sweeter place he and Charlie might have taken their tea out there, on a balcony with a view. Friedrich Engels, working just round the corner in Chetham's Library on *The Condition of the Working Class in England*, thought the river and its dwelling-places supremely noxious. Poor river, it had a coal mine at the very outset and more and more demands and abuses through the cotton towns below. All its tributaries harmed it. But there were blessings nonetheless, reprieves and survivals, woods, for example, beyond the sewage farm at Clifton, and bluebells in season, hyacinthine streams and pools, like a surrogate living water. For the body of the Irwell was largely effluent, it needed what humans spilled into it to keep going at all. The rain itself came heavily laden and before it reached the river must take on the further cargo of the gutters and the drains. The Irwell was never much of a waterway, and under the bridge and the sheer side of Telephone House there was little movement. Of his own accord, so to speak, the drowned man might have idled for ever in the dead stillness under Victoria Bridge.

The policemen took off their jackets and began to haul. In shirt-sleeves on that dismal perch they looked like snowbirds. The drowned man, fitted through the life-belt, rose in the water into a semblance of buoyancy, but very soon after that, when he was tiptoe on the surface as though they were puppeteers and now they would get him to dance, the operation went wrong. The deadweight of him was too much for their arrangement of ropes. He slipped from the ring and was upended, noosed tightly around the ankles, the ring

4

banging uselessly against his back. Water returned to the river from his jacket sleeves. We could smell it. There he hung, his clothes undoing around his midriff, hung and twirled very slowly, streaming. The frogmen assessed him. The police on the platform waited. It seemed his ropes would hold. It seemed they must risk it. At a signal, again they began to haul. Abattoir, martyrdom, circus, theatre, ascension. We were all very quiet. I decided I would tell the girl on the bus what I was seeing. I thought of the words. I felt certain she would understand what was happening to me while I watched. Suddenly there was a rush of things I must tell and ask the girl on the bus. Was her grandfather a soldier? Was his name in the book in the cathedral? And all the things my mother had begun to tell me, about the Blitz, how she and her best friends in Telephone House had volunteered to carry on working during a raid and the searchlights lit up the sky and soon they could hear the guns and the bombs. And her and my father courting: Ringley Woods, the bluebells, and how in the leap year 1936, egged on by the other girls, while the supervisor's back was turned, she phoned him at his work in the Post Office from hers on the top floor of Telephone House, and asked him to marry her. Things of that sort, so much, so many stories, all in a rush. By way of thanks for the poems of Wilfred Owen. Tell her and ask her. The drowned man twirled very slowly upside down in the lovely light of day, the water still running off him, a precious silver. And slowly he rose, with pauses, with rests in the air, hanging down, his hands come together like a diver's, everyone watching, all silent.

It was perhaps the beginnings of my father's illness that made my mother, that spring and summer, begin to tell me stories about the two of them in their early lives. He was slipping into something that neither of them understood and perhaps she wanted to assure herself of him by saying aloud how definite and luminous still their beginnings were. The remoteness of depression is hard to bear. Some acts of suicide in it may spring from the desire to be finally definite again. All the more definite around the depressive must the people who love him be, and perhaps that was an unconscious motive in my mother's stories: to make me her ally in knowing some things for sure. The cheerfulness of the girls high up in Telephone House was one such thing, how she proposed to him in the leap year with some of them watching her face for the answer in it and some further off watching out for the supervisor. And under the air raid all together, the lights and the noise, that was a brave thing to remember when it looked as though isolation by an illness might be coming up. But I liked best her assertion that on a clear day from the top floor of Telephone House she could see Ringley Woods where they went picking bluebells and came back on the bus with an armful and she slept against his shoulder in the scent of them lying in her lap like a child. And beyond Ringley, on a clear day, you could see the moors, level and high, and once up there, as is well known, you can walk out together for ever.

That spring and early summer, now I come to think of it, there must have been something about me that was asking for stories, because if it wasn't my mother telling them it was her mother, and I stood or sat or strolled between the generations of women and listened to whatever they wanted to tell me about the girls at Ermen and Engels Mill or Telephone House and courtships before the first war or the second, long courtships, engagements, marriages. I watched my father anxiously, willing him with my mother not to go absent on us, and my grandfather, 'blown to bits', as his widow said whenever she reached that point, said with a shrug, him, my mother's father, I was beginning to put him together again, his life till then, till the blowing to bits, collecting him up, so to speak, from her bits of story and the documents. So to speak. There is no liveliness of words comes anywhere near the life of life itself.

At the last, the drowned man's feet caught under the

platform and one policeman had to kneel, leaving the other taking all the weight. It was only then I noticed that he wore decent Oxford shoes. He turned my way, his tie hung over his open mouth. They meant no indecency, I am sure, but in getting their burden over the railing of the rickety platform they could not be gentle. They reached, heaved, landed him. He lay then over the railing, arms down and between his arms his head, the hair neatly plastered forward by the foul water in a v. He wore a suit. He was perhaps in his mid-forties. I could see him with a briefcase, conscientiously going to work and back. The policeman left him there, flopped, as though after a tremendous exertion mortally exhausted. They exited through the supervisor's office and soon returned with a stretcher. Then it was finished, the spectacle. The crowd remembered their own business.

I went for my bus, a 66, got the front right seat upstairs, and craned up to see the very roof of Telephone House. There was a white cloud or two, the high building seemed to be sailing. The bus filled up, mostly young women from their work, nattering and laughing. On the bridge the ambulance had taken the drowned man away; the policemen, still in their dazzling shirtsleeves, were having a cup of tea. Things were resuming, but not fast enough for Charlie. I doubt if he had watched the spectacle at all. He was in the road itself before the queue of buses, very agitated, tapping his watch and shaking his head. Suicide's one thing, but what about the buses? What about the timetable? His trouble was manifest and helpless. My pity, quickened by one thing and another, went out to him there on the public bridge in such an anxiety. He beckoned hard, stepped aside, we pulled away. I watched him lick his pencil and make the necessary note. Mustn't forget Charlie when I tell all this to the girl on the 42.

# Memorial

Caradoc's memorial service was a poor thing. In the little church there were more empty spaces than people. No one still studying at the College had known him. His surviving colleagues had never much liked him. He had published very little and on subjects they found distasteful. His rooms were in a separate house – a *petite maison*, the scurrilous called it – in the College grounds, and there was bitter wrangling over who should have them now. But the Master, new to the place and wishing to say something kind about him, ascertained that, by general agreement, he had been a good teacher; though even this, by the tone of voice in which it was conceded, sounded a rather louche achievement. Still the Master felt able to say publicly that Caradoc would be remembered with affection and gratitude by generations of undergraduates of the College.

There was tea in the refectory afterwards, but few wanted it. Most hurried away through the graveyard to their own affairs.

Odd among those attending were a man and a woman, obviously foreign, perhaps in their late fifties. They stood arm in arm at the very back of the church, the woman entirely in black, the man in a black suit and tie with a dazzlingly white shirt. They looked to be honouring an old code of conduct. Both were on the stout side with round and candid faces. They were weeping, their faces shone with tears. They stood arm-in-arm and, perhaps out of deference, let all the congregation leave before them. All saw their helpless faces, and looked away quickly.

It was warmer outside. The graveyard had leafed and flowered; it wore the scents of hawthorn and roses; in its silence there was birdsong. The foreigners stood in the porch. The man dried his wife's cheeks with a large white handkerchief, then dried his own. They stood there, at a loss.

From opposite ends of the graveyard, walking very deliberately, ignoring or not even noticing one another, two men approached them. Met on the flagged path, and faced them. They were perhaps in their late forties. Gino? said one. Lucia? said the other. The fair pronunciation of the names gave Gino and Lucia more hope than the two Englishmen, who introduced themselves as old pupils of Caradoc, could fulfil. But the four went out of the graveyard, turned left and in a café on the corner had tea and did their best to have a conversation.

Gino and Lucia spoke as if by force of wishing it they must be understood. They spoke in turn, a duet it sounded like, melodious, abundant, each heartening the other to remember and utter more. Their faces were so open, eyes and hands so expressive, it felt that in the transaction very little was being lost. Both Englishmen were thinking, How it comes back to you! Their stock, being revived, becoming more copious and useful.

Then quite suddenly it was over. Lucia began to weep again. Gino took out his large white handkerchief. The gist was easy to grasp: she had wanted him to die in her house, she had wanted to look after him to the end, she had wanted him in the little graveyard from where the snow, the fume and sometimes the creeping fires of Etna were to be seen by anyone looking up from tending a grave.

They waited together for the London bus. Lucia had a sister in Hillingdon. They would stay there the night. Then go home. Caradoc's old pupils waved them goodbye.

Then what? Neither asked. Heads down, side by side, they returned to the graveyard and found a seat against the far wall in a mild sunlight.

The taller of the two men began: It *was* you that night, wasn't it? But for answer he got a question: It *is* Jay, isn't it?

It was. I took a new name years ago. Thought it might change things.

Did it?

No. So just as well call me Jay. And you're Daniel, or you were then, and it was you that night. You and a girl called Merryn.

Yes, I still am. And it was us. We sat on this wall – nodding behind him – and looked out over there – nodding forwards – at his room where the lights were burning.

Thus introduced, they glanced sideways at one another, for a glimpse of the old faces. Then resumed, hands in their dark-suit pockets, staring forwards to the opposite wall of the graveyard, the five yew trees along it, the little gate in it, the College behind it, and the house and the room that had been Caradoc's.

Yes, said Daniel, we were out most nights, so it seems to me now, getting locked in, getting locked out, climbing over walls and fences, wading the rivers. The rules being what they were back then, we kept off the empty streets and browsed through the parks and gardens. The rules in those days being so ridiculous, if you fell in love and meant it, you went feral, there was no other way, you spent your days sleepwalking and at nights you trespassed. How we trespassed! And to get together in my narrow bed, under the maps that papered the sloped ceiling, what routes we had to negotiate quiet as mice through the grown-ups' private pleasaunces. And what risks to share an innocent black coffee on a roof under Orion who had seen many such as us but liked us specially, we fancied.

I didn't much like you when you arrived that night.

It was her idea, not mine. Back there – again the nod – they were pulling the Gothic mansions down to raise up blocks of science and we got in through the ruins, into the gardens, to steal their stocks and roses. We had armfuls, lupins too, and peonies and hollyhocks, and though we lost some climbing we still had enough for a wedding and a funeral when we got ourselves comfortable on that wall and she made me tell her again about Caradoc and Italy. I had told her before, but it was in bed and she fell asleep. I carried on. She slept and woke and slept and my voice went babbling on. It was then that I learned you don't need the whole story. Falling asleep and missing some, coming in later, forgetting where you were, loveliest is the voice, the bits and pieces of the story running on and on. But wide awake that night on the wall and staring at his lighted window she insisted I tell it to her again, at least an episode.

Tell some now, said Jay.

Did he never tell you?

Maybe. But tell some again. It's different, his telling it and yours. And different down the years.

He said he'd be passing through Florence at the end of June. Let's say the 30th, he said. Be there, he said, and I'll pick you up. Be there waiting at let's say 9 in the morning under Michelangelo's David (though I much prefer Donatello's) and I'll pick you up and take you as far as Rome. So there I was, and there he came, as the clocks struck nine, strolling across the square, smiling and looking very relaxed.

Yet here, said Jay, the buildings are as beautiful, the great domes and spires, the warm stone, the lanterns waiting for darkness, but did you ever see Caradoc in this place strolling and looking relaxed? Scarcely ever on the street at all.

I saw him once, said Daniel, soon after he had become my tutor, walking very quickly, almost scurrying, along the Broad and into the Turl. How strange he looked, out of place. I said to Merryn that it was like seeing a god, come down and managing the best he could. That was one of the first things I told her about him and it made her curious. Like a god, so out of place. But now I suppose I'd have to say he looked more like a man with a phobia, who couldn't bear daylight, traffic, the touch of people. I guess he was dashing to the indoor market, to the couple of familiar stalls, for a small shoulder of lamb, some cheeses, some fruit, to entertain a guest. I didn't accost him then or follow him, only watched, strangely intrigued and moved. It took me years to see that in the generosity of his entertaining must be included the effort it cost him to go out on the street and make a few purchases like any normal citizen.

But that night I sat on the wall here with Merryn and I tried to tell her what it felt like walking the streets of Florence with him, my teacher, my friend, become almost strange to me again because we were abroad and he was in his element and knew so much and imparted it in abundance, lightly. I didn't think of it then, it comes to me now, only now that he's dead and I'm sitting here looking at his room with you and the wall is behind me where I sat with her, this minute here and now it comes to me clearly what I felt that morning then. It was the rush of learning. It was the gathering force of the pentecost of learning blowing through me body and soul. Things he showed me then, enabled me to see and to go on seeing and see more and more elsewhere and down the years when he would not be there to show them. It was the continuation of his teaching in that room, his asking me questions, his clever inducing me to answer back, his getting me to ask and answer better, and his own questions and answers that would never let me rest. And the bottle of wine he bought, swelling in its straw basket, the cheese, the bread, the olives, the black grapes, his easy manners, how they liked him at the market stalls, how amiable he was and fluent in the language I had a few poor phrases of. I stood aside bashful, wanting one day to do likewise. I wanted his knowledge. Somewhere, nowhere, some remnant of the land of pastoral, we pulled off the road and picnicked under an olive tree. And that night in a restaurant in Orvieto he asked the waiter – yes, a very pretty boy – to tell him exactly how the little fish were cooked. And said pears were the fruit to eat with that particular pecorino cheese.

13

Yes, yes, said Jay. And eating pears and pecorino is like reading let's say Ronsard or Montaigne.

You ingest something. And being with a man at ease is a great gift in itself. He was bounteous to me.

So Merryn sitting up there with you and hearing all this and more thought she must meet the man and see for herself the way he worked.

She saw the light on. I said that was his room.

I was at the window. Perhaps you didn't see me. Certainly I had no wish to be seen. But I saw you two in the moonlight on the other side of these tombs up there sitting on the wall with your armfuls of flowers. I was thinking how unlike me you were. Caradoc was in his armchair behind my back. We were listening to Farandouri though neither of us knew a word of Greek. Listen, he had said, how she holds the lines — so steady. And I couldn't understand a word but I was listening well, if you know what I mean, truly in the heart, and looking at you two out there on the wall. And my loneliness welled up in me again and I could not see you for tears. Then came a knock at the door. I glanced at Caradoc. He raised his eyebrows. It was gone midnight. But he went and opened and there you were, like children with your silly flowers.

There was more, you see. I had told her more. In the end she could not bear not to know the man. I had told her that when we got to Rome and into the hotel and when he had gone out for a while, I don't know why, I began to be afraid. There were two beds, you see, but they were pushed together to be almost like one. In Orvieto they were far apart. But seeing the situation in that hotel in Rome I began to feel afraid that he would want to make love to me — though until then, and I don't just mean on the journey, I mean in all the months of my getting to know him, in the tutorials and going back later, quite late at nights, to his room up there, to carry on talking and drink a glass or two, in all that time and on all those private occasions, not once did he touch me unlawfully, as you might say, nor even make any suggestion, though, if I'm honest, I did quite often think he would. But in that room in Rome I was suddenly afraid, seeing the beds so close they looked like one, and I did a very bad thing: I pulled them apart, I made a gap between them, they were heavy to move, I felt very ashamed and foolish. And no sooner was I finished than Caradoc came back in and saw at once what I had done and a look went over his face, very hurt but then at once forgiving. And all he said was, Time for bed, I think. Would you like to use the bathroom first? When I came in again, carrying my few clothes in a bundle, he was reading a newspaper and didn't look out. And I was in my bed and turned away when he came back to his. We lay in the dark side by side with that ridiculous gap between us. He said goodnight to me and I said goodnight to him. Then after a little while, as though talking to nobody, he began telling me about Gino, how they had met in a bar in Naples where the conscripts hung out, Gino was working there, and how he had loved him at once and that same night they had found a place they could stay together. More and more, about the family in a village near Catania, the mother and father whom Gino soon very proudly introduced him to, their poverty, the struggle, their hopes in Gino, who was studying to be an engineer. And it was like with Merryn when I made up stories for her or when I told her the picaresque tale of Caradoc and the student engineer from a mafia village under Etna, I fell asleep listening, woke half-listening, slept again and he was still talking in the dark to me or to the ceiling. Next morning it was late and sunny before I woke and Caradoc had gone. I went down to the desk and they told me *il professore* had left an hour ago. They were gentle, they thought their thoughts, he was a familiar guest. They spoke slowly to me, they seemed to fear I would be sad. He was gone and had paid for two more nights in the room, so I should stay and get to know the city. And it was then that Merryn threw down her flowers, down into the graveyard, close by this seat, and took mine from my arms and threw them down after. And I did as she told me to: hung by my hands and dropped and stood below reaching up for her in her sandals, her bit of a skirt, her schoolgirly knickers, because she said the flowers had to be for him and for no one else, this teacher of mine, this faithful lover. I'm sorry now for intruding on you. But it had to be.

Jay rose abruptly, walked across to the far wall, passed between two very black and shapely yews, tried the little gate, found it locked, stepped back and looked up at the window that had been Caradoc's. After a while he returned and stood with his hands in his pockets looking down on Daniel. His hair was a tousled mop, boyish, but more grey than black. I don't mind about the intrusion, he said. But I do mind about the beds. On several counts. However, what's done is done and what's not done is not done. As to that night, I forgave you long before you left. What good was it doing me staring through the window at the pair of you on the wall? Does she still sing, by the way?

Yes, she still sings. I couldn't judge that night what the matter was, between you and Caradoc or in you yourself. But he was very courteous, as always. He gave us *sambuca*, do you remember?

All that palaver. The thin glass, the floating of the coffee beans, the setting fire to the spirit, the aroma, the bitter taste.

It was a wonder to Merryn. She's never forgotten it. The ceremony of it, the little dancing flames, she called him courtly lover and magician in one person.

Well, when you turned up like strays out of Arden I was on the run from the asylum, and Caradoc, while we were listening to Farandouri, was debating what to do with me.

And why had they locked you up?

Because I was mad. The College was going to send me down and I think that would have been the end of me, all the struggle my mother and father had to get me there, I'd have jumped under a train rather than go home that way and have

16

to look them in the face. But after some discussion the College deemed me mad and had me locked away.

Were you mad?

Well, a bit like you or not at all like you, I had a passion for climbing: cranes and scaffolding, but trees best of all. How I loved climbing trees! Caradoc said I was like the baron in Calvino's story, *il barone rampante*, and he bought me a copy and indeed I was, somewhat. My favourite tree was the beech in the College garden. Was there ever a tree like that before or since? I went back earlier today, just before that frightful service, and would you believe it, there is no tree — all gone, and only a ring on the lawn, a vast ring which was the shadow of its bulk, like the mark of a fort or camp as seen from the air in a drought when the present becomes transparent and you can see what was. I got up there most nights, doing nobody any harm. And I never hurt the tree, I loved it more than people, oh by far! Vast copper beech with long extending soughing and swaying limbs. Copper-black on a hot day, a heavy blackness, copper-red when you got to know the heart of it. Even in daylight there was always an opening on darkness for me in that garden and a darkening of the darkness in the night. And that is where I loved to be. High up, where the foliage broke like a sea monster surfacing and it was dappled with moon and stars. Doing no harm, not to man nor beast nor any living thing. Certainly not to the tree. But somebody must have betrayed me. And one night the Dean, damned time-server, damned slave in a living hell of his own making, stood there on the lawn with a flashlamp and a couple of porters, calling me in his castrated drawl to come down at once. Of course, I stayed where I was. That night, all the following day, all the following night. Then the Dean lost patience. He said he was fetching the police and the fire brigade. And I was tired and sadder than I'd ever been in my life before, sad as the tree was copious and dark, sad as its copper black was heavy, I was sad through and through, I had no heart for it anymore. And I leaned down till I could see his white face looking up, his pasty face, his hateful, chinless, spineless, gutless, feckless, witless, ugly mug looking up at me, and I said: Fuck off, Dean, fuck off. Absent thee from this pleasant place a while and I'll climb slowly down. But stand there five minutes longer and I'll jump. And off he toddled. He was out of his depth. I heard he wanted me sent down, mad or not, madness was no excuse for rudeness, so he said. But kinder counsels prevailed and I was transported to the nuthouse.

And that night you escaped?

It was child's play. Walls you and Merryn would have scaled in a twinkling and run along the copings of like squirrels. I was frightened. They were eyeing me up for ECT. They were saying I was a suitable case for treatment. So that evening I went through a toilet window and into the grounds and over a wall into some decent citizen's back garden and out past his bicycle and his coal bunker into the parks, for Caradoc's.

The graveyard was a warm place still, and lively. The two men in their suits were, with the yew trees, by far the darkest presences. Here and there, sitting against, lying upon, strolling among the tombs were the College's current generation of students, reading, dozing, talking animatedly. A couple quite speechlessly absorbed in one another; a young woman with an open notebook looking round at everyone else, at Jay and Daniel in particular perhaps.

Remembering the Dean, Jay continued, reminds me how much less I liked Caradoc when I saw him with his colleagues. He took me into dinner once or twice, I don't quite know why. Perhaps he thought I should witness these things. Perhaps he was testing me. If so, I don't know whether I passed or failed. I suffered, he must have seen that. I wished he would be more different, I wished some original local tone would surface in his voice, against their voices. But no, he fitted, his speech was theirs, his subjects and opinions were only theirs. And I watched – then as much as now – and my view was that they didn't quite believe him, they suspected him of dissembling, I even thought they must be leading him on, to see how well or badly he would do. And two or three times, until I told him I couldn't bear it, he took me along to watch him playing his part.

I went on a pilgrimage to Bardsey once. I thought it might help. I went on foot, I set off from here. And coming to the Lleyn, that pushes out into the sea like Italy, I saw I was very near Carmel, where he was born and grew up, and I made the little detour, to understand him better. Terrace houses, many ruinous, many for sale. The mines long abandoned, the sunlight slanting on the wet slate heaps, like the glances you see off a crow's wings. The chapels too grand for the few surviving streets. And looking back, the mountains. Did you ever see Caradoc's climbing books? Shelves of them. Did he ever describe to you Joe Brown's routes up Clogwyn? He was like a boy, a hero-worshipper, swearing he would do such things himself when he was a man.

By then I knew about Gino and had begun my researches, to try to find out more. And I had decided that Caradoc loved him especially because of his family, the hardship, the determination to fight back by intelligence and education, his loyalty, his passionate desire to help. And that during the talk at High Table and in the Common Room Caradoc must perhaps be saying to himself, It's all right, I have to do this, I'll get by, I'll get through, it's not for much longer and I'll load up my car with my books and my presents and head off out of this place, all that long way south.

You know more than I do, said Daniel.

I found out, said Jay. From Caradoc some things: about the Mafia, the bandits, the fear; about Gino's work with the Communists, his classes for children, the demonstrations, the fights. I found a photograph of a Communist Party march, Gino and Caradoc together under the banner in a crowd of men wearing caps, Caradoc in his suit and without a tie. He worshipped Dolci. That was a life, he said, a life you wouldn't mind people looking at. But I got little out of Caradoc about his own generosity: his arrangements, his regular payments, really his funding of Gino in the struggle. I had to go elsewhere for that. I went down there once. Not with him, on my own. I was on the edge anyway, out on the borders, and I think now that gave me a sort of innocence and perhaps protected me. For a while I think I was almost a Fool, with the privileges of that office. Terrible those villages under Etna, so ruinous and fearful. I'd arrive and see no one and knew that everyone was seeing me. I stood in that little cemetery Lucia wanted him home in. There were anemones and much of the bulk of Etna was white with snow. I'm glad she never saw our crematorium. I hope no one told her he dropped dead on the street.

Again he stood up, and did a tour among the graves. He looked odd and ill-dressed, his suit hung on him slackly, as if he had worn it for years and lost weight in it. Daniel surveyed the young men and women, looking for the types, the recurrent patterns of being young. The church was built in the twelfth century, the oldest surviving graves are of the late seventeenth, there are a couple of memorial trees in the far corner, for the first deaths from AIDS. The yews are as shapely as steady flames.

Jay came back, sat down again, stared up at the overlooking window and said: That night before you two arrived Caradoc had been persuading me not to kill myself. I know for certain that he did this with others too. I was round there one night, very late, when he got a phone call and said he must go and I could sleep on the sofa if I wished, he wouldn't be back. And I learned later it was a boy on the top floor in a big house up the Woodstock Road, on the window ledge with a razor – and Caradoc talked him in again, and out of the idea.

What did he say to you?

That although I was free to do it, my true imperative

was not to. That my responsibility was to stay alive so long as I might be useful. That although I was free to do it, I would harm other people – people who loved me – by doing it. I denied that I might be useful. I denied that anyone loved me. He said that I couldn't see clearly at present and that I had to trust somebody else's judgement until I could. He denied that nobody loved me. He denied I would never be useful. He took me in his arms and said that he for one would miss me sorely. Was that not reason enough to wait a while? I suppose you were already sitting on the wall by then. Soon afterwards I looked out and saw you. And then you arrived with your armfuls of flowers. I was weak and lachrymose and didn't want anyone but Caradoc knowing.

Merryn knew. I mean she knew you were weepy, but more that you wished no one but Caradoc to witness it. That was why she sang.

When the Farandouri came to an end there was a silence and Caradoc still hadn't decided what to do with his flowers but was standing with them in his arms rather gauchely and Merryn was sitting on the carpet with her knees up leaning back against the sofa.

My eyes were sharpened by sadness, I was weak and keen-sighted because I wanted to be persuaded not to kill myself. She had a scratch on her right leg, just below the knee, from all your climbing, I suppose, the blood had trickled down and dried in a brown line. There were seeds of some sort in her hair.

Elmseeds.

There were elmseeds in her black hair. Legs like a boychild's, scuffed sandals. Then she sang. It was like the Farandouri, I understood not a word, a different voice and a girl not much younger than me sitting there somewhere familiar in England but her singing was strange, so foreign, from long ago elsewhere. I half-thought I knew some words, but none either singly or in a phrase made any usual sense. But it was like the Farandouri, I felt its fingers clutching at my heart, but not so wistful, not tragic, it wanted something, it had energy, it was younger in spirit, it saw difficulties but no reason not to go out and fight them. And the sadness – there was some sadness – was more like an imagined possibility, what the cost would be, what your loss and regret would be, if you didn't fight bravely and win through to where you desired and believed you deserved to be. I discerned, perhaps more than you did, that Caradoc too was greatly moved. I like to think it reminded him of his own first language, that he had forgotten or suppressed. Even now I don't know what she sang. I've heard nothing like it since. What was it?

A troubadour song. Occitan, I suppose.

She knew songs like that?

Still does. And I'll tell you how. You're like me, you need icons, I give you this. She had classes with Mrs Delanty – another who never published, another every pupil revered – and one late afternoon it wasn't going very well, they weren't concentrating, perhaps they hadn't prepared it, the class was drifting into pieces. Then Mrs Delanty closed her book and told them quietly to close theirs. Listen, she said. And she stood up, put her arms by her sides – like a little girl at a party, Merryn said – closed her eyes, lifted up her face, and sang. A white-haired lady, her girlish beauty showing through the many years. She sang a troubadour song, though it certainly wasn't the troubadours that the failing class had been about. She sang. It was a Dawn Song, Merryn said: two lovers having to part after their stolen and risky night together. So Merryn learned later. When the song was finished Mrs Delanty opened her eyes, smiled at the class, said they should go now, she would see them at the same time next week and they would carry on from where they had left off. But that evening Merryn went to Mrs Delanty's rooms and knocked. Quite late, nobody did such a thing. Called in, closing the door behind her, she stood there. What is it, child? Mrs Delanty asked. And Merryn answered: Please, Mrs Delanty, will you teach me that language? I want to be able to sing that song you sang. Of course you do, said Mrs Delanty. And of course I will. We'll make a start tomorrow evening. Are you free at 8.30?

Jay stood up again. Paced around. Daniel observed his agitation, then looked away, over the yew trees and the wall, to what had been Caradoc's room. Somebody was standing at the window, looking down. Daniel had no idea who he might be, no interest either, except in the idea of a person, and years later another person, looking out and down over a graveyard in which the generations strolled, sat, lolled, conversed, made love.

Then Jay blocked his view and his thinking. So that was Merryn, he said. Caradoc was moved by her singing. He freely admitted that he found it hard to like the girlfriends of his young men but I could see that he did like her. As for you, I must say I like you better now. I thought then that you deserved neither Caradoc nor her. I didn't, said Daniel. I don't. You talked about Rimbaud, Jay said. You had just written on him and he was on your mind. You said it was a pity he let himself go. You said he should have bided his time. You said the *dérèglement de tous les sens* was an abdication of responsibility, he would have written better, more, for longer, for more people, to better effect, had he held on. And he should have known that, he was clever enough. You said it was a waste, it was all too rushed, the later poems already were a solipsistic cul-de-sac. I thought you very bourgeois.

I am. Petty bourgeois. Or you could say I want to stay alive, as lively as possible for as long as possible.

Sort of *bateau ivre* with life-jackets and the coastguard standing by?

Sort of. And here's a funny thing. That essay I wrote for Caradoc on Rimbaud, it was far too long, by the end of the tutorial I had hardly finished reading it. He said I should come back, come back that evening at ten, and we'd discuss it then. And that's when I began to get to know him. That was the beginning of what made him say he would meet me in Florence under Michelangelo's David and take me to Rome. I think he was intrigued that a boy of twenty wrote in favour of a sort of common sense. And this is the funny thing. I wrote at that essay all of the previous night and to stay awake I got myself something off somebody in College who supplied such things. I was high, my heart and my brain were racing, I had more ideas than I could get out through the nib of my pen, the one and only time I've taken any such thing, and I wrote in favour of not letting go, of holding back, of biding your time, of not giving in to the pull of unrestraint.

Jay sat down, patted Daniel's arm, left his hand lying there for a moment. Then he said: I never took anything, though you might think I would. I was always going up very high, and it frightened me, and down very low, and I grovelled there in terror. I never wanted any drugs. All I ever took was what they force-fed me in the hospitals. So perhaps we are more alike than I thought that night. Here I am still, large as life, all skin and bone but by no means dead. Plenty are. Plenty fell off along the way. Back then and since. I was with that boy who jumped off the crane in Parks Road. He thought he could fly, or didn't care if he couldn't. It was back where your ruined gardens had been. He landed on the scientific concrete. I was up there with him, not very tempted. I climbed down, saw the mess, crept into the parks and lay by the river vomiting. And several since, if not so dramatic equally fatal. The needle, the bottle, the blade. Gone, gone, the damage done. And somehow I didn't. I must have believed what he said: I might love, I might be loved, I might be asked to help and be able to. I drifted this way quite often. He always took me in. Make yourself at home, he said. I did, I had nowhere else. When did you see him last?

Daniel blushed. He was ashamed. Not long before he died, he said. I hadn't told him I was coming here. I had some business of my own. Then I met him by accident in the Lane.

He was at the back gate, you remember that door in the wall, he had his own key to it. He let me in there once or twice, as I'm sure he did you, he always made some comment and giggled. But when I saw him last I came on him suddenly and we were both embarrassed. He was fatter, his face had coarsened. Neither of us knew what to say to the other. There was some sunlight and he looked very ill in it, the flesh of his face all pocked and slack. I might say the eyes were still bright, very dark and bright, but they had withdrawn and were staring out as if from a hiding place, backing away almost to where his thoughts were. And his thoughts, like mine, were a long way from the speaking lips. I was thinking how much better he had looked in Italy, the sun was brighter there, he was on streets among people full in the public view, but he was fit to be looked at. Was it only because he had aged? I don't think so. After a little while I left him and walked away quickly. It occurred to me at once that I couldn't be sure whether he was about to go in at the gate or had just come out of it. If the latter, then we should at least have walked into town together; and he would be waiting there now, in the Lane, until he could be sure of not catching me up. Perhaps he was hurrying to the market, to buy the few things to be hospitable to a visitor, as he had been, often, to me.

I saw the same, said Jay, his loneliness, the wrecking of his face, but I swore not to let it matter. I would see through it to the spirit, as Troilus did through poor Cresseid's leprosy. And mostly I saw him indoors. He looked okay indoors. He embraced me, he welcomed me, he opened a bottle. I never saw him in Italy, though I hitchhiked the route he took every summer through France, all the long way down. I mooched around Florence where he picked you up. I can well imagine what you looked like under the statue, waiting. Be sure he saw you first. Be sure he was somewhere spying to see you first. And it rejoiced his heart to see you so burned with travelling, so lightly clad. And in his own good time he strolled across the square, to claim you, his waif and stray. And

25

I know which hotel it was in Rome, near the Spanish Steps, close to Keats's lodgings, he recommended it, should I ever be passing. I was passing, penniless, I saw it from the outside. I went on my way, all the long way down. And when I saw that graveyard under Etna I wished him safely home there when the time should come. For that was always the plan. When Gino met Lucia and when it came to marrying, he told her and her family as he had already told his own that his love for Caradoc might change but would never lessen and was a fact and a certainty and nobody could be bound to him who did not honour that. And they did. Gladly, simply, thoroughly they honoured it. He had a flat in their house. And every year, in his seasons, he would arrive with his reading and his gifts and made provision for the family and was godfather to the three children and when the first, a little boy, died he grieved with them and for a year wore a ribbon of mourning during all his teaching and all his College duties and nobody all that time once saw him smile. You have children, do you?

Daniel nodded. Two weeks after that night it was the end of term and I was very anxious. I didn't know what I dared ask of her. I was fearful. We were out at nights in the gardens and the parks, often by the river, following the tributaries to the big Thames, thinking of it leaving. And we were on the roof high above the streets and watched aeroplanes and shooting stars and the constellations travelling. And we lay under the maps on the sloped ceiling, they showed the possibilities, but I never dared say, We'll go there, shan't we, promise? She seemed free as a bird to me, by choice still lingering where I happened to be. I saw Caradoc several times, but never with her, and when he asked me what my summer was looking like, I shrugged and turned away. The term finished and she hadn't said even goodbye. But back home there was a note for me, waiting. It said: If you want me, I'll be in the Tuileries, by Maillol's La Nymphe, 9 July at 3 in the afternoon. And if you find me we'll go looking for castles in Spain. There's a particular troubadour I'm interested in.

Jay's smile was only faintly sardonic.

Then came again, said Daniel, again and more, the rush of learning. These hands – he raised them – these eyes – he looked into Jay's – and whatever and wherever the soul is, how they learned. I came into my own. Into earthly happiness. And you?

Jay shrugged, stood up abruptly. Time I was off, he said. The evening had lingered but was ending. The girl closed her notebook and with both hands rubbed her bare shoulders. At the gate Jay said, Some days I think there was only him. Others, I think he directed me into plenitude and it's up to me to grasp it, bear it, say how it was and is.

# The Man Who Said
# He Had Died

Pauline was very matter-of-fact about it. He left me, she said, because I wouldn't believe he died and came back to life again. Not that she went around telling her story, looking for sympathy; but if anyone asked, she told them why, and shrugged, and added, There you go, and looked whoever had asked her straight in the face with a look that said, And that's the truth, believe it or not.

Most people sided with Pauline and blamed Edward. She was a very down-to-earth person and now he had left her with two girls at university and all because she wouldn't believe him when he said he had died and come back from the dead and everything was changed. One or two women, even more down-to-earth than Pauline, said she was at fault herself for not humouring him. All men got funny ideas sooner or later and resurrection wasn't the worst he might have hit upon. Why couldn't she just go along with it until it passed and he got back to normal? But the general opinion, especially among the people Edward told his story to, was that all the fault was his and that Pauline would be better off without him.

Edward worked for the railways, in logistics. He had a pass for himself and his family, go where they liked, reduced or gratis, world-wide. Edward spent a good deal of time planning trips and Pauline did the provisions, when he told her. Off they went, man and wife and the two girls, or latterly just man and wife, long complicated journeys, often in great discomfort, but an adventure. When Eastern Europe opened up, Edward said it was a new lease of life. Very nice, said the hard-headed women who blamed Pauline for her disbelief. Quite a bonus in a marriage and now she's lost it. They had always thought Edward a bit funny, in his sports jacket, polished brown shoes and tweedy fisherman's hat; but not the worst man to be married to, not by a long chalk. He had an irritating voice, rather prissy; but he didn't smell of drink and not in a million years would you have thought him violent or adulterous.

Near-death and out-of-body experiences are pretty common. People it has happened to join clubs and chat for ever and ever on the world wide web. But mostly what it boils down to is that their hearts stopped, for one reason or another, and somebody kissed or shocked or thumped them back into breath again. Pauline knew all about that sort of thing from the usual television programmes and articles in magazines. Occasionally the brought-back-to-life said they had floated clear of the body and looked down on it from a distance. Some spoke of corridors or tunnels of light which they had entered, drifting, only to be fetched out again, regretfully. Pauline neither believed nor disbelieved these stories. She did not know the people, they did not insist from morning till night that she *must* believe them. Besides, Edward's experience was not like that. His was resurrection not resuscitation. He never said his heart had stopped and some medic or member of the public got it going again. In fact, when people suggested that, he got very cross; and if they reverted to it, as a likely explanation, and he heard from a third party that it was their decided opinion, he cut them off. Fewer and fewer were the people he would speak to.

Edward's story, which in a level and non-committal voice Pauline would repeat to anyone who asked, was that he had gone for his usual Sunday morning jog round the park and two thirds of the way through, climbing for home, he had suffered a sudden weakness, fallen to his knees, blacked out, and died. The next he knew, in the world of the living at least, a woman and her dog, a setter the colour of a centipede and just as disgusting, were leaning over him. He lay flat on his back, and when the woman asked was he all right he answered that he had died and come back to life again, whereupon she phoned for an ambulance. Called to the hospital, Pauline found Edward lying in his purple tracksuit on a bed; and he told her what he had told the woman and her dog. Pauline supposed he must have had a heart attack but a doctor, taking her aside, assured her that Edward's heart was fine, nobody had resuscitated him, he was fit and well, he could leave as soon as he liked. So Pauline, very relieved, drove Edward home, and her ordeal began.

Pauline had sometimes wondered, as any wife might, how she would manage if she 'lost her husband'; and when she heard from the hospital that he had collapsed whilst jogging uphill, she felt her love for him as a realization of the gap his loss would make. In the heart, she said, like a bolt of ice. She had long since got used to his fussy meticulousness; and the way he laid out his exceptionally neat fingers, when, as very often, he began an explanation or an argument on the premise that he could not possibly be wrong, even such mannerisms, enough to drive you insane, she had got used to and counted them in among the all-in-all of the man, whom she loved. When she thought of his sudden announcements that he had planned a trip to Thurso or Vilnius or Kalamata, and would she please pack the hamper, they seemed, as a serial and a still growing totality, a strange and wonderful benefit, even a characteristic expression of his love for her, that she would not have missed for worlds. And not long before his 'accident' he had, for the first time ever, announced a trip well in advance, as a present for her, indeed for both of them, something very special, a celebration. How pleased and twinkling he was when he made this little speech! They would cross Russia on the Trans-Siberian Railway, take a ship from Vladivostock to Los Angeles, cross America by Amtrak and the Greyhounds, and cruise home from New York on the Queen Mary. It could be done, he had worked it out. Most gratis, much cut-price, and even on the liner he had a contact who could get them a deal. It was to celebrate their silver wedding anniversary. How about that? But a week later came his 'accident', as she insisted on calling it, even to his face, even in the teeth of his ever more caustic rage.

In the first few days and nights after Edward's accident Pauline did as any wife might: she listened patiently, asked for details, raised no objections, uttered no refusal. She humoured him, and not for her own sake, to continue in the benefits of their marriage, but for his, to calm him, for she was still worried, despite the doctor's assurances, that his heart might be weak or his brain have a clot in it. So she asked him to tell her in careful detail about the sudden weakness two thirds of the way round his usual course, on the slope coming home. Had he felt tired? No. At all strange? No. Poorly? Absolutely not. And the weakness, was it around the heart, in his legs, in his head? Nowhere particular. Everywhere. A sudden total state. You fell to your knees, you blacked out? Consciousness left him, a fast and decisive erasure. Next thing, the woman, her horrible dog and her imbecile mobile phone. How long was the gap? Hard to say. Time over there, if there is such a thing, runs very unlike our sub-lunary, that's for sure. I suppose it does, said Pauline.

Why death? Why not just a black-out, a faint, a swoon? I knew, said Edward – they were at the kitchen table, he laid out his neat clean fingers – I know. That's enough for me. And, if I may say so, it should be enough for you. Pauline's resistance began when he said that. But she persevered in patience for a few more days. When you say you have changed, she said, please can you tell me what that means exactly? Edward began to be exasperated. I mean I am changed, he answered, utterly changed. Anyone would be, would they not, who died and came back to life again? Stands to reason. But Pauline wanted to be told what forms the change would take. How would people, and she, his wife, in particular, know that he had changed? I say so, said Edward. They'll believe me or they won't believe me. I must say I rather hoped *you* would believe me. All is changed. I am utterly changed. But will you leave your job? Will you give up the railways? Will the girls see a difference when they come home? I might leave my job, said Edward. I might not. It hardly matters. And as to the girls, I begin to fear they will be as obtuse and unbelieving as their mother.

Pauline's principle in the nearly twenty-five years of her marriage to Edward had been that they must not let the sun go down on their wrath. She had kept to it, perhaps in the old-fashioned fear that one or other of them might be taken in the night and the one surviving would be unable to forgive or be forgiven. And now, after Edward's accident, as though that rule were made of sand and the sea came in, it collapsed, it was flattened, there was no trace of it. They lay in bed in the dark, unloving, angry, and Edward in his finicky voice spoke upwards towards the invisible ceiling, aggrieved and charging Pauline with betraying him, failing him, failing in her duty to him, breaking her marriage vows. You want me obedient? she replied. What good would my obedience do you? I can't believe by obedience. And then she questioned him more closely on the weakest parts of his story and knew as she did so that all he heard in her questions was her tone of voice, she heard it herself, her own voice in the dark, not the tone of someone honestly asking in proper humility to be helped to believe, but one with no intention of believing, already scathing and deriding and only wishing to undo his own belief, so that he saw what a fool and a bully he was and would be sorry and ask her forgiveness, receive it, be reconciled and so get back again across the hideous fissure of his stupid accident, back to their proper marriage when she loved him despite his silly ways and they went on trips together that everyone laughed at but envied and thought rather wonderful. The spirit of her questioning being all

33

contrary and hostile, they got nowhere, she turned away and left him on his back complaining upwards at the ceiling.

After blacking out, Edward said, and before opening his eyes again under the concerned faces of the woman and her vile red setter, there was an interval, death itself, which he could, he claimed, in a certain sense remember. Indeed, without that memory he would have had no grounds for believing he had died and none for his conviction that he was utterly changed. But there Pauline saw his greatest weaknesses. Say what it was like then, being dead. Tell me. And what do you mean that everything is changed? All I see is that you have got more like you always were. You're exactly the same, only worse. Even at the beginning, in the first days and nights when Pauline was still being kind to him, humouring him, anxious for him, Edward had not been able to tell her in any concrete detail what death was like. Death, he said, seemed to have no spatial relations in it, there was neither a floor nor a ceiling, no ground, no sky, he did not part from his body into a relationship of above or to the side of it, and there was no light or dark. So death was not a location in space, but a state. And time, as he had at once asserted, did not exist and operate there in any way he or Pauline would have recognised. So he could not say and had no interest in trying to work out how long, in Pauline's down-to-earth terms, he had in fact been dead. The state itself then, how would he describe it? As sorrow, he answered, sorrow, regret, an aching sort of love becoming grief. For me? she asked. Were you loving and missing me? It was in me, Edward answered, that was all I was, sorrow and love and grief, in me but not under my name, and all for you, surely, since you are the only person I have loved liked that, but not under your name either. Pauline could not help being touched by this and later, when he had left home, it seemed to her that there, if anywhere, they might have found a ground to agree on, even some words, and she blamed herself and thought of phoning him to say so, but didn't, knowing he would want the letter of belief, the spirit not sufficing.

As to the change in Edward, there also his clarifications were feeble, in Pauline's view. All he could say was that having died and death being the state of love and grief he had tried to describe to her, he must from now on live his life accordingly and if she couldn't see that and couldn't or wouldn't follow him, he was very sorry for her, but so be it, if she was not with him she was against him. Then the crosser they got with one another, the more outrageous he became, every day on waking, all day long, last thing at night until she turned aside from him and slept. He asked in a hoity-toity voice who else did she know who had died and come back to life again? With whom else could she live a life in accordance with the truth of death as he, uniquely in modern times perhaps, had experienced it?

Edward left before the girls came home. Watched by the neighbours he moved out piecemeal by taxi, three or four trips; then finally on his bicycle, very laden. Parting from Pauline he assumed an expression more of sorrow than of anger and said, I have made proper provision. You will not want financially. In more important ways, of course, so his eyes behind his glasses said, her want would be terrible. He had rented a bedsit in the western part of the town where there had been bad flooding in the summer and nobody wanted to live. Handy for the station though.

So Kate and Emma came home for Christmas from their universities and found their mother alone. She had told them about Edward's accident and even about his delusion, but not how bad the after-effects had been. At first she was glad to have the girls to herself. She did not want him bullying them as he had her. Kate, in her fourth year reading medicine, was grateful for that great mercy, as she put it; but Emma, second year reading English, looked doubtful or even disappointed and Pauline at once gave her Edward's address and telephone number so that she could go and hear his claims and decide for herself whenever she pleased.

Telling the girls unsteadied Pauline. Was she not as

unreasonable as he was, in her way? Always fighting him and contradicting. Perhaps after all she should have swallowed her pride. Crawl to the Cross? said Kate. Not bloody likely. It was all bullying and nonsense, no one had to take such shit, and certainly not any woman from any man. Besides, said Kate, he wouldn't have believed you if you'd said you believed him. Emma thought the same, rationally. She did not for a moment believe that her father had died and come back to life again but she had spent the term reading Lawrence and the Last Plays and did profoundly believe in the possibility of radical change, new life and the soul's ever renewing adventure. Also she had fallen in love. So I know what it's like, she said. What what's like? said Kate. Emma shrugged, then questioned her mother more closely about the state of death, as her father had described it, and the change he claimed his remembering it had wrought in him. Why would you feel impelled to live utterly differently having experienced death as a state of aching love and sorrow? The connection was clear to Emma. You would resolve to purify your sorrow, she said, so that in it, when death came again, there would be no regrets. Love better, I mean, live better, more adventurously, regret, in women at least, being much more for what they haven't done than for what they have. Kate said very definitely that death was death, that was that, you felt nothing whatsoever, death as death couldn't be better or worse, you were dead, full stop. It's life I'm interested in, said Emma. So I suppose I'm speaking metaphorically. I suppose you are, said Kate. You should cut up corpses for a week or two, that would sort you out.

So it went on. Pauline was uneasy. And one evening at their meal, when, à propos of nothing, to no one in particular, Emma said, It is required you do awake your faith, Pauline covered her face and for the first time with any witnesses wept. Then the girls were shocked and closed around her in solidarity. They blamed him and damned him.

But it could not rest there. The absent man and his accident worked on the wife and daughters in feelings that changed by the minute. Each alone was troubled, but together they worsened it for one another. Emma said, I don't like to think of him on his own in that bedsit. Those streets are still horrible after the floods. And you think I do? said Pauline, beginning quietly. You think I like the idea of my husband on his own in a miserable room? Then white and furious, I love the bloody man! He said we were going on the Trans-Siberian Railway to Vladivostock and then on a boat to Los Angeles and across the USA on trains and buses and home on the new Queen Mary! He had worked it all out, for a celebration. All I had to do was say I believed him. Kate was livid. Did he try to bribe you like that? The swine, if he did. Pauline assured her there'd been no such bargaining. It was unconditional, she said. Swine anyway, said Kate. Unconditional! Who does he think he is? Unconditional obedience! Tyranny and servitude! I suppose he'll trawl around till he finds someone, Pauline said. Some woman. Emma said she could well imagine it. There'd be a few interested if he advertised. A stampede, said Kate. Especially if he mentioned his rail pass. No, I didn't mean that, said Emma. And again, almost talking to herself, she began musing on the pull, like a vortex, of the desire for radical change, the corn of wheat, if it die it bringeth forth much fruit, he that loseth his life shall find it etc etc. And she dwelled particularly on the sorowful regret that Edward had remembered in the state of death. What a potent injunction that was to live now in the desire for a death with no regrets! Yes, said Kate, we mustn't belittle it. The sexy thing isn't the rail pass after all. There'll be some dippy female who really will believe him, someone in her late forties beginning to wonder is this it, will life go on like this, will this be the best I'll get? My consultant's wife, still just about beautiful, she's started writing poetry, she's got that desperate look, she'd leave him without a backward glance for a man who said he'd died and come back to life again. She'd betray the world to save her soul with a man who said, Believe! But Pauline was thinking of Edward on his bicycle in his tweedy fisherman's hat as he set off wobblingly down the hill encumbered with belongings. She thought of his fingers, their subtlety of touch. I love him, she thought, what more does he want? Didn't we have fun together? I liked our life the way it was and might be. Come home, you unholy fool, let me persuade you.

# The Cave

Lou's sister phoned. Was she still seeing her funny chap? Lately he was all Maya asked about. Indeed, she had begun to preach, which Lou rather resented. But since she had no one else to discuss him – or it, the whole business – with, often she weakened and confessed. Yes, she said, I'm seeing him next week as a matter of fact. And what will it be this time? Maya asked. A longboat to the Arctic Circle? Lying on deck under the Aurora Borealis? Lou said it wouldn't be anything so idle but what it would be she didn't know. She never knew. That was what annoyed Maya. She said it was demeaning, always waiting for surprises, like a little girl, always waiting for the next treat. But she wasn't a little girl, she was a grown woman, time running out etc etc. Life's not all treats, you know. At which point Lou asked after the children. How was Chloë's piano? Did William like his new school? Was she, Maya, still doing all the fetching and carrying? How was Henry? Very busy? Was she seeing anyone else? As a matter of fact I am, said Maya. Time's running out, I do want a life of my own. And then she reverted, in what sounded like real concern, to her sister, *her* life, her infrequent meetings with the man she, Maya, thought very dubious. All I mean is, does he mean it? Mean what? When he takes you off doing these extraordinary things, is he serious? He's *very* serious, said Lou. Or rather, *it's* serious. *It* is very serious. But I suppose you mean does he love me, will he marry me, will we buy a house, will he have children with me, that sort of thing? You love him, that's obvious, said Maya, and if he doesn't love you he shouldn't keep doing things with you that make you love him

39

more. Obvious? Keep doing? More? Lou got tangled up and stopped listening. She wondered did men ever talk about women like that, hour after hour, about their women. She couldn't imagine that they did. She supposed some of them boasted. She couldn't imagine Owen talking to another man about her and boasting. For one thing, what did he have to boast about, in that sense? Maya, she said, coming back in, I sometimes think we're no better off than Jane Austen's women, and men aren't better off either, the way you talk. They mustn't do anything that might arouse in us expectations they cannot or will not fulfil. And if they do, they are bad men and we are fools. I only mean you should find out if he's serious, Maya said. Or what else is he after? Power? You worry me, Lou. You are on your own too much.

Lou was right to say that a longboat under the Aurora Borealis would not have been Owen's thing. Mostly when he wrote to suggest they might meet it was to do something he described as his job, or his job, 'sort of'. For example, during a bad fire on the moors he asked, the minute she arrived, would she like to climb up with him and see the damage? It was still burning when they got there and the usual roads had been closed by the police; but he knew a way round, from up wind, luckily enough, and they followed the fire as it cropped its way through the heather. Funny having residual flames about your ankles and kicking through hot ash. One discovery pleased him particularly. He had come across a poem about a hill fire in which the fire was described as advancing over all but 'leaving springs in hoofmarks'. In Lou's opinion, Owen did not give enough credence to poetry; but when they found several such damp survivals he had to concede that, for once, a poem told the truth.

Anyway, a week after Maya's phonecall, there they were, Lou Johnson and Owen Shepperd, in the limestone country and it was not going well. Miserably she trailed along behind him like a child in disgrace not knowing why, sorrowful and furious at the rules she did not understand but hated and despised anyway, whether she understood or not. Why had he asked her? Why had she been fool enough to come? They were trailing along the busy street of a small town and she supposed it must be back to the railway station he was leading her and there, courteous and cold, he would see her on to a train and that would be that. Well so be it. Still she was miserable.

Then suddenly he halted, turned to her and said, Forget all that. Here's this. And he took her first by the arm then very firmly by the hand and stepped with her off the busy street into an alleyway between two ordinary shops. The way was not surfaced like a modern street but roughly cobbled and before long not even that, the limestone itself was underfoot and the alley had become a track, rising. So the street had a very thin border, only one row of shops, and you could step between them, if you knew the gap, into this! Owen said nothing, he seemed to be concentrating. He had on his face the expression of a man concentrating hard to get something right, to make something come true under his feet and before his eyes. But he held her hand tightly as though that should be proof enough and she shouldn't worry he might rather be there concentrating alone. They went on in silence, the way climbed, soon it was more a deserted stream bed than a path, they climbed under hazels and alders, in a mossy light, and the noise of the town quietened behind them and below. The town continued in her consciousness for a while, lingering as a murmur at the back of her mind, then she forgot it. The first words he said were, The water's just underneath.

Stepping off a public street into a quite different space and time was something Owen had done with Lou before. Once it was in the spa town, in late summer. He had written and suggested they meet, she agreed, they met, they were walking along, it was going well between them, in a friendly sort of way. He seemed glad of the occasion, sure of it, and quite

41

suddenly guided her off the street through a broken door (it wouldn't open, they squeezed) into a long walled garden. The place astonished her. Only later, not having heard from him for weeks, did she again rather resent his ability to astonish her. Whenever Owen fell out of her favour she declared him, almost in her sister's voice, to be playing a very calculated game with her, the chief interest of which, from his point of view, was power. But the garden did astonish her. It belonged to a very big house whose many eyes and mouths were shut with steel against the vandals. Owen's interest lay at the far end, in the apple orchard. Scrumping, he said. Before the developers grub them up. And out of his rucksack he took several plastic bags and handed Lou a couple. The trees had been neglected, they wore mistletoe, moss and lichen on many dead branches as the marks of it; but nevertheless, keeping their side of the bargain, they had cropped. A few of each sort, if you wouldn't mind, Owen said. The old lady collected and some you can't find any more. Quietly they moved through the apple light plucking fruit that was shining pearl and shades of red and gold and underwater green. Owen could name some, but had a friend, he said, who would identify the rest and grow their progeny from pips. When he took out his notebook and became very serious, Lou drifted back to where the wreckage of a kitchen garden began and sat there, on the orchard frontier, under the last tree, eating an apple whose name perhaps only Owen's friend would know. The flesh and juice and sweetness without a name gave her a thoughtful pleasure that had an undertow of sadness, in full view of the stopped and blinded house.

And now, climbing the stream bed, Lou acknowledged that he must once again have schemed for an effect. Surely he knew very well where the particular gap was between the shops. But because of the bad mood and her trailing behind him dejectedly they might have forfeited the chance, their being in the stream bed after all was a mercy, and when he said that the water was 'just underneath' she felt a rush of affection for him and gratitude that he had wrenched himself out of his bad humour and rescued the good opportunity for them both.

The climb steepened, Owen went ahead. Then the course of the stream, the dampness, its covering of trees, its softening and adornment by moss and pennywort and fern, gave out and they had an open space before them and lapwings flapping up raggedly into a blue sky. Late afternoon. Some distance off was a grey-white scar. It's there, he said. What it was, Lou did not ask. I was sixteen when I came here last, he said, on my own. I doubted I would find the place again. I thought the gap would be filled in years ago. His happiness touched her. And the lapwing still! That's a blessing, they are so diminished nowadays. How I love limestone!

Owen lived on the gritstone, which has its own character and beauties. And – as he had told Lou more than once – he was content that the limestone should be some way off, within walking distance but still a sensible journey. It was a zone he could set off for and come into, a country of rock that changed from almost black through grey to white under the fleeting weather. He loved the shallows of water on the green grass in the sunshine after rain; the vanishings of water, its passage and collecting underground, its distant reappearances. All that and more, he said. Much more. And not that I don't love where I live.

Lou had gone there once, to Owen's house on the gritstone, uninvited, or at least without warning him. He had often said to her, Call in if you're ever that way, so one day she did, not having heard from him for weeks and without pretending that she had any other business in his neighbourhood. See how he pulls you, Maya said. But then she added, Your voice is funny. Is it bad again? Yes, said Lou it is very bad again. I thought the walk might get me out of it. So she bought the necessary map, drove for a couple of hours, left the car ten miles off, and walked. She did not expect him to be at home and was not even sure, the closer she got, that she really hoped he would be. Mile by mile the walk had inspirited her lungs, her voice came up, she tested it by singing. The walking itself – the movement, the attention – was so beautifully effective she began to believe she did not need him to be the object of it and, almost arrived, she had half a mind to turn and retrace her steps.

The village surprised her. It was intricately built up one side, the south-facing, of a narrow valley, the houses were fitted along terraces and access from level to level was by steep alleys and steps. Having no hope of finding his house, she asked at the shop, which was down below by the bridge. The woman directed her, and two or three gossipers looked on and smiled. It occurred to her that she had no real idea how Owen lived, not even whether he lived alone; but lodged now in the talk of the village she felt she had no option but to see her journey through. Besides, she was tired. The directions were inadequate, two levels up she had to ask again. A man who had been watching her pointed out the house, and soon she stood there in the garden of it, entering by the back gate not the front, and saw him in the window at a plain table, writing. For perhaps half a minute Lou had the advantage and considered him. She saw again – she had seen it often – how when he concentrated he seemed to need nobody and nothing but what he had in mind. He seemed in a circle of his own, and she stood outside, viewing him through the glass, banished. But then, not enjoying her advantage, she made a small movement of her hand so that he looked up, saw her, and she saw him not just surprised but at a loss, bewildered, fearful, as though appearing suddenly in his garden in the sunlight she was a phenomenon against which he was quite defenceless. It shook her to see him like that, and deeply confused her feelings.

By the time he opened the door, Owen had composed himself. But she had seen him strangely and differently, he knew it, she could see it in his eyes still, anxious, curious what she might mean by her arrival. But he welcomed her in and, watching him closely, Lou judged his warmth to be sincere. They stood in the kitchen, which was clean and bright, everything purposeful and in order, no clutter, nothing lying around. In style the larger room, where she had watched him writing, was much the same. There were many books, but neatly shelved; a few pictures, but with space around them; a plain brick hearth, nicely proportioned, with a fire laid in. Lou realised that she had always supposed he would inhabit such a house. It fitted her idea of him: that he was self-possessed, needed nobody, had things to do in a house conducive to doing them. But perhaps he lived like this by an effort of the will, by concentrating, by not allowing himself to be distracted? If so, then his discomposure, his look almost of panic when he saw her in the garden, must be counted a lapse, which he would duly make up for.

But how courteous he was, how glad she had sought him out! She must stay the night, in the morning he would walk back to the car with her, they would have at least half the day together. Such a treat! Lou watched him, he encouraged her credence. There was one spare bedroom. He apologised that it had no view – except upwards, to the crest of the hillside, sky, passing clouds. His – he showed her – looked out over the valley, received the sun. There was a guitar in one corner; a small table in the window; bare walls, one line-drawing of a nude, a girl walking away; the bed. The room was like a bedsit, within the house, as though he could withdraw there, to a sparse place, and be content. So, she thought, he lives alone, the way a man will live who is purposeful and self-reliant. The word 'economy' occurred to her, not as meanness, not even as thrift, but sufficiency, the parts fitting and belonging, like the features of his face when he was attentive in a conversation or set on a purpose, like his clothes, his body, his quick decided walk. Why should he want her or anyone else? He gave her a clean towel and she went for a bath. After it, back in her room, she wondered whether to change or not, and did then, into the red dress that hardly crumpled in a rucksack.

Supper was cooking. Lou heard Owen on the telephone in the kitchen. He seemed to be making an arrangement. She stood by the hearth and looked at the two photographs that were the only things on the mantelpiece: two young women, one from many years ago, in a loose dress patterned with what might be jasmine; the other modern, in the same style of dress, doubtless from a charity shop. Owen came in. Have you had to re-arrange your evening because of me? she asked. Yes, he said, and I'm glad. I was supposed to be keeping watch tonight, but I've swapped my shift, I'll do it tomorrow. Keeping watch? The Lady's Slipper, he said. There's a patch not far from here, I'll show you in the morning if you like. The last, or the first, it depends. We have to guard them all day and at nights. People know and would come and dig them up. So you lie out under the moon and stars and keep watch? It's my job, he said. Sort of. Once it was ospreys, now it's the Lady's Slipper. I see, said Lou.

Then Owen said, Can you see any family resemblance? He nodded at the photographs. Yes I can, said Lou. The smile, their eyes. The two women, side by side, looked out hesitantly and confidently, as though fearful of their own appeal, at whoever would look at them. They are both very beautiful, Lou said. She could remember Maya in that look, too beautiful, nervous at the power of it. Yes, said Owen. They are both eighteen. That one's my mother sixty years ago. The other's my daughter twelve years ago. Lou looked closely, from the photographs to him and back again. Yes, she said, I do see the likeness. And where are they now? My mother is in Manchester, I see her once a fortnight. Natalie, I don't know where she is. I never see her. Never? I did three times in the year of that photograph. I stood outside her college and watched her go in. But never since. I was afraid she would notice. Nor could I bear it. And I promised, you see.

She's not allowed to know. I promised her mother. She thinks the man at home is her father. He thinks so too. I see, said Lou.

Owen gave her some wine. We don't know much, do we? About one another, I mean. We don't ask, said Lou. I would always tell you if you asked. But saying that she thought, I'm an entrance into nothingness so put your questions softly or the earth will open up. But you, she said. I always supposed you must be very deep and now you tell me there's a grown-up daughter in you, so I was right. Owen shrugged. Except she's not, he said. Her absence is. I like you in that dress.

That night Lou couldn't sleep. The house was friendly, all its small noises were kind, the village felt homely, she could hear a stream, finding down to the river below. All evening he had been gentle, they were easy with one another, their talk went to and fro quietly and clear. Everything was kind. But the sadness came back on her, sadness and terror. She saw the two young women, girls of eighteen, the mother, the daughter, hesitant but sure of themselves, fearful of their beauty but trusting it, looking out. And herself she saw whirling in panic through a hole in the years into loveless space. She lay in the neat white bed in the hospitable room and shook from head to toe, she writhed, she dug her nails into her palms. Then she said aloud, This is foolish, he is my friend, I am sure of that at least, he will not take it amiss. She got out of bed and viewed her ghost in the long mirror naked, white, thin, clutching its shoulders. And at that she slipped on the red dress and went in to him. He was asleep. She woke him. Owen, she said, let me be with you, please. I can't sleep, I'm shaking to bits again. Hush, he said. Hush now. What is it? Come in here, we'll sleep.

In the bare landscape, in the expectation of the particular place ahead of her, Lou's feelings rose and widened. Between the two simple planes of earth and sky she entered a happiness she imagined most people had enjoyed, and many could still go back to, in childhood. The ground delighted her, the rock so evident through its pelt of grass, the blood-red cranesbill, the tufts of thyme and many more such graces over the vast deposits of sea-lily stone. And the sky, as a child might paint it, white clouds pasturing on blue, larks dangling. There's something else you don't know about me, she said. Owen waited. I was in the Bach choir once. Prove it, he said. Stand there on that pulpit stone and sing. Lou stood, folded her hands like a penitent, looked up to heaven and sang:

> When I was a bachelor, I lived all alone,
> I worked at the weaver's trade
> And the only, only thing that I ever did wrong
> Was to love a fair young maid.
> I loved her in the wintertime
> And in the summer, too
> And the only, only thing that I ever did wrong
> Was to keep her from the foggy, foggy dew.
>
> One night she came to my bedside
> As I lay sound asleep.
> She laid her head upon my breast
> And she began to weep.
> She sighed, she cried, she damn near died,
> She cried, What shall I do?
> So I took her into bed and I covered up her head
> Just to keep her from the foggy foggy dew.

There she halted. Owen's look halted her. In the silence they heard the larks again, the irrepressible leaps and falls and leapings again of song. And something else, still faintly, ahead of them on the higher ground, they heard water.

They climbed. Soon the way levelled across a broad terrace where it was damper and there were orchids, tight magenta spires, and also the yellow bog myrtle; and this moistening, where the water sank, was the sign that they were getting closer to the place itself, the cave, where the water issued. Owen's few words ceased altogether. Lou paused to let him go ahead. He shrugged, made a little gesture of apology and helplessness. He was hauling back the years in broad daylight, even before they reached the cave the boy he had been was repossessing him. But Lou was not put out, she gathered her own happiness down from the sky and off the open country into this young course of water that they were climbing to the cave, its place of issue, that Owen had remembered and wanted her to know. She waved him ahead, content being in herself. The water babbled and sparkled, this was its phase of passage under the sun and moon, after the cave and before the yellow and verdant and magenta dampness, the sink. She followed Owen, who had more years in him, she watched his stepping up and up against the water hurrying down at him, higher and higher he stepped, to the cliff itself, over which the water leaped and offered itself as a rope, a silver ladder, for him and her to climb. She would always see it thus: the clear hank of living water let down over the scar for her to climb, to the phenomenon the man she loved remembered and had wanted her to see.

Owen stood up on the brink. From the last foothold, splashed by the toppling water, Lou got two good handholds, two good grips, each into wet clefts, her fingers feeling rock under the moss, and heaved herself up and through in one quick movement of pure ability and lightness. And there they stood, on a broad and stony and flowery ledge, the water sliding fast towards them, towards its fall, and nothing now ahead of them but the cave.

The cave stretched all across and came down at either end. Naturally, it resembled a mouth, but not one screaming, it was not open wide enough for that; but sighing, gasping, moaning, in pain or pleasure, yes, open that wide. The breaths coming out of it were cold. Even where she stood, on the brink with Owen, where the stream hurried over, Lou felt the cold breath of the cave. Doubtless it carried on the cold slide of water. She and Owen had that water between them, steadily fast, sliding between them to the edge, only a narrow divide they could have taken hands across. She turned from facing the cave to facing him, and saw that he was watching her very closely. They were high up, they might have relaxed side by side, looking back down the way they had come, all the way down to where the path went into the dark foliage and dived as a stream bed, dry or damp or flowing, steeply back into the river-level town. Instead, he stood staring at her, waiting, and Lou understood they had not yet arrived. The cave was astonishing in its spread, the water hurrying out of it was lucid and beautiful, the climb had been a joy; but still they were only on a threshold. Listen, he said. Then she listened to what she had been hearing, without knowing, for some minutes or perhaps for years: the sound of the cave, audible outside in the sunlight but coming from far, far in, from inside, in the immeasurable bulk of limestone behind and beyond the cave, from deep in there. That's what I heard when I came here on my own, he said. In a way I've been hearkening for it ever since. And I wanted you to hear it and myself to hear it again now with you. Then he reached across, handed her over the fast shallow stream, to his side, and led her in, under the quite abruptly down-sloping roof of the cave, in till they stooped, in till they crouched, and where they could go no further, in the angle of roof and floor, there at the slit, the flat aperture, where the water emerged, they made themselves small and sat.

Though you could hear nothing else, the water behind the slit was not deafening, not at all; its force lay in the certainty that its origins were remote. When you see a star, you know that its light has travelled years to your eyes. Similarly this noise, to their ears: from remote space and time. So the commotion they could hear was the long-after sound, carrying in it the remembered horror of the making. The water, that, far back, had been in there at the making, slid out in absolute silence, shallow, clear, very fast, and bubbles rode on it, clear domes travelled out of a zone of utter darkness into the cave-light on a sliding fast surface and very soon, silently, popped, and the air in them joined the air that Owen and Lou, bowed over them, watching intently, breathed.

In the way that human beings are bound to, Lou was thinking, What is this like? And ideas came to mind, rough gestures towards the thing itself: like a heart and a pulse, though not of any beast she knew; like an engine, the thrumming of a steady – but varied – working; like an oven, a furnace, if you could think of its cold as heat. But it was easier to compare this thing whose utterance was close and that was really of the earth, to phenomena she would never be anywhere near and was at liberty merely to imagine. The background noise of space, for example, the aural context of all the galactic debris still dispersing. So Lou spun ideas, as any human would, to try to say what the sound of the cave was like; but in the midst of her ideas, despite their interference, she knew with a thrill of horror, that what she was listening to, though nameless, was familiar. So reading a poem, often what dawns on you is a thing you knew already but had forgotten or didn't know well enough and now the lines with a vengeance will remind you and make you know it this time close and true.

Owen looked mesmerised, entranced, as though his first and remembered deep impression was deepening further now and more than he could bear. Lou touched his arm, and he started. She pointed towards the daylight at the mouth of the cave and after a little moment, which seemed not a reluctance but a coming to, he nodded and followed her. They went out to the brink and sat there looking over the open land, still sunny, down to where the little town must be.

What did you do when you came here last time, Lou asked, all those years ago? I ran away, said Owen. I wanted to sleep in the cave, I had ideas of that sort. But as soon as I lay down there was only that noise behind that slit. I couldn't bear it, so I decamped. Lou said nothing. After a while Owen said, I was going to ask what you would like to do. If we left now we could be back in town before dark and perhaps find a train or a bus. Is that what you want? Lou asked. If you were here on your own again, what would you do? I don't think I'd be here on my own, said Owen. But if I were, I think I should try to stay. Then we'll stay, said Lou.

Where they sat, the water toppling over made quite a loud and cheerful noise; but behind them, as they watched the shadow extending slowly over the open land towards their heights, the noise inside the cave became, if not louder, certainly more insistent. Why did you want to listen to it again? Lou asked. Because, Owen answered, I've often – and in some periods constantly – wanted to live as though I could always hear that cave. I don't want to live forgetting there's a noise like that. I mean, in some ways it isn't so very mysterious. Somewhere inside there must be a waterfall, quite a big one. Very beautiful no doubt, if things are beautiful that nobody can see. And what we can hear is the chute, the impact, the milling, the overflowing of water through tunnels till it finds that slit. All magnified, echoing, distorted. After heavy rain it would sound different. After no rain different again. But essentially the same, for all its variations, and always strange. Like the flight of the stuff of the universe: you might grasp the principle, but the act of it, the working out, is infinitely strange. But I can talk like this because we are sitting here together facing away and the sunlight will last a while longer. Up close, in the dark, when I was a boy I understood nothing at all, I heard the noise, only that. And it would be the same today, I guess, up close in there on my own. I thought we'd sleep in the mouth, said Lou, nearer the open air. I thought the same, said Owen. Still it will be cold and loud.

The shadow was climbing. They moved along to the far corner of the cave where, as you might say, upper lip and lower met. Owen dug out from his rucksack first a bag of food, then an old army blanket. This latter resource Lou smiled at. I've got something similar, she said. From Marks & Spencer's. Not so serious, but very handy. She produced it. We can lie on that and have yours over us. She went back to the stream, filled her water bottle, and returning saw, first, that he had also fished out a botttle of wine, and, secondly, that, above his head, under the coping of stone and fern and moss, a wren had gone in to nest. The smallness of the bird — she could almost feel its heartbeat — and the constant booming and droning from in the cave, the two together, brought a rush of tears to her eyes, and she knelt down by Owen in a state he could perhaps only guess at, to take the cup of wine.

They were still in the sun, but not for much longer. She watched him eyeing the shadow. She wanted him not to worry. I see it will be cold, she said. But it isn't now. So they ate and drank on the ledge, without haste. But then he was brisk, stood up, said they must get ready, and walked away, round that edge of the cave out of sight, she supposed to pee. She went round the other corner, taking her washbag, and met him back at the stream where it toppled over, and face to face across the water they cleaned their teeth. Very domestic, he said. Then back in their alcove he said she must put on everything she had with her, which she did, or almost. And when they were on her rug and under his blanket, lying on ferns and their heads on the rucksacks, and the wren chirred loudly against the steady engine of the cave, she said, Funny how I put on clothes to go to bed with you. Then she added, I'll tell you something, though my big sister told me I shouldn't. Why did she tell you you shouldn't? Owen asked. She said I'd be more in your power if you knew. I see, said Owen. Don't tell me then, if you believe what she says. But you're not in my power, I don't want that power. Whether or not, said Lou. It's nothing much, only silly. Before I come and see you, because I never know what we'll do, I always go and buy myself something pretty, just in case. Like your red dress? No, for underneath. I see, said Owen. But you don't, said Lou.

The thing is you don't. No, I never do, he said. Now, for example, said Lou, I'd freeze to death if you did. All the same, said Owen. What else does your sister say? She says I should ask you if you are serious. But you know that I'm serious. That's what I tell her, said Lou. I tell her you are *very* serious.

Night moved in quietly and very gradually. The evening let go its colours, their great variety, into the state of pallor into which the dark could seep. Stars flowered delicately on a fainter and fainter wash of blue and pink and green; then hardened, began to glint and pulse, on the risen tide of their own element, blackness. Under a house roof or under the street lamps you never see them coming into their energy. You have to be out, lying under them, aware of the thinness of the habitable skin of the earth, and the stars in a dome come crowding over you and the spaces between them fill with black infinity.

Sheltered from half the sky under their eave of rock, Owen and Lou had the cave behind them. They lay in the mouth of it as though in the bowl and under the lid of a half-open shell, and the din of the engines of water, as everything else was hushed, entered their consciousness through tunnels in the rock and tunnels in their ears, totally. Lou doubted whether thoughts and the unspeaking voice you employ within your head would be at all effective, as a self-assertion, against that constant pulse. She understood why the boy Owen had fled and wondered where out of earshot he had gone and shivered. Her face was cold but in his arms under the blanket in all her clothes the rest was warm. After a while she said, My sister says we never do anything ordinary. She says it's not grown-up to only do extraordinary things together. Your sister..., Owen began. Then he asked had she, Lou, ever been underground, really underground, in a deep cave, and put the lights out? Because if she hadn't, they could do that together one day, if she liked. He knew somebody who would take them down. I mean so you can see a true

54

darkness. Really underground with the lights out you can't see the hand in front of your face, put it as close and stare at it as hard and for as long as you will. Lou said no thank you, where they were now, together with the noise of it, was dark enough. Owen agreed. I thought I had to, he added, for my work. I was with someone who knew about the creatures that can live in dark like that. They are white and don't have any eyes. I thought I ought to see them so he took me down and showed me how they live. You and your work, said Lou. Yes, said Owen, and the reason I wanted to hear this cave again is so that I won't forget how much there is on earth we'll never see.

Lou wanted him to say that her being there with him was some consolation, at least, for what he couldn't see; but he stayed silent, the silence filled up with the noise and soon she said, You see a lot, you understand the way life hangs together. I hadn't thought much about the web of life till I met you. It's torn, he said, it's tearing worse and worse before my eyes, day and night, we mend what bits we can but it's all a rearguard fighting, little halts we make now and then that feel like victories, but the way is hurrying to ruin as everyone in the business, whichever side they're on, knows very well. His voice was level; a level sadness. And in the end what does it matter? That in there, that machine, will go on in some shape or form whatever we do. When the accident of our being here is cancelled out, what's left will start up again without us, by the old laws. Which is another reason for always being able to hear that noise. They are the mechanics that will survive us when by our doing – melting the ice, raising the seas, opening the deluges of the firmament – we have helped them wipe us out. And there we are.

Owen was a long time silent. They both were. The pulse of inhuman life in total darkness continued unperturbed. Lou began to be very fearful. Something more cavernous than he seemed to have any inkling of was opening up in her, as she had feared it would. But then in the same level voice against the cold breathing of the cave he said, And of course it's loveless. That's why I came to listen to it again. Beautiful it may be, intricate and powerful beyond our imagining – but loveless. It is sentient life that loves, in varying degrees, we humans most. Every creature fears and in various ways, many finer than ours, they know. But we love most and know most, the most connectedly. We know the damage, for example. So we can't watch ourselves, the accident, hurrying to ruin without grief. Going back by the old mechanics into the old chaos of fire and flood, is sad to watch. No other thing on earth feels sad like that because nothing else on earth can know and love the way we do.

Frightened by a gap in speech, because it filled up with the churning of the waters behind the cave, Lou asked Owen what he knew of his daughter. Nothing, he said. Her mother stopped writing to me twelve years ago. Really I don't even know whether she's alive or dead. Did you love Natalie's mother? Yes I did. And did she love you? She said she did. But she wouldn't leave and come away with you? She had one child already and she loved her husband. So you love your daughter and you never see her? Yes. And can you do anything for her? Her mother wouldn't let me. She said Natalie must never know. Not even when her mother and father and the man she thinks is her father are dead must she ever know. But those photographs on your mantelpiece? They're not there usually. I only put them out every now and then. And when you appeared so suddenly that day I left them there for you to see. No one else sees them.

Lou dwelled on Natalie, on her mother and on the man she called her father. She felt anxious for them, as though they had been entrusted into her thinking, and were vulnerable. They floated on a lie, the truth, falling from heaven, would sink them. Lou imagined them floating on the surface of the underground roaring in a bubble. And bubbles in hundreds meanwhile rode out through the slit on the cold rapid slide of water, lasting in the lighter darkness until they popped. And warm against the man, Lou must have slept and breathed with him a little of the air shipped out from inside in those hemispheres.

Some while later, sleeping very near the surface and the waters under the earth seeming louder and louder, Lou became aware that Owen was speaking, but to whom, if anybody, and whether in his sleep or waking she could not have said. The voice was close and rapid and even if she were indeed the one addressed, still it felt like eavesdropping. She could not unhear it, any more than she could unsee the sight of him through the garden window the day she suddenly appeared; the words and the sight accrued to her like a power she had not sought but could not disavow. Perhaps he had been speaking for some time and only now, surfacing through their broken sleep, could she hear and understand. I was very young, he said, and perhaps when she said she would keep the baby a secret, though I did love her, in some part of me I thought this lets me off, I can start again and live my life on my own and no harm done. I suppose a woman always knows how much she will love her baby but perhaps a man does not, even if it's a love-child, perhaps he can't imagine how he will love his child and be loved by her or him and be fastened in life-long. Or perhaps he can, said Lou. Perhaps he sees as well as the woman he slept with sees. And so you didn't insist very much when she said the best for all concerned would be you keep her secret and go away. We kept in touch, she wrote me letters once a year at least. And then soon after Natalie's eighteenth birthday came that photograph and a note she was starting art school in Newcastle on a certain day. I stood five mornings there, it was only on the third I saw her and on the fourth and fifth again. That last day was very bad. I saw her and it went through me. I thought will I ever see the girl again? I left the place, I was almost running down the street, away, and then I stopped and turned and walked very slowly back and there she was, coming out again through the big glass doors, with a look on her face as though she had forgotten or remembered something. And stood on the top step looking down at me, into my eyes, in a puzzled sort of shock. And when I think of it now there was nobody else around, only her and me, and the noise of the street or in my heart and head was like the noise in there, in the dark, behind that slit. After that her mother never wrote to me again and I kept my side of the bargain and never tried to learn about her further life. Funny to think of her, said Lou, going her ways in the world and you going yours and never crossing. If there was a god with nothing better to do he might have amused himself with your lines of life. Yes, said Owen, I read of a man who met his daughter abroad somewhere and fell in love with her and neither knew. They slept together on an island for a week or so and he begged her to marry him and it was only when she agreed and they went home that piece by piece the evidence of who they were came in. Is that what you're frightened of? Lou asked. You've seen her, you've got her photograph, it could never happen. Not like that, it couldn't, not like the man on the island, said Owen. Not in ignorance.

Lou pondered this; the cave too, so it seemed, mulled the business over, but indifferently, only as an engine, on and on. Like bubbles riding out on the fast cold water, the image of the girl looking down and the man looking up, both seeing deep into one another's eyes, became very clear to Lou and she said, perhaps aloud, perhaps already asleep and to a man asleep, Like falling in love, I suppose, there and then, the way it happens to some people, the lightning, so go your separate ways and trail the earth apart and you will never forget her nor she you. She slept in Owen's arms, the furnace of cold in the innermost heart of rock continuing to roar and to breathe little bubbles into the human world. Meanwhile outside, above, the stars pulsed on their black infinity.

Sleeping, Lou acknowledged more thoroughly than she would have cared to do in daylight that she and the noise in the dark behind the cave were old familiars. Owen had said he needed to hear it again, to be reminded that such undergound noise was there; but Lou, brought to the site by him, lay sleeping-listening to a thing she had known for years, and what appalled her now was how much deeper into it a soul might go. Suppose, she thought, or thoughts took hold of her and swirled her round and sent her out under the squeeze of rock as bubbles into the world where humans live, suppose it's all like that, only a mechanism and whether we live or not it will go on and on and whether he loves me or not is neither here nor there and I might as well be the water falling from a terrible height that he says must be beautiful, if something nobody sees can be called beautiful. Dread filled her up, the trembling took hold of her, deeply asleep she felt even closer to the noise, deeper down in it, staring to see and seeing nothing, eyes wide open and seeing not a thing but knowing that creatures were in there with her, white as death, white as the underbelly of a flat-fish, big, flat, fast and blind, their eyes over millions of years of useless effort having evolved away. Lou tried her best to answer back, she babbled all she knew by heart and many good new things occurring to her while she slept, she pitched them all in her small human voice against the never-to-be-exhausted fund of noise within the cave. Then failing, so she felt, defeated, she gave up making sentences and screamed, widened her eyes and screamed and screamed.

Hush, Owen said, hush now, nothing's amiss. It's only the noise. We're safe out here under our blanket, you and me. Feel my heart, she said. Whirring like a wren. Was it like that night in my house when you couldn't sleep? he asked. Worse, said Lou. Your lovely house, I could hear a little stream falling down to the river by the bridge where I asked the gossipy women how to find you. But in me nevertheless in your friendly house, to my shame, oh it was very bad. She was quiet, she listened to the noise, the churning, milling, steady mechanical cold breathing. Was I talking? she asked. Yes. Could you understand? The words, I could. What words?

What did I say? I'll tell you one night when we are quiet, if you want to know. Sleep now.

Sleep rose and fell in her, in levels and layers with the noise of the underground waters. Sometimes her sleep felt threadbare, and she shivered with cold; but in other passages, Owen wrapping her more tightly perhaps, she went deeper under, and found it not only warm but strangely tranquil too. Later, when she thought of this sleeping with him, these depths of warmth and tranquility seemed to her quite peculiarly blessed. Hopeful too, that she could sleep with him like that. And another thing: every time she surfaced and said a few fragments more on subjects troubling her, he answered at once, just where she would have wished him to, so that her feeling, later, was that he had been attentive all night long, not awake necessarily, but so tuned to her sleeping, its rise and fall, its shallows, depths, fretfulness and calm, that whenever she needed him listening and answering, there he was. She remembered very little of what in the latter part of the night they had exchanged in the way of words, but the sense of it all, of their embracing and sleeping and speaking while the vast heart of the back and beyond of the cave pulsed, throbbed, thudded and dispatched its flotillas of bubbles into their breathing space, the sense of all that, she would never forget.

The light crept up as delicately as it had faded. Lou became aware of it as a faint alteration on the lids of her eyes; she opened them, dozed again, opened them next on a hazy visibility. The wren churred loudly and flitted. Lou found that her right hand was gripping quite hard into the clothing over Owen's heart. And in a rush of happiness back came a memory of the strength of the grip of her fingers in the clefts of moss and rock when she hauled herself by the last body-length of the let-down hank of pure water in one light movement through and safely up.

She felt for Owen's cold face, the rasp of beard, and

further, for his eyes – first one then the other they fluttered at the centre of the palm of her right hand. He eased himself free, wrapped her more tightly, put on his boots and a hat, and left. The blanket alone was by no means enough. So much warmth in a man. Still she lay, watching and listening. Outside was lighter, but misty. Under the coping, the ferns were beaded. The breathing through the slit of the cave issued over her cold. And she exulted – to have kept warm, like a bird, like a small animal, to have slept on a ledge with the din of the underworld droning all night in her ears, her and the man, with his arms around her, warm enough together, surviving.

When Owen came back he appeared strange to her. He was bare-headed and his hair, shining with droplets of mist, had a grizzled look. But he was grinning like a boy. See here, he said, see what I've found. She sat up and peered into his proffered hat. Berries, like big blackberries, the drupels with a grey-purple bloom over them, like plums. Dewberries, he said. I hoped there might be some. He laid them by her, she took one very gently between three fingers and a thumb, examined it, its collected succulence. Dewberry, she said, and popped it into the warm room of her mouth. Meanwhile Owen dug out a small gaz from his bag and brewed a mug of black coffee. Boy scout, she said. Hunter-gatherer in the fog. She loved him when he couldn't help showing he was pleased with himself. After the small ceremony of breakfast, she asked him did he have a towel in that bag of his. He did, he produced it. Now go for a little walk while I see to myself.

First Lou went to the back of the cave where the clear water slid out with the bubbles. She made herself small, to get as close as possible, and listened. Listened hard. It was a pulse, a great heart beating and pulsing, it would live for ever. So the rock-earth respired, air riding on water came forth. Then she went out, taking her bag, to the brink where the water fell. She could see nothing ahead or below, only mist. But the mist, not so very high above her, was colouring faintly blue;

and above that, very distinctly, were larks. Quickly she undressed, ran off to the far corner, squatted like a beast, ran back to the water, stood in it, stooped and with copious freezing handfuls sluiced and washed herself. Stood towelling then on the brink, facing out. Nobody sees me, she thought. Like the chute in the dark in the cave. And here I am, fit to be looked at, and shivering for no other reason than that I am cold. Then she put on the underwear she had bought for their meeting, then her jeans, socks and boots. Next the red dress, and over that her sweater and fleece.

Owen came back. They packed. Owen, she said, can we walk all day now? Do we have to go back into the town? I don't really want to climb down the waterfall. Not that I couldn't, you understand, but it was so lovely climbing up. I was going to say, said Owen, that we can walk across to the gritstone from here, if you like, all the way back to my house, if you would like. I looked at the map while you were seeing to yourself. That is exactly what I would like, she said. And will it be warm? I'd say so, he said. In an hour or so. Good, said Lou, I want some sun. I know I look funny at the moment, bundled up. But things will improve as we go along, you'll see.

# Phantom Pain

Yes, she said, I'm the last. That's why it's only neighbours coming to fetch me, I've got no relatives, I'm the last.

Mother didn't seem to want to drink any more so I took the plastic beaker out of her right hand and set it down on the tray. The hand remained on the bedspread, the fingers still enclosing the space vacated by the beaker. I believe I noticed that. Then I forgot.

Your mother doesn't say much, does she, said the woman in the next bed. No, not now, I answered. She used to though. She used to be a great talker. Well she's a very nice lady, the talkative woman said. I can tell you that. She was sitting up straight on the bed, not in it, and watching down the corridor for the neighbours coming to take her home. I don't belong here, she said. I belong in Salford. I was on holiday, would you believe it.

I was holding my mother's left hand in my left hand and stroking it with my right. I was looking into her face and wishing she would look at me but she had her eyes on the corridor where there was the usual coming and going. At least she is paying attention, I said to myself, and her eyes look almost the same as they always did, very beautiful, but sunk in under the bone of the sockets now, sunk deep in, far back under the bony hood, and from back there still watching. And I was supposing that none of it made much sense to her, neither the WRVS trolley arriving with tea and snacks, nor the trolley with the prone white figure on, shoving away at speed.

Yes, said the Salford woman, you get a good view from here and it's a lovely day by the looks of it. The old volcanoes, the yellow gorse, a child could draw you little hills like that, the sky so blue. A few weeks ago there was a sort of mist of bluebells in a skirt or apron around each hill, a sort of vapour that became substantial, a substantial blue, the nearer you approached. There's a castle up there, I said. You see that tower? That belongs to it, the ruins are in the place between the hills. I know, said the woman, I came here once. I was going there again last week when I took bad.

I was impressed by the old woman in the next bed, sitting so upright and holding forth. She looked rather like a watch-tower still more or less intact, her face was big and broad with a bad complexion, quite ugly really, but you couldn't help admiring it. The two other women in the ward were fast asleep, sunk right down below the level of their bed-ends and invisible to me. Opposite the Salford woman the bed was empty. That was Mrs Williams, she said. Poor soul. So if the woman from Salford hadn't been so talkative we should have been very quiet in there, which I might have preferred, since my mother wasn't listening to her but looking at the comings and goings on the corridor. But I was listening, though I kept my eyes on my mother's face.

Yes, said the talkative woman, I'm eighty-seven and nobody left. My husband died seven years ago and he was the last. So there's only neighbours fetching me and I hope they remember to call at the B&B and collect my slacks or I'll have to leave here in my nightie with my bag of pills. You're well off for pills, I said, glancing her way. I am that, she said, and tipped them all out in her lap. These are for my thyroid, these are on account of my pacemaker... One by one she put them

back in the plastic bag, each with a little rattle. Some I don't
know what they're for. But they keep me going, I suppose.

I raised my left hand into my mother's line of vision. She
contemplated it. I wanted her to look at me and not be
watching what was going on by the nurses' desk and along
the corridor all the time. And her eyes did come my way,
looked into mine, and her look for a moment hesitated sadly.
Then she smiled.

You'll be her son, said the talkative woman. I can see the
likeness. Yes, I said, I am her son. And my wife will be along
in a minute. She's gone to buy some fruit. And was that your
brother and his wife come visiting yesterday? Yes, it was, I said.
That would be them. She knows who you are still, I suppose?
I disliked the woman from Salford when she asked me that. I
saw in her face that she thought the answer must be no. So,
Yes, I said, she knows who we are all right. And the day before
yesterday, was that your daughter and her husband and their
little boy? I can see the likeness now. Mother, son, his daughter
and her son. That would be them, I said. There's no mistaking
them. And I touched my mother's face so that she must look
at me and listen when I said: Sam was here on Saturday, wasn't
he? You remember Sam, don't you, mother? I felt the woman
from Salford watching us, to be proved right that my mother
did not know who we were. But her voice when she
interjected was a gentle thing, woman to woman or mother
to little girl, at any rate all kindness. He sang you a song, your
Sam did, didn't he? He sang her a song. Stood by the bed and
looked her in the eyes, she looked at him, she listened, she
watched him, there can be no doubt, he sang his song for her,
two verses, concentrating, and smiled, well pleased with
himself, when he was done. Enjoyed it, didn't you? the
woman from Salford said. I saw her face light up. Beyond any
shadow of a doubt. Her face lit up and she raised her hands,
to clap. Didn't he, mother? Didn't he stand over there on your

right side and look you full in the face and sing his song? She shook her head so very slightly I took the sign to be wonderment, not a negative. Wonderment. Wondering. Was it only she was wondering what on earth I meant? Or wondering was it truly as I said it was? And her hesitation, that wrings my heart, was that the passing over into the wonder of it, the wonder that he stood there by her bed and sang his song and earned her quiet applause? Again I vowed there would be no more interrogatives in my speaking with my mother, no more asking her could she remember it. From now on only the steady assertion: it happened, you were there. Fact upon fact, such a multitude I could tip out for you and fill your lap to overflowing, all our doings together on this earth, a multitude of stories and every one of them is true. Cupping your hands in mine, you will believe me. Slightly, very slightly, she shook her head.

Yes, said the woman from Salford still waiting for her neighbours to come and take her home, he was a lovely boy, your little visitor, six next birthday, so they told me when I asked. He reminded me of our Michael at that age, the same clear skin and his eyes were that same dark blue. Rising six, and all we had of him was the same small number of years again.

But at that moment, distracting me from what the talkative woman had begun to broach, my mother did a very strange thing. She had looked away again to the comings and goings on the corridor and I continued in my contemplation of her face, pleased by its attentiveness, saddened by its disregarding me, when suddenly all her attention lapsed, the will for it died in her, a small shudder passed through her or perhaps she shook herself very slightly as though to be rid of something, and the vacancy in her look filled up with sadness. I was about to speak, ignoring the Salford woman's broached remembrance, when my mother herself seemed to remember something. Again the small shudder. And very slowly she lifted her right hand, still shaped around the absent beaker, very slowly and carefully as though she must not spill what it contained, she raised the phantom glass to her lips. It was an exact reproduction, as a silent actor might have mimed it. Then her lips felt for the rim, her hand performed the necessary tilting, and only then, as though the liquid shocked her by its palpable absence, did she halt, startled, and seemed to wake and looked to me for an explanation and then shamefacedly she smiled.

Twice we went up there, the Salford woman continued. She was looking through the window at the two gorse hills between which, invisibly, the ruins of the castle stood. We came here for two holidays, you see. The first was after his little sister died, as soon as I was fit to travel again, my husband brought us on a holiday here, me and our Michael, the three of us, so we might begin to get over it, as he said. And the second was seven years after that, when we were as over it as we'd ever be, and we came again to the seaside here and for an outing one day climbed up again to where we had been before, between those hills. Michael was twelve then and a famous climber of rocks and other difficult places and no sooner were we in among the ruins and I was getting my breath back and getting the bit of a picnic out than Michael vanished and the next we saw of him he was up there on that hill, the near one, do you see, above the castle and far above our heads. And Father and I stood in the ruins underneath and he stood up there in the sunshine in his red shirt waving down to us and shouting, Mam! Dad! I can see them big mountains! And I was fearful and begged him to be careful and to find an easy way down and come and eat the picnic I had made. But I needn't have been fearful, he was as nimble as a monkey, and down he came in no time and hugged us, both of us, and said he'd climb all the Himalayas when he was a man. And seven days later he was dead, and it wasn't his climbing rocks and mountains I should have been fearful of.

I'm sorry, I said.

My mother's hands were lying together on the bed disconsolately. They had fallen open like a broken bowl and she was looking down at them as though they were a mystery to her. As though, if they were hers, she had no idea on earth what she might have done with them.

And now I'm the last, said the woman waiting to be taken home, and soon I'll be done with thinking about it or trying not to think about it. Our Elaine was bad, I thought she would break my heart, but she didn't, because we still had Michael, I suppose, and when we didn't have him to love for both of them then it was worse and worse. And my only comfort since it happened has been that nothing worse could ever happen. Because twelve years is a lot of life to remember, there's a deal of a lot of things will keep coming back to you as sharp as needles when you've got twelve years of a life to keep on mulling over. That picnic for one thing, up there in the ruins between them little hills, you might spend a day over that, remembering and thinking. I used to wonder how a thing that wasn't there could hurt so much.

I'm very sorry, I said.

I mean the things he did but also the things he never did but might have done. With our Elaine, of course, there was nothing to go on, she never began, but Michael was already taking shape. He'd have been as old as you are now, I guess, you won't mind me saying so, and who knows what he might have done with the years, one friend of his became a doctor and another's an inspector in the police. I could stop myself dead on the street only suddenly thinking what he might have been. A famous mountaineer at the very least.

Then my wife arrived. She came in with the neighbours who would take the Salford woman home. No, they hadn't collected her slacks from the B&B, she would have to go out in her nightie with her stick and her pills. But you see worse sights than that in the sunshine nowadays. They sat, one either side her bed, all nattering. The man said he fancied a stroll along the prom.

My wife had brought some raspberries, which she washed at the sink. Mother seemed to have forgotten her hands, she was watching my wife at the tap under the window, for her coming back. I went and borrowed a saucer from the WRVS and we put a good few rasperries in it and laid them down like that, in a soft mound, on the resting place of my mother's open hands. And from there we fed her and ourselves. They were wonderfully sharp, an acute sweetness. Her mouth received them at intervals, one by one, and between-times I suppose she forgot what the taste was like. So she smiled and widened her eyes whenever it came again.

I set the empty saucer on the tray and took my mother's empty hands in mine. Listen, I said. At home the raspberries were behind the rustic where the roses grew. You gave us a bowl and sent us to pick them for an afters when Dad came home for tea. The bowl was an ordinary white one that you used for baking. I remember pulling them off the stalk with three closed fingers and the thumb, I remember the feel of that, and how white the little stub was when the raspberry came off. We ate a lot, of course. We looked into the heart first to see if any grubs were there, and on the outside for any greenfly. And if they were clean we put them in the bowl, or ate them, as we liked. Little brother can't remember, I have asked him, but I was old enough to remember and I do.

69

Because that day I'm thinking of I squashed some raspberries in the palm of my left hand and with this finger on my right hand I painted a line across his throat from ear to ear, as though it had been slit. Quite realistic, so it seemed to me. And then I slobbered his face and my own hands with juice and told him to lie across my lap and act like he was murdered. You and Dad were on the lawn by now, on the other side of the rustic, I could see you through the roses. He had just come home, he had his arm around your shoulders, and you were looking our way into the raspberries, smiling and any minute you'd be sure to come and find us. I remember that best of all, being on the very point of being found by you and what a fright you'd have and when you saw it was all a joke how you would laugh. It gave me a funny feeling between my legs.

The talk around the Salford woman's bed had stopped.

Then you and Dad came close and I stood up red-handed with my little brother in my arms all slobbered with raspberry blood and with his eyes shut tight like he was dead.

That's how it was, I said, on that occasion, mother. And the look of you went through me like a spear.

You say so, she replied. So I believe you.

# Wishing Well

Happiness. Some lines came back to him: 'What are we? Beings of a day/ Shadows of a dream. But when/ The light, god-given, the light/ When that comes/ Brightness is on us, brightness/ And life is lovely.' And so it was: light coming, alighting, playing over all, but over the two of them in particular, like tongues. Wellbeing – in which he was aware of the passing away of trouble and tension, so that although light had indeed come over him, it was also like passing out of a sunlight that had been too brilliant into a grateful shade and suddenly feeling, under a dappling coverlet of leaves, a release and a relief, so that the features knew, with a shock, how tense and strained they had been and for too long. Lightness of spirit.

He looked about him. Rhos in summer is a busy place, busy and ordinary, and everything he looked at pleased him, especially the little harbour which had not made any effort to keep up with the world. He liked that. And that they were strangers here and he could sit with her at a table in the public view and take her hand when he pleased and they could stroll along.

She watched his enjoyment. He was quite transparent. She saw quite clearly what it felt like in him as his feelings climbed and held and he looked about him, pleased. He saw her watching. He knew that her own enjoyment at that moment consisted mostly in being amused by the sight of him. But he was not downcast and felt he could carry her away with him on his feelings, just as soon as he wished.

There's a lot you don't know about me, she said.

He was grateful for this topic into which he could direct his happiness. He answered that he was glad, they were at the beginning, it was an outset, he loved outsets, he would learn and learn and the more there still was to know about her, the better.

When I fell in love with you, she said, it grieved me that there were so many years of your life before my time, that I could never belong to and I could only learn about if I asked you and you told me.

Telling is good, he said. For both of us. When I tell you things you didn't know, I feel I hardly knew them myself before I told you. It's as though they are only becoming clear to me now, in the light of you.

And then – because of course this was at the heart of his happiness, this was lighting up the ordinary seaside town, lightening his spirits, relaxing the strain that for so long had tensed his features – then he couldn't hold back and he said: And after tonight, after we've slept together, it won't grieve you any more, once we know each other like that the rest won't trouble you, you'll see it the way I see it now, life for the asking, more and more, nowhere refused.

She looked at him wonderingly. Such innocence. He seemed to walk on faith without fear of disappointment. The very spectacle of him made her fearful. How was any mortal supposed to live up to a part in that? Then she thought him not innocent but, for all his intelligence, obtuse; and beginning to say, I hope you won't be disappointed, she felt almost a wish that he should be, that he should grow up, and she halted the sentence, shaking her head. And perhaps he was right. Certainly she had no more worries about the place. The place they had decided on was certainly right, she was on firm ground where she had feared she might sink in. That was one good stepping stone, she would believe him, the other stones would be there, step by step.

She stood up. I'll go and pay, she said. When she came out again she saw a hesitancy in his manner, as though in the brief absence her lingering anxiety had touched him. She took him by the hand. The well, she said. I have to show you the well. I have to begin showing you and telling you. Today's the day and tonight is the night.

Coming back is risky. He was glad to be a stranger there, with no memories. Soon she let go of his hand and walked apart, wholly given up to an anxious looking. This wasn't here then, she muttered. The sea came right in. To him the wall, the railing, the further defences were unexceptionable. But she said crossly, as though he were to blame, It was a shore, the sea came right up. There were floods, he said. You told me about them. They had to build a wall. Yes, yes, she said, they had to. Don't they always have to?

They had walked too far. She was wringing her hands, almost in tears. Don't say it's gone. Nobody would do a thing like that. Chapel and well. Nobody would raze a chapel and fill in a well. She turned and walked back, hurrying away from him. It's here, he said. He had to shout after her. She had hurried on. How lovely. He was leaning over the railing, looking down. The tiny humped chapel, squat and solid, crouched under the wall, out of sight of the road, like a shell, like something that would have housed a naked hermit-crab. Between it and high tide ran a bulwark of quarry stones.

But it was on the beach, she said. Just above high water. Not protected at all. Why does everything have to be protected? Once or twice the sea came in. I know that. And my father told me he had read of other occasions. Seaweed on the flagstones, salt water on the fresh under the altar. But they cleaned it out. The sea went away again. The freshwater well renewed itself. Stink of salt and weed in that thick shell for months. Like being in a sea-cave. But it freshened again, the sun came in, a breeze, people brought wild flowers. Why put a wall around it? He shrugged. Things are getting worse, he said. You know that. The floods further up the coast were terrible.

Slowly she was reconciled. She took his hand again.

Come and see, she said, come down. I'm so happy that we are here together and I can show you the well.

*Temenos*, a little precinct – which he liked. She clung to her picture of a sacred house on the beach, just above high water, but conceded that the enclosure was decent. Inside, the memory took her by the throat, seized her around the heart with a hand of ice, the hairs on her neck stood up 'in holy dread'. One window by the altar, another in the north wall broadside on to the sea, a saint in each. An utter simplicity. It was a cave, a shell, the carapace of a spirit, furnished humanly with a table and a few chairs, not asking to be thought beautiful. The thick walls, rough as the hands that had fitted them, enclosed a presence of – of what, exactly? Human impress, people at their most serious, their most given up and most wishful. She went on her knees and pulled him down by her, not at the altar – which she disregarded – but at the well beneath the stone roof that the altar made. A square of clear water, as though a flagstone had been removed and there was the water, quietly arrived and waiting. She dipped in her hands, raised them up to his mouth. Drink, she said, drink and wish hard. He did as she asked, all the water, he lapped at her wet palms, drank and loved her and wished hard, looking into her eyes over the bowl of her hands. He had never seen her so sure and demanding. Now me, she said. Offer me. So he did, raised up some water in his cupped hands to her mouth. She drank, wished hard, looked him hard in the eyes.

Then she stood up, as abruptly as she had from their café table, and took him to the window that looked out towards the sea. The window was thin and the saint himself, in the coloured glass, rather blocked the view. But it was not so much a matter of looking and seeing, more of listening, of her murmuring and his listening.

We played down there, she said. You and your friend? What was she called, your friend? She was called Awen. A name like yours, he said. We were very like, she said. We came after school when the evenings were long and at weekends summer and winter when we chose. Nobody minded in those days. She was from here, I was an incomer, but I learned her language at school and together we never spoke anything else. Except we had our own speech too. Speech within a speech, foreign and secret. We used that sometimes, for the things which mattered most. When we found anything especially pretty we brought it in here, splashed it from the well, and laid it on the altar. A flower you mean? Or a shell? A shell, a flower, a starfish, a bit of whitened wood, anything pretty or especially strange. We wetted it and laid it on the altar under that saint's window. Nobody minded in those days. And if we found any creature that had died we brought that in too, splashed it and buried it outside, close under the western wall, and made a little mound of stones. An oiled-up seagull, a fish, even a crab or a rat, anything that had lived the way humans live and was dead. We looked out for such things as keenly as for pretty things fit to go on the table top. And always we drank, lifting our hands to one another, just as you and I have done now. And every time we drank we looked each other in the eyes and made a wish. There's a lot you don't know about me, and one thing is this: that I am afraid my friend Awen is dying. Do you have a pen? Do you have a scrap of paper? I didn't think I would do this but now I feel I must.

He carried a pencil. It fitted into the spine of a handy blue notebook. He tore out a page, handed her the pencil, she used the altar as a desk and wrote: Please wish for my dear friend Awen who is very ill. She folded the note and slotted it in among others in a sort of lattice on the south wall.

Now come out, she said. I want to show you the sea properly, not through a narrow window. But as soon as they were they out and had climbed over the rampart of new rocks and had broached the empty sands, she halted, turned to him and alarmed him by her helpless agitation. What is it? he asked. Oh, I should have written it in Welsh, she answered. But more people will understand it in English. But it's closer to her in Welsh. And it may work better. Do it then. And he handed her the notebook with the pencil fitted in. Can I even? Do I even know the words any more? Try. She closed her eyes, faced him, waited. Then said in a rush: Gwnewch ddymuniad i Awen wella – mae hi'n sâl iawn. Good, he said. Now go back and write it.

It seemed he waited quite some time. When she came out of the chapel she was barefoot, carrying her shoes. So he took his off also, stuffed the socks into them, laced them together, watched her cross the rocks. Your notebook is full of things, she said. So much I don't know. Then she took his hand and led him – so it felt – out where the sea must be.

I came out here with my father once, she said, with Awen, he walked between us, holding our hands. He didn't speak Welsh, though he knew many of the words because of his studies in local history. It was strange to be with Awen speaking English. My father asked her questions. I could tell that he liked the way she talked. She was very pretty. You would have liked her too. My father had read that before they built the chapel on the beach they built one out on the flats in what was then a forest. He asked Awen was it true. She said she believed it was. My father wanted to see evidence of the forest, if not of the chapel, and on that afternoon when, according to his chart, the tides were exceptionally big, he took us out, the two of us, to have a look. We walked and walked, like now, the sea was quite invisible. We were the only people out. I don't think he should have taken us there, do you? But he consulted his watch very often and kept an eye on the horizon, where the sea must be. And at last we did come to the forest, the stumps and traces of it, a sort of herd, emergent or disappearing, over a vast area of sand, as I remember now. We shan't go so far today. I'm not sure of the tide. But another day when the tides are very big we'll work it out exactly and I'll take you to where you can see the stumps of that great forest, if they are still to be seen. The sand moves, you know. It covers and uncovers. But the tide comes in very fast. Faster than a man can run, so my father said. He told us that out there in that vast graveyard of a forest. I don't think he should have told us that, do you? He told Awen particularly. I didn't like him doing that. So if there really was a forest, he said, perhaps there really was a chapel too, with its own well, of course, like the one on the beach. But we'd never find it, he said, not in a hundred years and we looked every day. Stones under the sand, a mouth of fresh water stopped up under the sand. My father! There was still no sign of the sea. You could almost believe it had withdrawn for good. But my father said we must go home. By his calculations we were still entirely safe, but we must go back in and not linger.

When we turned, then I was frightened. The shore looked to be infinitely far away. I couldn't make out the chapel at all. The distance looked to be quite beyond my strength. But Awen seemed unconcerned. She laughed and looked up at my father and he held her hand very tightly and said nothing to worry about we'd be safe home in no time. My hand he held tightly too, but I felt he hadn't even noticed how frightened I was because he and Awen were being so jolly together. We were the only people out there, the only upright things in all that flat space. You'd think with your own father if he said nothing to worry about, you'd believe him, wouldn't you? But I kept looking back, to see if the sea was coming after us, faster than a man could run.

My father said the chapel out here was the first building and the chapel on the beach just above high water was the second. And the third, he said, was a proper church, at Llandrillo, about a mile inland, on a rocky hill, quite safe from the sea. I knew about that church already. Awen had told me. And I knew something else as well, that she had told me. And suddenly out here on the sands, in English, she told my father the thing I thought was a secret between her and me: that a tunnel went from the church on the hill to the chapel on the beach, an escape way to Ireland, when the old believers were in danger from the new. I heard her tell him that in English when I had kept it secret even though he was my own father and I knew how much it would have interested him. And indeed he was very interested. He stopped dead in his tracks out here on the sands and said, Goodness me, what a thing! We must find it, this tunnel, you must take me and show me where you think it is. We have found the forest together, and we believe there was once a chapel in that forest, and now you tell me there's a secret tunnel from the chapel on the beach to the church on the hill, so certainly we must go and find that together. I was hurt by Awen. Across him, I said to her in Welsh, You shouldn't have told him that. It was our secret. Why did you tell him that? But all she answered was, Will if I like. And we set off again, him between us, and I couldn't get over it and hoped the sea would come at a lick and drown us all.

Then there was worse. Much worse. My father was very interested in wells and had visited a number of them along the coast and inland. It's true this area is especially rich in wells. Wishing wells, he said, I'm a great lover of wishing wells. And then Awen said, Wishing wells are one thing. But I know a cursing well. That was the worst. Never in my life, before or since, have I hated anyone as much as I hated my friend Awen when she said in English to my father that she knew a cursing well. The tunnel was one secret. We hadn't been able to find any likely flagstone in the floor of the chapel, nor any suggestion of an entrance behind its south wall above high water, but we were planning to make a thorough search at Llandrillo, both in the church itself and in the graveyard around. We had hidden torches and a special notebook up there ready, in a grave whose lid was loose, under an elder bush at the bottom of the slope. When she told my father, all the fun went out of that. But the well, the cursing well, was the secret of secrets. We only ever spoke of it in our tongue within the tongue, our speech that nobody on the planet understood but us. And there she was, in broad daylight, in everyday English, ready to tell my father what she knew. Don't tell him, I said, in the secret tongue. Even in Welsh he would not have understood, but I said it in the secret tongue, to impress on her the seriousness of the matter. But she smiled me a bad smile and grinned up at him and answered me in English just the two words: Why not? The well was on her farm, she told him, at Llanelian-yn-Rhos, under hazels, holly and alders, where the stream started, at the bottom of the steep field, and it was the most famous cursing well in Wales, or had been until the Bishop forbade it and smashed the lovely stone bowl of it a hundred years ago. Now hardly anyone knew of that well and nobody who came looking on his own would ever find it, it was on private land, her land, and hidden away, but she would show him, my father, whenever he liked, since he was so interested in wells.

She stopped. We've come out too far, she said. We must go back in. I don't know about the tides. I believe we are nearly out where the forest was. The sea is so fast when it turns and starts to come in. He was not so bothered, not about the sea. Did he not believe that tideflow came faster than a man could run? Perhaps he did, but he was sunk in her, how travailed she was, how girlish and much older than a girl, how it was welling up in her through the deposits of the years, through her eyes and through her mouth. He was beginning to see what love would be like, with her. So he stood, looking neither out to where the sea must arrive from, nor in towards the chapel where they must return, but only at her, at her face, at her standing disconsolate on the flat infinity of wet sand, holding her sandals, wide-eyed and as if in shadow in all the sunlight. I'm frightened, she said. I'm frightened out here. I'm all alone, you know. Some days it's like a black cloud around me, head and shoulders. You are going to have to look after me. Come in now, let's go and find the place where we will stay tonight. There's more, you know, about the cursing well. Above it the air is peculiarly healthful, they say, because the airs that come in off the sea meet there with those that live over the land. And there's more about what we did at the cursing well together, Awen and I, raising the water to one another's lips, the way you and I did at the wishing well. Much more. And what I did there and said there and wished there on my own one day, on her private land, unbeknown to her, in that deep hollow out of sight. There's a lot you don't know about me. Come back with me now quickly. There are things I can't say in the daylight, but I will say them in the dark when we have slept together.

# Witness

The school itself had belonged to an industrialist. It was his home. He moved smartly west before the Russians arrived and died many years later in the bosom of his family, before the bad things about him became known. His children and their children had a harder time. The eldest son very determinedly, through much hostile bureaucracy, went back to see the house he had spent his childhood in, and saw it full of schoolchildren, Grete being one of them perhaps. Had he come back a few years later he would have found the place empty, he might have gone from room to room, tried to put himself together. The school had moved, under a new dispensation.

Before passing to the industrialist the big house had been in one family for nearly a hundred years. They were well liked locally, in a respectful sort of way. Their land near the city, most of it forest, was a remnant of the many thousands of acres that, until 1919, they had held in Mecklenburg. They lost that remnant, the house and the forest, in the mid-1930s, to the industrialist, whose interests coincided with the Party's.

When Sam and Grete met – end of May 1990, on the terrace at Stratford, during the interval of *Richard III* – they did not begin with that history. Grete liked the look of him (he was staring into the river) and came over to ask, in very clear English, could he explain to her where Gloucester had come from, so to speak, in the dynastic struggle. She knew Brecht's version, of course, but had only once read Shakespeare's, in

German, years ago, too early. And she added that she could not afford a programme. Sam did his best. She thanked him; and said in a matter-of-fact voice that she had sat all afternoon by the Avon and not since she was a little girl had she been so happy. They met up afterwards and continued talking. He was at university in Manchester but had friends he could stay with in Warwick, she had a B&B in Stratford. In the event, they ignored these possibilities and wandered around till very late, then hid behind the church and dozed there chastely. By then he had confessed that he was writing a Ph.D. on forced labour under the Nazis. But all of the East interested him greatly, he said. And how people managed under one regime or another. So here I am, she said: the word made flesh. And she added, My mother was a Christian, it was her way of answering back. My father's was Esperanto. I see, he said. But you mustn't like me just for things like that, she said. I don't, he answered. I won't. He liked her for her intensity and candour. His eyes had never looked into eyes as darkly bright as hers. Her thin body felt concentrated keenly on a purpose.

At first when they slept together they scarcely slept at all. The occasions were rare and their hunger for the pleasures of one another felt insatiable. But almost as keen was their hunger to talk. West and East they were new-found-land. And when she worried – or pretended to worry – that he loved her because she was living history, he answered that he was too, whether she cared for that in him or no, he was citizen of a land of failure, betrayal and numerous enslavements. She agreed, but countered that in her land the betrayals, failures and oppression had been worse, far worse; and that its future looked only differently unpromising. Their own future, on the other hand, looked boundless and abundant.

On Grete's second visit to Manchester Sam promised her better accommodation for the few days, in his new bedsit. But when they came back from the airport together, the place had been burgled, burgled and trashed. He stood with her in the wreckage. The wreckers had ignored the stereo, worth very little, but had cleaned out the CDs – jazz, blues, world music, much it would be hard to find again, for years the gaps would strike him with a little recurrence of grief. His books and papers were all over the floor. They had come in through the window, stepping down on to his desk. The page he had written last – on Russians worked to death by I.G. Farben – had a bootprint on it, large and very dirty. I ought to frame that, Sam said. Frame it and put it on the wall. It might keep me real. But the worst was when he turned to the bed. He saw Grete's framed photograph flung down there. The thought that they had touched it made him sick. Then he saw that they had stolen her gift to him, a little Chinese good-luck charm, an old man in wood with a fish slung over his shoulder, they had taken it from the bedside table. Grete had not seen a man so hurt, not since her father had stood before her finally and admitted that her mother was dead. Remembering that occasion, feeling the difference in degrees of loss, she was kind to Sam, but brisk. You don't need a charm, she said. Whoever did this does. And I'll find you another one. And as for the music, did you not promise me we'd travel the world?

Instead of going to bed, they cleaned up together thoroughly, he fixed the broken window lock, and soon, but for the losses, there was no sign of any violation. Then they went out, to see more of the city. He showed her the room in Chetham's Library, where Engels had worked, by the foul river. Then the place of the Peterloo Massacre. After that they crossed the river into Salford, where his family were from. They got bombed out, he said. The planes came up the canal and the railway line. In all that area only one named street remained, all the rest had gone, long since gone, in the clearances, under the Thatcher new enterprises, themselves now already derelict. Grete and Sam walked in the sun, talking, talking. The vanished past was itself a territory, they felt rich, in a free exchange.

That night, speaking softly in German, Grete told Sam about her school, the big house that had belonged to one of Hitler's industrialists and before him to a landowner from Mecklenburg. And that when the weather was kind her mother would sometimes be waiting for her after school and they would walk away together into the forest for an hour or so. Her mother carried a picnic in a wicker basket, under a blue or red check cloth. It might be apples or small sweet plums in the season, and always a slice of cake, lemon or chocolate, just made, and a drink in a special bottle. They walked through the forest to a clearing, in which there was a house, quite a substantial house, all of wood, and empty. And they sat on the wooden steps of the verandah, and had their picnic. The removal of the check cloth, the laying of it down, the setting of the things upon it, all was performed in silence. Then they might talk, but never very much. There was birdsong, there were fiery-black squirrels, now and then a deer. But Grete particularly remembered the stillness, nobody else ever came. Once she asked her mother why the house was empty. Who had it belonged to? But her mother shook her head, to mean that she did not know, or did not want to be asked. After a gap of years, after the death of her mother, Grete went back there on her own. She had trouble finding the place. The clearing was scarcely a clearing any more. The house had been broken into and had begun to tumble down. Grete turned and walked very definitely away. Then she asked her father who the house had belonged to. He was evasive, but she insisted. Altogether, after the death of her mother, Grete *insisted*. Jews, he said at last. They lived there, or went and hid there. They thought they might live out the bad years, I daresay. But somebody told the Gestapo. Or so I was told when I was growing up.

Soon after this admission by Grete's father, the forest itself began to disappear. Mile after mile it was felled and transported. Then the scraping for brown coal began. The house in the clearing went away with the topsoil. Where did the birds and animals go? And the stillness over the picnics in the clearing? Mile after mile, deeper and deeper, the mining pushed. It came within earshot of the school. Soon there was only a poor cordon of forest between the children and the excavation. They could hear the machines. They became accustomed to the noise as dwellers by the surf cease hearing even that. Instead of the forest where I walked with my mother, there was a hole, said Grete softly in the dark. The biggest and ugliest hole in the world, spreading from my schooldays, further and further, deeper and deeper down. And still? Sam asked. Of course still. Except there's no work now, only wreckage in the hole.

At the end of the year Sam went to visit Grete in Leipzig. He arrived by train from Berlin. The station amazed him, so vast, dirty, purposeful, bustling, the travellers, the arrivals and departures, all the business seeming filmed in a hurried black and white. Don't get to love it, said Grete. Next time you come it will be a shopping mall. But there'll still be trains? A shopping mall, with trains offstage somewhere. Sam told her about Berlin. He had walked the corridor of trees and ruins along the broken wall. There were still rabbits in the Potsdamer Platz. Rabbits and gypsies. And in the middle of it all he saw a man painting the ironwork of the old U-Bahn exit. The exit reminded the world of tunnels that still existed. There in the very middle of a savage park, the reminder! Like a spring, surviving, about to be unstopped. Nice way to think about it, said Grete. But also they've found the old Gestapo cellars, Sam continued. There's a sort of archaeological dig going on. It was a torture place. People can visit. I didn't. I wanted to see the decades of ruins and trees, before they vanish.

Grete loved her city and wanted to show him. They walked miles across it and rode its trams to and fro in brilliant cold sunlight. Water and forest ran through the heart of it, such a healthful vein, surviving, indeed growing in strength. She took him to the Nikolaikirche, where she had stood in the crowds every Monday, all leaning their quiet force against the untenable state. And the broad boulevard, the inner ring, where they had processed in thousands under the Stasi windows and in the end, growing bolder, stormed the place, believing it defended, expecting violence, finding it abandoned. When Grete recounted these things Sam stared like a child at her. And he thought again: The creature hath a purpose, its eyes are bright with it. He asked was her father ever with her on these big occasions. In spirit he was. I'm with you in spirit, he would say to me, she answered. He was working. He is an anxious man. My mother would have been there in the spirit and in the flesh, at the Nikolaikirche week after week and in the Stasi corridors. So I was there for her as well as for me, in the body and in spirit.

Grete's father still lived in the family flat. One Sunday she and Sam crossed town from her student bedsit, to visit him and stay the night. He was indeed an anxious man. The *Wende* had thrown him out of work at once. He was in his fifties and looked to have little chance. But he re-trained, working almost maniacally at it, and got a job programming and fixing computers with a firm in Munich. Every Sunday afternoon he set off down the motorways; spent the week in a hostel with men half his age. Sam liked him. He put his heels together and bowed when they shook hands, almost giggling with nervousness. My English is very poor, he said. But your German is very good. Then he said something that made both the children blush. You and Grete, he said. It is the coming of the brotherhood of man. He said the sentence first in German, then in Esperanto: Vi kaj Grete, vi estas la alveno de la kongregacio de la homaro! Grete will have told you about my Esperanto. It was my dissidence. And he smiled a little smile that on a less anxious face would have looked like smugness. Sam said it was strange – then he corrected himself – it was *sad* that a regime professing fraternity should have been so unfriendly towards Esperanto. Indeed, said Grete's father. They spied on us. They spied on everyone, said Grete.

Where two or three are gathered together in my name, there shall the Stasi be in the midst of them. So my mother said. Her father excused himself. He must get ready for his drive to Munich.

That night Sam said, Your father is a lovable man. You think so? said Grete. Really, you think so? Of course I think so. For a while she was silent in the dark. Then she said, I don't like him driving so far every week. And to the young men he works with he must seem very strange and stand-offish. He has nothing in common with them. Then she laughed. We are the coming of the brotherhood of man, you and I, Sam. So we are, said Sam. The coming of the sister- and brotherhood of humans beneath the visiting moon. Then she told him another thing about her mother. There's such a lot still to tell you. She worked in the community creche. There was one black baby. All the years there was only one black baby. He was the son of a pair of students from Mozambique, about the only place in Africa we were allowed to have fraternal dealings with. But his mother and father disappeared. Perhaps they went back to Africa, perhaps they went West. So my mother looked after him. In the end she brought him home, he was my little foster-brother. He was called Tobias, or my mother called him that. And when she pushed him in the pram through our neighbourhood the neighbours looked away, they would not speak to her. Except that once a man came close and spat into the pram. I was there. My mother slapped his face. There on the public street she slapped that big man's face.

Grete had no idea that her mother might die. On the morning in question she said goodbye to her as usual but came home from school to an empty house. When her father appeared after an hour or so, with Tobias, who had been left at the police station, he said it was nothing to worry about, she had to spend a night in hospital, she would be home next day, or they would all go and visit her. In fact she had died in the ambulance. It was years before Grete could forgive her father his evasion. He said she would understand it one day.

Sam was silent in the dark, thinking of that. Perhaps he slept. But then, perhaps after a while, perhaps in no time at all, he felt Grete clinging to him very tightly and heard her say, Sam, you do love me, don't you? I'll never get a job here. I'll come to England and train as a teacher and we'll live together. You do want that, don't you? He assured her that he did. Good, she said. Good. Because I have heard of something and I want to go and see is it true or not. There's only you in the world I'd go and see it with. I'd have gone with my mother if she hadn't died and I hadn't met you. But she's dead and I love you so tomorrow we'll go and see whether this thing that sounds unbelievable is true or not. I think it will be true if we go and look together.

Next morning Grete took Sam first to her old school. It was playtime, the children were running and yelling around the yard like enchanted animals. They're the last year, Grete said, the place shuts next summer. Then she led him the way she had walked with her mother, from the school gates into what was left of the forest. They could see the light ahead where the trees gave out. They passed a square settlement of low huts and houses, some derelict, others quite cheerful with gnomes and geraniums. Tobias lived out here for a while, said Grete. To think, he said. It was a satellite of Sachsenhausen, said Sam. Foreign women, communists mainly. They worked for the industrialist who owned your school. You find things out, said Grete. Then the trees finished and they saw the wasteland. Grete had described it more than once, but the reality, even to her, was a shock.

The hole was terraced along the contours, further and further, deeper and deeper, year after year. It, and the air around it and above it, had filled with silence, the silence of afterwards, of what continues and must be contemplated after the thing has been done. Absence; fact of the deed; the long thereafter. Terracing is a lovely art, so clever, so caring, so tuned to the slopes of a terrain. Terracers want to make

88

platforms to plant on, build on, live on, and ways of going along and up and down between them. They work tactfully and the hills allow it. But this was a working of the land to death, it was the will to barrenness unleashed to run its course. The tools of it lay on the finished ground, rusting. Take it in, said Grete. Look and look. As far and deep and wide as you can see. Indeed it went further than eyesight. Mournfully the spirit supposed it must last for ever.

Grete took a paper out of her pocket. Sam saw a rough map. She was concentrating hard, glancing from the map to the land and to the map again, narrowing her black eyes, shielding her sight from the brilliant sun. I think I see where, she said. I think I see how we get there. She took Sam's hand. Who gave you the map? he asked. Tobias, she answered. Who else?

All around the rim, snaking for miles, were concrete posts and wire. They carried notices of prohibition and death. Left, said Grete, seventeen along from that leaning one. The wire was vandalised or rusted through in many places, but at the seventeenth post there was a welcoming gap. And really it's to show us where to start, she said. They had to get down, vast step by step, and the stepping down took them further in, so that they were crossing as well as fathoming the hole. The map gave them the start and the general direction, but the connections from level to level had to be discovered, the old routes having fallen in or having been blocked by the machines that had made them. Roughly the way was zig-zag. Grete seemed to be trusting her instinct, almost remembering, and it was Sam who first noticed the cairns: small mounds of stone or some arranged wreckage of iron, wood, rubber, glass, either the earth's body itself or the machinery of its violation that had been used to make small waymarkers at the head of each new diagonal down. Tobias, said Grete. That's his doing. He is guiding us. And she made a sort of greeting and acknowledgement with the fist of her left hand.

The coal had been near the surface, their descent

through the strata of sand and gravel did not take long. Sixty million years in no time at all! The ledges were rather like shelves on which specimens of the strata – abandoned diggers, broken trucks, futilely lifted conveyor-belts – were beached and displayed. Or it was a battlefield, a rout of tanks, guns, transport and soldiers' paraphernalia. Or a camp, its workplace and its pit, big enough to enslave and disappear the world. Wire, concrete and wire. Hideous however you looked at it, dead-planet and spectral. But their descent was not in the least like tunnelling. They were not leaving the sunlight and the sky. The heavens seemed amplified by the vastness of the dead excavation. Going down was eerie because of their own smallness. They had a troubling sense of what they must look like viewed from high above. Step by step diminishing, degree by degree going down and further in, all by their own locomotion, on legs, with an occasional steadying by hands, spying ahead with eyes, thinking and wondering, they magnified the feeling of their own going out of sight. At the same time, if they shook off that perspective and fixed wholly on their own purpose, they felt a bud- and seedlike concentration of individual life.

They reached the floor, the last wide level. Here there was nothing. The machinery of work had been hauled up and out. They could see now that, entering and descending, they had come into the sealed end of a vast horseshoe. Most of the excavation stretched away north and, because of the extending sky above it, looked to go on for ever. The stepped walls either side made a long embrace. For the first time they felt fearful. Is this it? Sam asked. Is this what you wished to show me? Not yet, Grete answered, whispering, afraid she might echo and the giant open-ended theatre overhear. She looked again at the sketchy map. Two hundred metres. Then Sam noticed the coal itself, the undug floor of it, ridged up into an arrow-shaped cicatrice, man-sized and pointing. Tobias, he said. Only think of him down here on his own. I suppose he was on his own? He was, said Grete. They began counting their strides but could soon make out their objective and hand in hand ran towards it. Here we are, Grete said. This is what I believed would be here.

It was another horseshoe, about thirty yards long, about ten yards across, an image in extreme miniature of the colossal shape at whose southern end it lay, the ground around it rising in a lip. And the small horseshoe held a crystal-clear water. This is the start, said Grete. Or one of the starts. According to Tobias there may be dozens of them. But this is the one he found and told me about and that I wanted to see the truth of with you. The water was icy clear and still, but with a trembling in it, a thrill of continuous quivering, and that was the spring, rising, donating, becoming a well and a pool. Grete kneeled down, leaned over. Hold me, she said. Sam held her at the hips, she leaned over and in and down and extended her hands, put out her long fingers, immersed their tips, he brought her up wetted, and kissed the cold water on her nails. Then, sitting on the brim, they ate the bread, cheese and apples of their picnic.

Think of my mother and me, said Grete, up there somewhere, on a forest floor, in a clearing, on the wooden steps of an empty house, in the upper air and the roots of trees feeling down for a water like this one. Tobias says that in not many years the entire excavation will fill from springs like this. There will be a weight of clear water where there was a weight of topsoil, sand, gravel, rock and coal. Tobias works for the mapmakers. They are marking these waters in, as already arrived. There is one in Mecklenburg as large as a town, with sailing boats already on it. Breezes and sails and thousands of clamorous visiting birds. They know Tobias by now. They give him the future parts of their maps to do. He is very thorough in his researches. He promises only what he truly believes the earth can deliver. There will be several such lakes under the skies. The waiting shapes of them are on the maps, attested by Tobias, my black foster-brother.

Grete's whispering voice excited Sam. It was the voice

she told him her history in, at nights. He wanted to make love there and then, on the lips of the rising spring, in the vast derelict and replenishing horseshoe, under the infinite cold bright sky. But she was sensible, said they would freeze, said they would go to bed at home as soon as they got back.

They began the climb, which looked infinitely arduous. Sam babbled his thoughts, though he needed his breath for climbing. If it was full already we'd go up naked hand in hand and very fast in a stream of bubbles. When it is full we'll come again, we'll find a rowing boat, we'll row out to where the house was in the forest in the upper air. We'll be over the horseshoe which will be as far below us as the clearing in the forest is above us now. He felt the life of water, all the seeding it contains, all the beauties it draws to it, the mirrorings of trees, of rainbows, of moon, of a dizzying number of cold bright stars, of their dust falling in showers whenever the turning of the year desires it.

# The Shieling

They invented a place. It was far away from here, indeed from anywhere, high up, at the limits, like a shieling. He particularly liked the word 'shieling'. A bare place, as far up the valley as you could go and the house itself very simple. In reality such dwellings, the shielings, are only for habitation in the summer, the brief summer; but theirs they allowed themselves to proof almost snugly against the winter months. In winter, the long winter, this place of their invention would be needed most. So he fitted a chimney that drew remarkably well and built a hearth out of the rough stones that were lying around. There was little fuel, of course – a few almost petrified roots very hard to saw – so when they climbed to this place at the top of the valley they always carried a billet or two of firewood in their packs. He liked the word 'billet', in that usage.

Not that they ever did climb to it, not in the flesh. It was a place for our thoughts and dreams to go to, she said. A sort of safe house for them. Not for us in the flesh. Why the need for such a place? She asked me did I understand the word 'dejection'? I replied that I did. Well, she said, when he saw me in my state of dejection, or more especially when he had to leave me in that state, he begged me to try to lift my spirits by imagining a place where it would be easier to breathe and where my voice, which in the dejected state seemed to sink far into my chest, might revive and come forth again. Will you be there too? she asked. Will we be quiet? He said he would, of course he would, sometimes at least they would be there together and, yes, they would be quiet. He said it would do her good to imagine herself in a high and remote place where the air was a joy to breathe and him there with her, sometimes at least, quietly. In fact he was the least restful of men, could never sit still, must always be anxiously ordering things, in a pre-emptive sort of way. You don't trust your life, do you? she said. Which means you don't trust us. Often, when I think of you, of your anxiety, I get so nervous, for you, for us both, I would almost rather be in the state of dejection, where I don't feel anything much. This hurt him, like a reproach, and he answered back, to hurt her too, that whenever he dreamed of her it did him more harm than good. When he told me how he dreamed of me, she said, what night dreams and day dreams he had of me, I was very hurt. He saw me taking somebody else's arm and turning away. He saw himself coming to my house and getting no answer and standing there on the step like any hawker. It hurt me terribly, she said. I was all the more dejected. Why could we never be a reassuring place for our thoughts and dreams of one another?

In the shieling, she said, we had only the necessary things: a bed, a table, two chairs, the few things wanted for living there a while. Even books, we had very few, nine at the most, that was the rule, if we added one, we must take one away. In truth the shieling was a sparsely furnished place. And it seems they were never there for long, not even in thinking and dreaming did they absent themselves for long. Nor did they allow themselves to be there together very often. I said I'd have thought it would do them most good to imagine climbing to the shieling, opening it up, making it homely again, together. She blushed like a girl, agreeing. Nonetheless, she said, the times when they dreamed or thought themselves there together were few, mostly each went alone, the long and arduous climb, the opening up, the settling in, was solitary. And I wondered how that could help, did it not rather make things worse, to climb in thoughts and dreams to their shared invention, and be solitary in it? But she said no, certainly not for her and she truly believed not for him either, did being in the shieling alone, she without him, he without her, make their situation worse.

The virtue of the place lay in its being their invention, in their having made it so clear on all the senses, everything so solid, necessary, useful and to hand. Therein lay the virtue of the place, she said. And she added that she loved the word 'virtue', when it had that sense. How she smiled, how her face lit up when she confessed to me in a rush of words that even in the busy city where they were obliged to meet, in all the noise and trample of other people and in all the anxiety of clocks and timetables, if they began to dwell on the exact shape and colouring of a particular hearth stone in their shieling, on the wooden handle of a knife and its cheerful mismatch with the bone handle of a fork, dwelling on those and any dozen other concrete facts, they could abstract themselves completely and were as happy as children in the details of their invention. 'Dwelling on' is a lovely expression, don't you think? Dwelling on and in: the indwelling virtue of the place.

So either might sit down at the table with or without a fire and sleep alone and wake in the bed alone, and still there was virtue in it, great power to help. And at the table, moving aside the plate and the glass, he wrote a note or quite a long letter for her, or she for him, to find, having climbed alone, pushed open the door and paused, before stepping in. Or laid a book on the table from the frugal library (whose contents changed according to mood and need) and put a slip of paper in it, to mark a particular page, and a scribbled word: Read this. Tell me what you think.

Sometimes instead of a note or a book she left him a picture, either on the table or stuck above the hearth. She was good at art and might have drawn and painted him an abode as complex and intriguing as the castles and palaces on hilltops in the background of renaissance paintings: delightful winding roads that climbed to safety on snow or blue sky, distracting the mind from the foreground martyrdoms, allowing it rest and peace. But all she ever did for him, knowing his mind and his desires, was the place of their shared invention, each time with some alteration that she knew he would notice and trusted he would approve: a rowan by the front door instead of a hawthorn; harebells in the window, not heather. Once she added a small knoll, to one side and a little forward of the shieling, on land they thought of as theirs, and laid steps up it, so they would have a vantage point. He was glad of that and wondered how they had ever managed without.

From that invented hillock in warm weather either might watch for the other coming, she explained, such a clear view they had down the long valley, and there she stood, or he stood, watching for the friend. How slow the approach was, how long a time elapsed between the first sighting and the first embrace; but that interlude, though the feelings lifted as the climber inch by inch drew near, that long space of time had no anxiety in it, not the least, it was all sureness, confidence, step by step, minute by minute, becoming ever more precisely flesh and blood and bone, a confirmed familiarity, the person as trustworthy as the place itself. And there again, she said, looking at me very closely to be sure I had understood, in that too the virtue of our invention was proven. I was helped alone and I was helped when I thought of myself on our vantage point watching his slow arrival.

When they were together in the shieling – only ever for two or three days at the very most – then of course they made love; but when she told me this she said how much she, and he too, for that matter, preferred to say 'we slept together'. She was pedantically anxious that I should understand her in this and that I should not deduce anything false out of her distinctions. I understood that she wanted me to know that the pleasure they had given one another, the love they had made, was intense, and her body and soul would never forget it; but I also understood that in the whole invention their thinking and dreaming of sleeping together had even greater virtue, was even better able to help. That was what she dwelled on in her dejections, and what she urged him to dwell on in his constant anxiety and restlessness. She said to him: I am someone you can go to sleep with. And if you wake in the night you will hear me breathing quietly in my sleep. Think of that. Your hand will be on my breast. You will feel how contented my heart is. Dwell on that.

There was more, much more. You must remember that their shieling was an invented place; and an invention, even one confined to simplicity, austerity, necessity, might be elaborated for ever by two people who have a vital interest in it. She spoke of the deep contentment there was in sitting face to face at the table, writing. How one looked up for a word and with a shock saw the other likewise listening and waiting. And this happened alone in the place, she said, as often and as easily as when they thought or dreamed themselves there together. Then the subject took hold of her, the words came tumbling forth from her like the stream they had to climb to reach the shieling of their invention. More and more she found to say – and how I encouraged her! – on the subject of a place so simple, so bare in its appointment and decoration, so frugal in its amenities. All her girlhood awoke in her when she told me what was there, what might have been there, how free they were, within the strict forms laid on their desires, to add and subtract, to change and to innovate, and all their doing, saying, sleeping and dreaming in that place I felt it binding me to her, as her listener, for ever. For example, she said, there was a window at the back of the house. Through it we could see the stony ground, the screes either side, the lingering snow, the gap, the col, the windy exit from our valley over into the next.

Their place reminded me of many places, needless to say. I located it easily in three or four different lands; felt I had been there; felt I might go there again; but on the one occasion when I asked her would she name the place, her looks froze against me, as against an indecency. I blushed in shame, I begged her forgiveness. After a while she forgave me by resuming her voice. Forgiveness was a part of the place, she said. 'Forgive and Forget' might have been an inscription over our door. I believe it was for a while. We imagined several, and swapped them. My favourite was 'Let Be'. I don't like forgetting. I like to think we could remember and forgive. But I especially love the words 'Let be'. The gesture of the shieling was that, therein lay its great good. I mean, she said, the hand raised in greeting, open to show peace and welcome, but also, because of who we were, because of what we were like, it was the hand and the fingers that will be raised and extended to touch the lips of the friend when he or she is full of doubt and fear and the words better never said, not needing to be said, are rushing into utterance and the hand very gently stops them: There is no need, let be.

I think she could see that my indecent asking after a name for the place still grieved me, because of her own accord she added something more (and other) than I had asked for. Once I did come to such a place, she said. By accident really, by folly and passive drifting and failure to watch my step. I was with somebody who was very fond of me and I liked him well enough or I should never have been there with him, I suppose. We were walking, it was his idea, he said he knew a place he was sure I would like, it would lift my spirits, he said. I doubted it, I very much doubted it, but I had no energy in me to say no. I had lost the cure of my own soul. We were climbing and came out of a forest and quite suddenly – I had not paid attention – there was a wide valley stretching away and above us, narrowing to a col. I seemed to be dreaming, I let myself trek in a dream by waterfalls and by rowan trees, a long long climb, in silence, like the wraith of myself following a man I liked well enough and who I knew was very fond of me. She paused, she looked at me with more trouble in her face than I could bear to witness. I put up my hand, I extended my fingers, gently, gently to stop her voice. Then she shrugged and said, I'm sure you can guess the rest. We came to the ruins of a shieling, the stones of it were tumbled down and all around. It was a shieling at the very limit of tractable land, where the bare rock began. How I wept to see it. I turned away. I left him standing there in his poor ignorance. I made back down the valley on my own. I was inconsolable. Still am in fact.

# Petra

I was there on the quay when she arrived. Most boat days I went down, I liked to see who came and left, and that day, towards the end of March, it was her, arriving. In fact, I 'handed her ashore', across the gap. She had the camera around her neck and a small rucksack on her back. Otherwise all I noticed was her beauty.

Young people did arrive at Gerwick now and then, in the so-called season, and even some older people who could not bear the thought of getting old. They stayed a day or two, then left for the hinterland with all their gear. For a few years they were mostly Dutch. Word must have gone out, perhaps in an article or even a book, that you could only reach us by boat, which is attractive to a certain sort of person.

Petra wasn't Dutch. She was 'East European'. Most people thought she was Polish; but Granny Mac, who got very fond of her, said Estonian. She told Felix she knew the Baltic pretty well. What does it matter? A long way east of Gerwick, somewhere not at all like Gerwick.

When I handed her ashore (I like that phrase) she thanked me and asked did I know where she could lodge for perhaps a week. Her English was flawless, her accent as delicately strange as the aura of beauty around her hair and her cold face. 'Flawless', not a word I use much, fitted Petra well, in most respects. Frightening, really. Quite inhuman, some of the women said. I directed her to Granny Mac's, though in those days there were many places she might have tried. That's what the locals did back then, when there were travellers arriving in the season: let rooms, let the whole house if possible, lived in a caravan if necessary, to make what bit they could while the less inclement weather lasted. But Petra went off to stay at Granny Mac's, across the harbour, her neat and white abode, only a step from the little white headland chapel of Mary Star of the Sea. Everyone on the quay, half a dozen of us, and the two boatmen, stopped still and watched her go. I felt as I often felt, that they didn't like me and now especially not since I had touched her hand and spoken to her and directed her to lodge with Granny Mac. But Colvel, edging his tractor back for the pallet of fresh kegs, said, Very nice. A good start, I should say. By which he meant perhaps that a season starting with her must bring us all prosperity. So there she was, Petra, landfall, four weeks ahead of the swallows.

Merrick wasn't on the quay that afternoon. He never had anyone to meet, rarely anything to collect, and, unlike me, he didn't interest himself in other people's business. So I saw her beauty long before he did. In fact I met her again next morning near the shop and asked her how she had settled in at Granny Mac's. Very well indeed, said Petra. What a kind lady! See the pretty skirt she gave me! It was long and red, almost down to her ankles, quite heavy, I should have thought. It belonged to her daughter, said Petra. And then to her granddaughter. 'Pale' is not the word for the colour of Petra's skin. 'Pale' usually suggests that a darker colour would be healthier. Her skin was white, of a whiteness that did not suggest a want of colour. I assumed without question that all her body would be white like that.

How I miss Gerwick! More than I've ever missed any other place. When I wake in the night, which is often, the best thing I can do against misery and panic is to summon up Gerwick, the opening, the place of landfall. The small port is a gate into the hinterland, vast acreage of streams, trackless moor, sudden lakes and pools and the ramparts of mountains at the limits of vision. The village wrings your heart by its smallness as an outset, soon quitted. Or come down off the mountains and the moors – people do, weathered and made strange by days without human proximities – and stand at the harbour, at the flat end of the water-enclosing horseshoe, and from there it is exit, putting out, going forth, and access through a silent herd of islands into an ocean and the intimation of absolutes. Sky and the heaving level of water and between them the winds. Daylight is a kindness out there. It shows you the waters of the earth and the sun in the firmament, but conceals the rest, the infinity. A moonless night gives you more of the truth, quite enough, more than any human, viewing it honestly, can bear. Try lying in a small boat under the still hurtling debris of the makings of a universe, the flight of more stars than there are grains of sand, which are the ruins of the body of the earth, the bits of quartz and mica of her stone. No wonder I loved the garden on the slopes behind my house in Gerwick! Didn't I make it with my own two hands, yard by yard, terracing it into existence with all my strength and gentleness, till plants could hold and grow and the birds come and visit and sing in the shelter? And loved my workroom too, my window over the horseshoe harbour, half a circle of big light, and the cosiness when I curtained it and lit the lamp and sat among my books, late evening, and could concentrate. Solitude was my companion in the house. Ate with me, slept with me, woke when I did, and thought too much.

When Petra asked me about the community, about belonging and fellow-feeling, I answered candidly – she encouraged candour – that I was happiest in my garden or my workroom or in my small boat fishing or alone in the wilderness climbing a stream up to the ruined shieling and beyond to one or other of the many lakes. Of course, I knew *about* people, everybody knew a great deal about everybody else, but that of itself wouldn't make a community, would it? If there was a disaster, a flood, say, or a bad storm, danger and damage, everyone would pull together, of course they would. And for a death, especially anything unusual in the way of a death, most of the living would turn out and trail from the house in question to the windy churchyard, goes without saying they would. What more do you want? I suppose you feel a bit above, said Petra. She was standing in my bow window, where I sit and work. Up here, I mean. I began to distinguish between superior and peripheral, but soon desisted, not liking my tone of voice. Petra, in my experience, often had that effect. She listened to what you were saying – in fact, she *watched* it – with such close and impartial attention, if you weren't absolutely sure of yourself, your voice gave out, you shrugged, waited in silence. She photographed my view. The camera was always with her and she never asked permission. Above, she said. Just literally so.

From my window I could see most of the comings and goings of the place, and whenever I spotted Petra leaving Granny Mac's I'd make my way down and bump into her near the shop – 'accidentally on purpose', as she said, which I did not deny. There in the street – not a street at all really, just a public way among the few houses, joining the shop, the pub, the two arms of the harbour, the church, and soon giving out – Petra asked me who people were and what they did, and I told her, or began telling her and elsewhere later would tell her more until she knew all I knew and soon knew things I didn't know, that she had got from other sources, interesting things that she imparted to me coolly. After five or six days, when I was wondering how long she might still be with us, we were in the churchyard together, she was facing the sea, I was facing the land, and I noticed Merrick with his gun and his dog on the first rise, the first high line of the heather, behind the village, striding across. I nodded upwards. Have you met him yet? Would that be Merrick? It would. No, I haven't, yet. But Granny Mac had told her things about him, good and bad. Oh you must meet Merrick, I said. For a fair picture of the place before you leave, you must pay him a visit. And I showed her the way that led to Merrick's house. Not above, not superior, but outside, that's for sure, and without a view, unless he climbs up there, which he often does, every day in fact. What does he shoot? Petra asked. Hoodies and blackbacks. He says they take his chickens.

The next time I saw Petra, for all the spyings from my famous window, it was early April, warm. She was coming out of the shop, carrying an old-fashioned wicker basket, still wearing the skirt Granny had given her but now with a man's collarless shirt to it, the sleeves rolled up, the flaps outside, pale blue on the red, very effective. That Merrick's? I asked. Yes, she said. I'm lodging with him now. But Granny says I must come to tea whenever I like.

I was thinking about Merrick and his history. I nearly told Petra she wasn't the first, but I checked myself, thinking it might show me vulnerable. Fortunately at that moment Felix rode up on his tractor. Morning you two, he said. Nice shirt. And he leaned over as if to look down the front of it. Petra smiled and photographed him, and I knew why. It was the manifest inability of the spirit in him to live up to his position of advantage and to fill out his jocular words with confidence. The gap, the failure, plain as day! I nodded, Petra smiled again, and Felix swung the sack of post off the bonnet and passed with it into the shop. Why is he called Felix? Petra asked. His mother loved Mendelssohn, I replied. She hoped he would be a musician. And his father hoped he would be lucky and build them a bungalow in their old age. Petra photographed me and I knew why. But I was right to say 'fortunately' a few lines back. Most people in Gerwick were glad to meet Felix. It perked them up, they felt better about themselves. They looked around them, as soon as he had gone, for somebody to relate the encounter to. You were asking me about the community, I said to Petra. Felix is very good for it. Be in the pub one evening when they are talking about him. How they like one another then! He's the lynchpin. You know the word? Petra frowned. Of course I know the word. But a lynchpin is there, in the middle of the wheel, the wheel falls apart without it. Lynchpin! Felix is like the negroes hanging in the trees and all that chortly fellow-feeling swilling around under their feet. Let's not exaggerate, I said. I have that photograph with me wherever I go, she said.

Felix came out of the shop. I noticed that he had mended his glasses with elastoplast. You two still here? he said. People will talk. He drove off. Is it true he sleeps in the shed? Petra asked. Lots do, I replied, in shacks and caravans, when they can let their rooms. But yes, Felix sleeps in the shed out of season too. Either because Grace won't have him in the house or because he likes it better in the shed. I had kept my tone neutral but she asked, Which, in your opinion? The former, though I wish with all my heart it were the latter. I have a view of Felix which disqualifies me from fellow-feeling in the pub. He was on the ships, you know, on the high seas, he worked for Cable and Wireless, many times he sailed around the world, he was useful, he's seen things people here couldn't begin to imagine, he's – But Petra held up her hand. You're pleading, she said. You don't need to. Where is his shed? Let's walk by that way.

I often met Petra in the churchyard. I liked it out there. The church is the only completely pleasing house in Gerwick. Solid, neither squat nor too heavy, all of it fits, all is in proportion. The neglect in my day was grievous – fallen gutters, broken windows, damp plaster – but the building endured, close by the sea, on its acre of flat ground, quite separate from the dwellings. How I miss that place! I always wanted to be buried there. I'd do well at nights to think of the graves in their safe enclosure and not the immensities of ocean, sky and moor.

I always looked to see what Petra was wearing. Once her black hair was in a red kerchief I recognised as Merrick's. Better on you, I said. I never liked it round his scrawny throat.

Other times, as the weather got warmer, she wore blouses he'd given her, or skirts, that had belonged to his wife or his eldest daughter. When she saw me looking, she nodded and smiled. Really, she was too beautiful to look at and from her and Merrick I turned away to the gravestones and told her a few more stories in a rush. Poor Foster, I said, cut his throat on the train coming back from the war, last stop before the port, by all accounts. And there's Betty Seton, who walked into the sea one winter night, and that's her father Frederick next to her who died in his bed with his right hand on the bible at the age of ninety-one, before they found out anything bad about him. Petra listened and once or twice photographed me. I'll stop if you're not interested, I said. No, go on, she said. Of course I'm interested. It's just that I can't see them but I can see you.

I reverted to this a few weeks later. We were more intimate by then. Not that Petra needed intimacy before she would be candid. There on the quay, the first day, I might have asked her anything and, looking me in the eyes, she would have answered carefully and truthfully. But that afternoon, when I had known her a little while longer, we were in my room, at the window, looking down on the comings and goings of the place, and I said, You're not really interested in why people do things, are you? A bit I am, but not the way you are, she answered. I'm sure you lie awake wondering why I sleep with Merrick but I never wonder much about things like that. Who knows why people do things? I'm more interested in what they look like while they're doing them or when they're thinking of doing them or when they have. It's the look of the things and the people that interests me. Do you understand? I know you think you and I are two of a kind, and in a sense we are. But at bottom we're not. You couldn't do what I do, try as you might. It scares me sometimes that I can. But there we are.

Felix, I said, with the post. Murdoe the coastguard going in for his brandy. I expect his flies are open and Mrs P. will ask him to adjust his dress before she serves him. Granny Mac with flowers for the chapel. Archie with a customer for once. Where's Archie from, by the way? Petra asked. Birmingham, I said. Did he arrive here looking like that? More or less, I said. Him and his lady wife. It was a sudden decision they took one morning in a house very far from here. Falconry! Now why? Archie's a very good example, Petra said. Why ask why? There he is, looking like that. I asked had she met Doreen yet. I'm having coffee with her, said Petra, as soon as Archie has well and truly gone. Their front garden, I said, where he keeps his birds, is the saddest place in the universe. You must tell me which one you think Doreen looks like most. The scops, I'd say. Archie was striding away, the baffled hawk on his shoulder, the customer waddling after. It's about now they realize their mistake, I said. Must go, said Petra. She kissed me on the cheek, the suddenness of her face, its whiteness, light as snow her lips.

Petra was right. I did lie awake in my solitude wondering why she slept with Merrick. She could have lodged with Granny Mac as long as she pleased, so why go off to Merrick's? Now it is well known that some young women will sleep with older men who are rich and powerful for the material advantages it may bring them. But Merrick was penniless and had no material power. Nor was Petra interested in such advantages. I can imagine that a young woman might like to be seen with an older man, especially an older man the worse for wear, because he will set her off nicely in the public view. But that couldn't apply to Petra either. Everyone knew she was lodging with Merrick but nobody ever saw them together. Of course they knew how wrecked Merrick looked and how beautiful Petra was so that in the mind's eye at least, if they coupled them up, she would shine forth. But Petra had no such vanity. The simplest explanation is her curiosity; and in his case it couldn't be satisfied by having tea with him and taking photographs of him in his habitat. She couldn't just visit him as she did the others. She had to move in. She had to see his face up close when they made love.

When I put this to Petra – we were in among the graves again – she shrugged. Maybe, she said, as though obliged to consider some third person who didn't much interest her. Okay, I said, I've got another theory, it occurred to me last night. The young woman with the older man delights in realising how pleasureable she is. Making love, she thinks, Oh how he is enjoying me! Oh how enjoyable I am! It delights her to feel how he desires her. She does not even wish him to be considerate and attend to her pleasure. Really all she wants is to be enjoyed. The unlikely man, he might be ugly and old, the man who can't believe his good fortune when she favours him, he is most likely to give her the deep and peculiar pleasure of knowing how desirable she is. Petra took a photograph of me waiting for her response. Then she said, You and your reasons why. Turned away, faced out to sea, rested her bare left hand, the long white fingers, on the pleasingly curving top of Sidney Oliver's stone, and said, Suppose she loves him. Have you thought of that? I admitted that I hadn't thought of that. Just an idea, she said, drifting away, her long blue skirt, sea-blue, sea-green, brushing the lichened stones. I walked after. Two elderly visitors, entering at the iron gate, will have thought we were quarrelling. By the far wall, its soft pink tamarisks, Petra halted, I stood behind her, I said, You know Granny Mac's granddaughter is a prostitute? Yes, yes, Petra said. In London. She told me the morning she gave me the red skirt. And the newspapers sending a gang in a speedboat to photograph Granny and ask her what she felt? Yes, said Petra, turning round – I had no power at all whenever, after an interval, moon behind cloud, she turned her face on me – And how she opened the bedroom window and levelled Mac's shotgun at them and said she'd blow them to the devil if they didn't get out of her sight. I wish, oh I wish, said Petra, that I had seen their faces then! She's got Tammy's photograph on the mantelpiece, and the little boy's too, who has a black man for his dad, as everyone in Gerwick knows. How soon before you know all there is to know, I said, and have seen all there is to see? Typical of you, she said, to suppose I am only collecting and will have enough one day.

My bedroom was rather dark but I never minded that. It looked over the garden I had made on the west- and south-facing slopes, the small theatre, warm and moist, into which the birds came, the hedgehogs, the shrews and mice, a badger now and then or a fox, I could stand at the window for hours looking out and down. By craning up and away you could see the ridges of heather and gorse that were the borders of the wilderness. We stood in the window once, Petra and I, not looking into the garden nor up towards the hinterland, but at some photographs of Merrick. We were standing in the window for the better light. These, she said, he thought you would recognise. I did. They were taken on the little white beach just north of the harbour, below the land Merrick and his wife had begun to work as soon as they arrived. At that time they were friendly towards Gerwick and he and Julie and their first girl Beth were seen around on the quay and in the shop like anyone else. They gave a party on the beach, all welcome. There you see Merrick, bearded like Che, boyish as Dylan, smiling over his guitar, on a camp stool by a fire. Julie was singing. She had the purest voice I've ever heard, steady and sure, with undertones that blinded your view of her with tears. So it was, truly. And see how glad of his life he looks! And no wonder, labouring for his family all the hours God gave, with a vision, with principles, full of love and faith. There were several photos of that famous occasion, Julie with Beth in her lap, Merrick listening; one of him arguing in a smiling passion. None of you, said Petra. He said he had none of you. He said you were the photographer. Can that be true? I gave up soon after, I said. It made me smile to see her almost asking why. Let me see him now, I said. She showed me, in black and white: Merrick asleep naked, the sheet across his waist like the sheet you draw back over a face after an identification; Merrick, icon of disappointment, at a window looking out. And so on, a dozen such. Well? she said. As you know, I said, I couldn't do what you do. I can hardly even bear to look. Yes, yes, she said. But it's the same man isn't it, the one you took, the one I took, you'd know him for himself, wouldn't you? Does he ever sleep easy? I asked. What can you do for his nightmares?

That was Petra's first time in my bedroom. Her second, and last, was in the late summer. Again we were standing at the window and I, pressing my forehead against the glass, had got into a monologue on the subject of my garden, the pleasure it had given me in the making, the pleasure it gave me still, at any hour of the day, and even at night, under the moon and stars, if I couldn't sleep and stood there watching, when Petra said, There's Merrick. She had not been looking into the garden but up and away to the high ground and spotted him striding along with his gun and the dog. I didn't mind. He was a fine sight, up there on the ramparts of the mind, the gun shouldered, in clear silhouette. What's his gibbet like nowadays? I asked. Blackbacks, hung upside down by the feet. How big they look, crashed like that. The hens doing well? They are, we ate one yesterday. Does he still have that lever thing, by the stone steps into the barn, to break their necks? He does. I took a photo. Then he gave me the hen to pluck. Funny, the heat of her.

Not taking her eyes off Merrick, Petra said, By the way, Felix took me somewhere very beautiful, to a small lake he says no one else knows about. I looked into the warm hollow of my garden, listening. He took a notebook with him and a compass, but no map. He said he had found the place many years before, when things started going wrong with Grace and he would sometimes go off on his own towards the mountains. He said he had often thought he would walk and walk and not come back. I watched him pushing up his glasses and poring over the directions in his notebook. He said the place in question was as near as he would ever get to paradise and he wrote very careful directions in a secret notebook to prove to himself, when his life was more like hell, that the place really existed, only a couple of hours behind the village, and he knew the way. I took a photo of him peering at his bad writing and looking very worried and mumbling to himself. He hadn't been back for many years, only once in fact, to write the directions in his little book.

I moved my forehead to a cooler patch of glass. At first the thought of it was worse than Merrick – whom her eyes never left – but after a while, credit where credit's due, the beauty of it crept over me, the pathos, the charity, the gift, the requiting, and I listened wholly in the present tense, which was itself a great blessing on me.

They were small landmarks, Petra said, a cluster of rowans, a ruined sheepfold, another stream coming in from the right or the left. He would read a passage, consult his compass, and we made another hundred yards or so. Once he muttered, Cleft rock. And I pointed to it. He was sweating and out of breath and the worry on his face got worse and worse the nearer we came to the last page of his directions and the place itself on the earth. Finally he put away the notebook and the compass and set off quickly to the left up a rise, as it seemed to nowhere in particular. I let him go ahead, I was thinking what his face would look like disappointed, but when he turned he was radiant, such a boy. Still here! he shouted. Still here!

Merrick had gone. Petra leaned her forehead against the window, quite close to mine, and continued her narrative very softly. I climbed up to Felix and stood by him and saw the water on its level under a heathery slope with only hills and moorland beyond and all around it for ever and ever, quite shallow water at the near side where we stood, a thin beach of fine shingle, but with sedge and many white water-lilies approaching from the far side. And this, the strangest thing, the water, which took its colour, a golden darkness, from the peat floor, wore on its surface the blue sky. Truly, the sky, the blueness, appeared to dip into the water, through the surface and some way into the depth. A lake of blue sky. That attracted me. Did you swim? I asked him. Yes I did, he answered, all on my own, and floated out there in the middle and stared at the sky and thought of not ever coming in.

So Petra set down her precious camera, undressed and stepped through the shallow water, first on shingle, then on a soft peaty mud, waded till she had depth enough, then slipped in and swam. Felix stood by her clothes. She swam right across, through a watery illusion of blue sky, to the fringe of white water lilies. The lake was as smooth on her as silk and, so long as she moved near its surface, warm; but if she stood, treading water, her body below the waist, reaching down like the fork of a root, felt, so she said, an uprising of cold, truly, she said, as though she were tapping it. But the surface was delightful, she idled there on her back.

Then, so she told me, came another phenomenon, stranger and more beautiful even than the mirage of sky. From nowhere, out of nothing, a mist formed, a soft warm mist, and drifted over the surface of the water, overlaying it but leaving the blue sky visible in the heights. Felix vanished. The mist rolled over her, warmly. He called to her, she answered, each invisible. Their cries were disembodied, birds might have uttered them. Petra lay on her back, moving as little as possible, and Felix could not see her, he could see the blue sky above her and she lay in a drifting light grey shroud, a stratum of air and light and water, in a sort of sleep, calling out to him now and then, not words, not even his name, but notes, like a plover's, a golden plover's, as though she had been enchanted. She had no wish to come back, she said, but did so after a while. Rolled, turned and made slowly towards him, guided by his cries.

The drift of vapour thinned, Petra stood up, there were wisps of it still around her, clinging, parting, dissolving. She waded from the lake. His face! she said. Alas, my camera was on my pile of clothes.

I often think of Felix standing on the bank of his paradise water and Petra wading, emerging, towards him. Since she could not photograph him I made the image of him myself, his mended glasses, his drinker's nose, the abject tilt of his head, his big and helpless hands. Like that. But also like the ship's boy sent up to the crow's nest, to watch, and when he came down, so the poet says, his face was wet with tears. Petra turned to me, to see how I had taken her account. Much like the ship's boy, I expect.

I wonder how you would stare, she said. I ignored her. Reminds me, I said. There's a place just south of here, quite easy to get to if you know how, where you can swim with the seals. I used to go two or three times every summer. No one else ever there. Just me and the seals. They're very curious, they let you get quite close. I've been meaning to ask you would you care to come? I must see what you would look like, she replied. She moistened her lips. Once I was there in a mist, I continued. There's a rocky island where they congregate, a little way out. That day in the fog I could hear them moaning. Did you ever hear seals moaning? Like nothing on earth. Sit on the bed, will you, said Petra, this end, facing the pillows, and carry on telling me about the seals. No, I never did hear them. Tell me what they sound like in a fog and what they look like in sunlight when they wait for you swimming nearer and nearer. My big brass bed. I sat leaning against the bottom frame of it, facing the empty pillows. Close your eyes, will you, and carry on telling me. She was behind my back, in the space between me and the window. I did as she asked. Julie used to sing about the silkie, I said. That voice of hers. Do you know the song? I can't sing but I'll say the words. Petra moved round, I felt the bed take her weight, heard the shivers and trembles of brass, as she leaned back. I sang in a tuneless monotone, a flat chant, about the silkie, who came in from the sea, out of the rocks and fog where they copulate and moan, and took up with a crofter for a while, in female shape, until one morning she walked on the shore with him and her human babies and heard the moaning at sea and quitted them there and then. Now you can open your eyes, said Petra. I did. She was sitting on my pillows, naked, with her camera. She took me at once. Oh the light's so good, she cried. The window light. More, oh a few more! She drew up her knees, rested an elbow on each, her arms slanting up to an apex over the gap, her eye behind the camera, its eye seeing exactly how I stared.

Gerwick was an unstable place. People blew in, were enchanted, began a new life, hung on, fell away. The effort of it all defeated them. How to live the new life? How to make a living? An artist moved into an old boathouse and painted sunsets; his wife – much better than me, as he liked to say – put the local flora on mugs and tea towels and sold them in the shop. A writer converted a barn, to write a novel (*the* novel) in; but the barn took years, he wrote notes on converting it and sold them, in a little book illustrated by the artist's wife, in the shop to the visitors. All had to feed on the visitors, vacate their homes, live in a shack or a caravan, cook fry and hold forth about the beauties of the place. Can't beat it. Nowhere like it. Couldn't live anywhere else. Some sort of solvent ran through Gerwick. A girl landed, the man of a house fell in love with her, she evicted the wife who scooped up the children and left. Or a man: the woman of a house fell in love with him, they ran away to elsewhere, to start again, taking her children. And the drink, always the drink; at Colvel's loudly, at home in silence or muttering alone. The long winters, the melancholy. Left to themselves, nobody new and beautiful and interesting blowing in, around Christmas husbands and wives had suddenly had enough. Jean Colvel went to Edinburgh, to be with the grandchildren. Nothing personal, he said. She just prefers them to me. Grace said she'd go back to Brighton unless Felix agreed to sleep in the shed. He agreed. She made it quite pretty for him, proper curtains, a heater, a little television. Setting him up in the shed got her through the winter. The silence at nights in winter was overwhelming. I used to lie awake thinking any minute now someone will scream, very long and loud, and everyone will hear it and think, That could have been me. No wonder we looked forward to the visitors, arriving enchanted, telling us, the locals, how lucky we were, how it tempted them, how they'd been thinking for years they must get out and start again, how they admired us for doing what they hadn't had the courage to do. We hated the visitors, the effort it was every morning to smile at them over the fry. One of Gerwick's best fellow-feelings sprang from hating the visitors. Place to ourselves again, we'd say, when, later than the swallows, the last of them departed. Thank God for that.

I went down to meet the launch. No one arriving, a few hanging around to leave. I didn't wait. On the way back I met Felix. I hadn't seen him to speak to since Petra told me about the paradise lake. He halted, as though there was something to say. His face in the mornings never looked good, so many little broken veins and his eyes behind the glasses wet and desperate. I suppose Petra was between us, unspoken. He made his usual joke about me having nothing to do. And that was that, he drove off. I hadn't been able to see the vision in his face, not while I was looking at him, but heading for home, suddenly I saw it, the stare at beauty stepping towards him out of a place kept secret in his head, through years of humiliation, as paradise. The broken material of his abject face made new. I could see it.

Back here I stood at the window, trying to settle. I saw Petra come out of Granny Mac's, embrace her on the doorstep and walk away quickly. She was wearing the clothes she had worn that day in March, before any of the gifts, and carrying her camera and the small rucksack. Down the south side of the horseshoe, she came towards me; went out of my sight under the few harbour houses along the curve;

reappeared walking quickly, down the north side, away. She stepped on to the launch, which left at once.

I lay in bed for two days, hugging the pillow on which, so I fondly imagined, still clung her feral scent. Then I thought this won't do. Carry on like this, come Christmas you'll be dead. I dressed, shaved and walked out to Merrick's. Many years since I was there. I came in through his fields, remembering. Docks, nettles, bracken everywhere. Pigsty, donkey shed, sheep pen and byre, all ruinous, vanishing, the stuff of archaeology. The wind-pump, that he had set up himself to draw their water, was toppled. Then I heard the dog, squealing and howling. She was locked in a cubbyhole under the stone barn and a note on cardboard nailed to the door. Please feed Pippa. The nail was enormous and driven in so hard it had passed right through. Pippa looked crazed. The chickens were scrabbling free all over the yard. In the kitchen I fed Pippa and shouted for Merrick. Then I had to go through the house, even his bedroom, the women's clothes on the bed, calling his name. Nothing. He was always careful about his gun. He kept it locked in a cupboard under the stairs. The cupboard was unlocked; no gun. I ran down to the beach; no boat either. So I went to tell Murdoe, paid a retainer as coastguard. I had to wake him, he was still pretty drunk.

It was misty next day. I thought I'd walk to the beach I had told her about where you could swim with the seals and hear them moaning. Many years since I was there. It came back to me, the rise as you draw near, the excitement, the brink of vision over a low cliff. The beach is only a scoop of white sand and the mist, drifting in, almost annulled it. But I got down without much trouble and stood at the edge, the small waves coming in as softly as breathing, lapsing with a sigh, breathing forward again. The seals on their rock in the fog were as I had remembered them and told her about and sung in my tuneless voice about before she told me to open my eyes, a moaning and keening, more lament than love but with some of the love-tones too, the moaning in little breaths, as though continually surprised by the depths of it, then keening, only that, a wailing and sobbing. I was quite determined to do what I had said she would surely love to do, swim out to them. I undressed and stood there, the water lapped my ugly feet. I stood till I was quaking with cold. Then I dressed and slunk off home.

The next day, still misty but with a strong sense of blue sky above, I thought I would take a walk into the wilderness. Years since I was there. I looked out my old boots and even found the ashplant I had liked to walk with, packed some provisions and the map and my compass, and set off. I felt sure I'd be able to find Felix's lake. I guessed he had borne away north from the biggest of the streams. Truth is, I had quite forgotten how hard that terrain is, the tussocks so bad my ankles twisted at every step, bog up to my knees before I noticed it. I bore away left up a likely stream. I was recalling my first sight of an otter in that country, suddenly hurrying ahead of me up just such a steep water, surprisingly bulky, shouldering forward and up at great speed and away. My foot slipped, I fell, grazing both wrists and hitting my knee. The retreat was very laborious and painful, but I made it back to Gerwick by the late afternoon. On a curious impulse, limping badly, blood on both hands, I stopped at the gates of Archie's bungalow, a thing built before we were designated an area of outstanding natural beauty. Archie was seated in the immense window, in all his gear, the leather, the silver buttons, the epaulettes, the plume, the tassels, the breeches, reading a newspaper under a tasselled standard lamp. The owls and raptors were in the garden, each chained to its perch. They looked at me, in absolute silence, all turned their faces, flat white, big-eyed, savagely beaked, and contemplated me. Archie called the place a sanctuary, and it is true there were some the Duke's keepers had tried to poison or shoot, a harrier or two, an osprey, a golden eagle. But what was he doing with an eagle owl and a snowy owl in his suburban front garden? I knew he liked to stand among his birds, fully costumed, and walk from one to the next, calling them by their names. Flat white faces, strange, strange savagery, every one chained to an ornamental rock or a rustic perch at the feathered leg, just above the talons. Then Doreen came into the lounge with a cup of tea. Scops was indeed the one she most resembled. She saw me at the gate, she and Archie together beckoned me most warmly to come in. But I made a gesture with my ashplant of having to be on my way.

The currents on that coast have a life of their own. No one can work them out. It was a week before Merrick came in, sixty miles to the north. In an access of fellow-feeling Murdoe called to tell me. He stank, the breath he made the words with was heavily laden, his flies were open. Seems Merrick rowed out – he never would have an engine – very far, shipped the oars, lay back, put the gun between his legs, bit the end of it, and fired. Then drifted for a week till a crabber spotted him and towed him in. The gun and the blackbacks. Dear Mother of God, said Murdoe. I thought I'd come and tell you. Thank you, I said.

Lately when I think of Gerwick, when I wake and think, I concentrate on my back garden, the slopes, the moist hollow, altogether my best work. I think of a colour – white, say – and one by one dwell on all the flowers of that colour, in their seasons, in their ways of being. A pool and overflowing of snowdrops; a bush of white roses; white stocks (their scent at my bedroom window); a white lilac; the white-rock and alyssum that I induced to thrive and topple in profusion over a brink of the hill's implacable stone.

# Regrets

In the last years of your life — the last ten, the last twenty, perhaps even the last thirty — you begin to think: I hope I get through to the end without doing any more damage. And if your special risk is saying rather than doing, then it's the deathbed itself you grow fearful of. What if I lose control? What if I wander and say something terrible, that will undo everything, cast a new light on everything, and in that light they would look at me and I would look at them, and with that look I should have to leave them, disappointed.

We had this conversation more than once; in fact, we had it quite often, if I'm honest. Mostly I knew when it was coming and I'm bound to say the very thought of it made me uncomfortable and I'd have avoided it, had he let me. But he insisted, and I went along. Or we'd be together somewhere on some other business, having quite another kind of conversation, and suddenly his look would change, he was at the mercy of his subject and I was alone with him, no chance of an interruption and at his mercy. I pitied him. His whole bearing suffered an alteration. He hunched to one side, he pressed his left hand hard at the back of his neck, as though it were there the subject had landed, squatted and was riding him. One time I thought — and I believe I even said aloud — You look like a gargoyle. He did too: like something *made* to be ugly and risible, spouting whatever the heavens tipped on him. So I pitied him with a little thrill of horror and disgust.

He confessed to me — but I'd have guessed it anyway — that

he read the newspapers every day of the week including Sunday almost only to learn had anyone suddenly been arrested for a crime committed years ago. When he found such a case, and nowadays they come up pretty often, he cut it out with a pair of scissors he used for nothing else, and put it away in a box file that was nearly full. After he had read it, of course. The way he told me the stories he'd just read you'd think he was himself the man in question: the terrible pleasure, shame and fear and loathing and relief. For surely, he said, it must be a relief when in the end they come and knock on your door and ask, Are you this man? The end of years of waiting. On the other hand, I said, it is the start of something just as bad. He agreed that a long public crucifixion would be no fun; particularly not if in the meantime, during the many years of waiting, you had become loved and respected in your home and community, as was often the case. Often, he said, it's something they did in their twenties, and after it nothing of the sort ever again; and for twenty, thirty, forty, fifty years, you were moving on, making your way in life, doing some good. And all the while the one bad thing was waiting, you and it were waiting, for the day a police car pulls up at your door. By 'thing', I said, by 'it', you mean a person, you mean a he or she. Yes, he said, someone you damaged.

I was round at his place, in the kitchen, having this conversation. Catharine was out. He said she'd gone to an exhibition, she wouldn't be back, and either side the kitchen table with the box file between us we were having our conversation when the doorbell rang and he stood up to answer it, leaving me. See for yourself, he said.

The box was sepulchral, the clip that held the cuttings down was as tense and sudden as a mouse trap. Take your fingers off, if you weren't careful. I was very careful. The cuttings went back thirty or forty years. But they were not in any order. From which I deduced that he was forever looking through them, re-reading one or another of them, and laying it back on top. So far as I could see, but really I'd have needed longer to be certain, there were no camp-guards or killers of Jews and partisans among his cases. And the normal murderers, if you can call them that, all seemed, at a glance, to have been hauled forth to answer for a crime of passion. As you'd expect (these days) there were a lot of priests; but about an equal number of ordinary fathers whose offences were not a benefit or a liability of any sort of public office or profession. But in nearly every case, so far as I could tell, it was the lapse of time that had attracted my friend's attention, the gap of waiting between the crime, if we are to call it that, and the having to answer for it. I say 'crime, if we are to call it that' because some of the cases that affected him most (he had marked them with a red pencil) were those which at the time had not seemed a crime to either party; but only later, often much later, one of them, the younger one, brooding on it, festering in it and as the climate of opinion about such matters changed, suddenly went public and denounced the malefactor. A headmistress, for example, was brought to court in her mid-fifties for seducing a pupil of fifteen when she was in her thirties. There was a photograph of her leaving court on her own. She looked like someone touched on the face by a hand whose fingers had the power to kill the soul. That was one of the cuttings he had marked in red.

I heard the front door close but he didn't come back to me. I read a few more reports, but began to resent being left there to sift through his obsession. So I snapped the clip down, closed the box, and found him, as I expected, skulking in the lounge. I must say his appearance rather disgusted me. Well? he said. Well what? I said. And I said I had to be going. I didn't want to be there when Catharine came home.

They invited me round now and then. Catharine says will you come and have supper with us, he would say. I suppose she felt sorry for me being on my own. I went; but I must say I was always glad to leave. They sat either end of the table and

123

me in the middle. Often in the silences they looked at me, both of them together, their eyes met on my face. They looked as if they wished I would make something happen, but without much hope that I would. I looked from one to the other, then down at my hands which were probably lying on the table cloth, rolling a bit of bread. Once in a silence I made a creature with my bread, a sort of mandrake, a forked thing, and sat it up for all to see. Bad manners really. Later I had what you might call an after-feeling of the pair of them closely watching me.

I'm a childless man. So far as I know, at least. Nobody has ever summonsed me for maintenance or knocked on my door claiming to be my grown-up son or daughter. I've never had one of those sudden letters you read about. But the sort of conversations I've been describing do make you uneasy for a while. Bound to. Which is why I avoid them if I can.

I suppose Catharine must know about his box of cuttings. Hard to keep a thing like that a secret from your wife, I should have thought. I said to him once – to torment him, I suppose – that all he seemed to worry about was getting through to the end, as he put it, without doing any more damage or without being named and shamed for whatever damage he had already done, when really he ought to be worrying about what might come out after he was gone and what damage that might do, not to him, of course, but to his loved ones, as he called them. He looked glum. There was a case the other day, I said. A grandfather dying at home in the bosom of his family and a woman in red stands up at his funeral and says the old devil interfered with her when she was a little girl. Where did you read that? he asked. I didn't see that. It upset him to think I'd seen something he hadn't. Can't remember, I said. Perhaps I dreamed it. You know what I'm like. But the point is, I said, you should get rid of that box of cuttings before you go. Or people will be bound to draw the wrong conclusions when they find it.

He and Catharine had a child called Amy. She left home about a year after I came on the scene. And they had another girl living in the house, a bit older than Amy, who was practically their daughter, the way she lived with them. She was called Beatrice, and we hardly overlapped at all. She left some months before Amy. So it must be twenty years he and Catharine have been without them, in that house too big for a solitary couple. Amy and Beatrice are not their real names, by the way. I thought it best to make them up.

The reason why I don't like going round there for supper (though I always accept) is the atmosphere. Catharine is quite a good cook really – a lot better than me, at any rate – and I know she makes an effort when she invites me round. But she loses heart. Often she can't eat it herself, which isn't very encouraging. He eats all his and I think if I wasn't there he'd eat up hers as well, the way he eyes it. He's very mean. His best friend, which may well be me, couldn't call him a generous man. The wine, for example, which I suppose is his responsibility. The wife usually leaves it to the husband, so I believe. With a decent glass of wine you don't mind what you're eating. At least, that's how I help my cooking down. But at their place it's always been open a week. Red or white, he brings it out of the fridge with a stopper in. And that's what we get. I honestly think it makes for vindictiveness, wine like that, fetched out like that, never a new bottle of anything any good.

I don't know what it is he's done and is so worried about. I mean his box of cuttings and his one topic of conversation. Nothing, would be my guess. I've read that a man can become obsessed about anything, for no reason; or for no reason you could call halfways adequate. Once he did say something, but not enough to explain his collection of horrible revelations and court cases. It was some while ago and I was round there for supper. I was surprised they asked me again after that. But they did, and before very long. What I call the atmosphere, why I don't like sharing a meal with them, was worse after his sudden coming out with something. It became more of a burden – a burden on *me*. As though they were looking to me for another confession. I don't mean one of my own.

What he came out with was peculiar enough, in its way, but nothing likely to interest the Law, I shouldn't have thought. Only a family matter. I was in my usual position between the two of them, him at the end on my left, Catharine on my right, and no doubt I was fiddling with the doughy bread, as usual. He never made much of an effort, he always looked the same, not quite his carpet slippers but pretty near. But Catharine always put something nice on. It was like with her cooking. She made an effort, then somehow lost heart, couldn't quite believe in it. I looked at her with pleasure, I must admit. In fact on the evening in question I was feeling very sympathetic towards her and quite antagonistic towards him with his miserable wine and the same old pullover. She was wearing what I suppose you'd call a forties dress – like something a young woman with real flair would have spotted in Oxfam, knowing it would suit her exactly: calf-length, short sleeves, loose around the bosom, quite low-cut but decent, silky, a soft green. I can't say it suited her exactly, but it was very touching to me at least, because it was the sign of her having made an effort. She wore a necklace with it, of stones of a darker green. Catharine is very slim and neat. I've seen her from the back occasionally and thought she might be a woman half her age. But her face is a sadness to me when she turns round. There it all shows.

Anyway, we were having a sort of conversation about what we'd done with our lives so far and whether we thought we'd do any better in the time remaining. Catharine had pushed aside her plate, most of her portion uneaten, and her hands were lying together, open, on the cloth. I've always admired her hands, the plain ring scarcely trespasses on their beauty. It wasn't much of a conversation because although she and I were doing our best he would contribute nothing but facetiousness. In the end it wearied me and I asked after Amy and Beatrice, to change the subject. Fine, said Catharine. So far as we know. He said nothing. Then she looked very coolly at him, and then almost confidingly at me, and said, Perhaps you regret what you haven't done more than what you have. Perhaps women do, at least. I could see the face under the face, so to speak – what she looked like before all the disappointment, before I knew her. The eyes showed forth, but the skin also, cheekbones, lips, chin, the whole expression, briefly returned, like a ghost visiting. She smiled and asked me what I thought.

I was about to answer. At least, I was thinking what kind of answer I could possibly make, when he, on my left, speaking to me, said in what I call his gargoyle voice: Talking of Beatrice, she stripped off for me once. I told her to, and lo and behold she did! He was grinning, sour as his wine. I glanced at Catharine. She looked like that headmistress leaving court. Yes, he said, I caught the pair of them in our bedroom, dressing up. Then he glanced Catharine's way. I don't believe I ever told you this, Catharine. I believe you were out at one of your exhibitions. And I must have omitted to tell you when you came in. Then he leaned back and faced the two of us very affably. There they were at your dressing-table, Catharine. Our Amy was sitting down and Beatrice was standing next to her in the mirror. That was how they saw me coming in, in the mirror. They didn't look a bit embarrassed. They were both wearing your things, Catharine. Beatrice had a dress on like the one you're wearing now. Might even have been that one, for all I know. After grinning at me in the mirror for a minute they turned round, Amy on the stool, Beatrice standing up, and Amy said, Don't look so shocked, Dad. It's all right. Mum said we could. But I wasn't having any. Well I say you can't, I said. And I looked at Beatrice and I said, That's Catharine's. Take it off. Then she turned her back on our Amy, looked over her shoulder at her and said, Unzip me, will you, Amy. Your dad says I've got to take it off. So Amy reached up and unzipped her, she turned to face me, sort of wriggled her shoulders and down it came, with a sigh. He grinned. He liked saying 'with a sigh'. That'll do, I said, glancing again at Catharine. She was watching him. No, no, he said. Better hear the rest. I don't like to leave things undone. And he took a gulp of his mean-spirited wine. And damn me, he continued, if she wasn't wearing your bra and knickers, Catharine, and your stockings too. Mum said we could, said our Amy, but I said, Well I say you can't. They're Catharine's. Take them off. So again Beatrice turned her back on Amy. Undo me, will you, Amy. Your dad says I've to take them off. So Amy reached up and unfastened the strap. Thanks, said Beatrice. I'll manage the rest. Which she did, oh indeed she did. She managed the rest. Funny I've never told you this, Catharine. Can't think why I haven't. It was the year before she left us. Beatrice, I mean. A year and a half before our Amy left us, to join her wherever she was.

I began saying my goodbyes. Catharine begged me to stay. She said there was a pudding still, one I specially liked. But I said I was very sorry, it was time for me to go. And I did go and I left them to it, whatever it was. Walking home I decided I must do more for Catharine, if I possibly could. I didn't like to think of her alone in that big house with my peculiar friend. So I often said to myself that surely I could look after her more than I did. But I was fearful of doing more harm than good and in any case by then it was too late.

# Purgatory

1

Soon after his wife left him the Reverend Peter Simple began to have conversation with the Devil. Dr Lyons, a no-nonsense sort of man and very active in the parish, said not to worry, men of his, the Reverend Simple's, age (45) and in his situation (deserted) mostly had some such thing to put up with, not often the Devil nowadays, but some such cross. We'll keep an eye on it, he said, doctor and vicar, and if it gets much worse, if you start *seeing* him, for example, come back and we'll have another think. I'll never move now, said Peter, more to himself (or the Devil) than to Lyons. And why on earth should you? Lyons asked. You're needed here. You'll not stop the voices by jumping ship. I wanted Toxteth, said Peter, or Burnley, Salford, Brixton, somewhere like that. Instead I got Penton Mewsey with Duxford and the three Slaughters. Twenty years. And twenty still to come, said Dr Lyons, ushering him out. And don't forget Saturday, litter blitz, we meet outside the Post Office, ten o'clock sharp.

Penton Mewsey is a pretty place. The church, Mary Magdalene's, has stood for eight hundred years and in its list of vicars there is hardly a gap, wars and plagues and doctrinal mutability notwithstanding. Be honest, said the Devil, you like it here. You like old buildings. You like being able to sit in the House of God day or night, whenever you please. Peter conceded that he had grown fond of the church and of the acre around it, the yews, the lichened graves. And the moor, you love the moor, saved for the parishes by Dr Lyons and

129

other tireless activists, you love being out on the dire moor
and in the wild wood any hour of the day and night,
whenever the fancy takes you, the Devil said.

Penton Mewsey has the stone, the famous honey-stone,
that holds the warmth of summer days through the lingering
evenings into real darkness under visible stars. Duxford,
Penton Mewsey and the three Slaughters have five perfect
churches built of that stone, holiness gone into it like the sun.
And they have several good big houses with walled gardens
too, and hollyhock cottages, ancient wells and artefacts, scents
of roses and stocks, thatch and barns with faithful swallows,
and two or three rookeries, communities within the
community. The motorway, pushed aside to the east, is
nonetheless easily accessible and the railway line to London,
passing on the west, has been saved for the breadwinners by
public-spirited men and women all along its route.

You don't know when you're well off, said the Devil. I
wanted Brixton, said Peter. I might have made a difference.
Doubtful, said the Devil. Besides, as the Bishop told you,
there's soul-work everywhere. It pained Peter to be reminded
of his bishop. It pained him to remember his fellow-ordinands
who, knowing his bent, had laughed like gargoyles when they
heard he had got Penton Mewsey with Duxford and the
three Slaughters. To chasten your spirit, they roared, to test
your faith and charity. Anyway, said the Devil, I'm very glad
you're here. There's several people in this place I wouldn't
want in Hell. I rely on you, old chap, to get them into
Heaven. Don't call me 'old chap', said Peter. You know I can't
stand it.

For some months after his arrival in Penton Mewsey
Peter had asked everyone to call him 'Pete'. But nobody
would. All the women and many of the men addressed him
as 'Vicar' or 'Reverend Simple'. A few men managed 'Peter'
and later, especially when they wished to correct him or
secure his support for one cause or another, they called him
'My dear Peter', often putting an arm around his shoulders as

they did so. Testingly at first, then with complete confidence, the parishioners of the five churches claimed him as one of their kind. And he let them. For some years, perhaps ten of the twenty already served, he had honestly believed that somewhere in himself he still possessed his own soul, whatever they called him and whatever assumptions they made. Then over ten more years that faith dwindled. I'm too conciliatory, he said to his wife. That's my trouble. That's one of your troubles, she replied.

Apart from jogging, which since his desertion he was close to giving up, Peter's leisure activities were much as they might have been in the civilised eighteenth century. He cultivated his garden. He studied the natural and local history of his parishes, adding or correcting a detail here and there. And in all weathers he went for long walks. Even before his children and his wife left home these walks had mostly been solitary. To recuperate, he said. From what? his wife asked.

Peter's favourite haunt was the site – a clover bank, a few courses of stone, a cressy well – of a place called Purgatory. In his fief of five parishes, after much searching, he had found nowhere more remote than Purgatory. There the motorway was inaudible, unless the wind blew strongly from the east, which it almost never did; and the only man-made things in the sky, and only on Sundays, were gliders, white, silent and graceful in their slow circling descents. So Peter came and sat on a stone in the remains of Purgatory whose name, attested in Domesday, pleased him. Very fond of ruins, aren't we, said the Devil. Bare ruined choirs, that sort of thing. Peter said it fortified him, sitting for an hour or so in the scant ruins of Purgatory. Birdsong, the spring water, a rabbit now and then... Of course, said the Devil, you'd rather be in Salford, but coming here, kneeling at the spring, thinking your thoughts, under no flight path, civil or military, hearing no traffic, seeing no chicken battery, it's a good second best and it does give you strength to face your early morning ladies.

Early Communion was indeed a trial of Peter's faith and

charity. He savoured the words, Take and eat this in remembrance that Christ died for thee… Drink this in remembrance that Christ's blood was shed for thee… but the actual earthly presence of Mrs Evenlode, Mrs Charnley and Mrs Bassett, his three takers, their indecent beatitude, their thin voracious mouths, their ringed and jewelled claws, their drapes, disgusted him. God forgive me, he said to the Devil, I wish they'd catch the bird flu. But they never missed, the weird sisters, month after month, in the cold early morning church, Peter's ladies kneeled and he helped them to the Saviour.

Then on a Sunday in late May, first after Trinity, not that it matters, at 8.21, with his back to the crows (as he unkindly called his communicants), raising the chalice, Peter felt, like a thrust through his left side, the certainty that he was being watched. Eyes, staring eyes, down the leper slit, a famous feature of the church of Mary Magdalene in the village of Penton Mewsey. Eyes. Peter saw the eyes and they looked into his. The wine, not literally blood but symbolising blood, suffered a moment of turmoil in the chalice. Turning, Peter administered a sip of it to Mrs Bassett, Mrs Charnley and Mrs Evenlode, the white linen in his hand. And the eyes watched him, he could feel them. He got through the service – we most heartily thank thee, for that thou dost vouchsafe to feed us – the ladies noticing nothing. Often he had felt they noticed nothing. He officiated, of him in his own person they were oblivious. Often he had felt, I am not really here and, It does not matter whether I am really here or not, I officiate, I stand for something. But the eyes down the leper slit fixed him in his proper self, no doubt of that. When the church was empty and the phrases of the Blessing were fading from the air, Peter turned in a hurry to rejoin the eyes, fearful they would have fled and he would have no reassurance they had ever been. But there they still were, staring. He could not have said were they hungry or amazed, angry or pleading – only that they were fierce. Who are you? he asked, leaning close. What do you want? Can I help you? They made no answer.

Peter backed away, willing the eyes to remain. Then, passing out of sight of them, he ran down the aisle, out at the south porch and through the grass and the graves round the north wall of his familiar church. But he was not quick enough – except to see a bulky creature, a man, dark-skinned and naked, already beyond the graveyard wall and lumbering through a field of early potatoes all athwart the ridges, towards the wood. It was an early Sunday morning in late May, the kind of morning the villagers had in mind when they congratulated one another on living in paradise.

There was no presence at the leper slit during the 10.30 Communion. Peter expected none, still he kept glancing where it would have shown. At the door he shook hands with the congregation, declined three offers to lunch (since his desertion there were always some) and in the big vicarage kitchen he warmed up his soup from the day before, took a glass of wine with it, and sank deep into the privacy of thinking about the eyes and their blundering owner fleeing towards the wood. His passionate reverie was interrupted by a phone call from Dr Lyons asking jokily had he started seeing things yet and very earnestly might they meet before long – would Wednesday at 6.30 suit? – to discuss what to do about the Post Office? Yes, said Peter, wishing Dr Lyons in Hell. Till Evensong, in a violent agitation, he dug at the vicarage garden and re-read an article by one of his predecessors, the Reverend Elijah Strange, on the old leper hospital attached to Mary Magdalene's. Strange, disagreeing with earlier authorities, located it in the wood not on the moor. But that was in 1837. No one since, as Peter well knew, had found any stone of it for certain anywhere.

Evensong was very beautiful, the sun streaming in, the choir swelled by songsters from the three Slaughters, but there were no eyes at the slit. Peter felt possessed like a man suddenly in love, changed by a great secret, and still moving among people who presumed to know him well. He filled out the usual prayers with a fervour quite private to himself. He saw the fierce eyes of his visitant, then the bulky flesh, naked, dark, nearly black in its dirt or natural pigment, making across the potato ridges into the ancient wood.

The wood, recorded in Domesday, the biggest in the county, had birds and beasts in it, but also some humans from time to time. Lovers went in there; the intrepid Mrs Shabbington, in khaki, led her painters into the very heart of it, especially in winter, to open their eyes to the silvery beauty of old man's beard; every week of summer Professor Poyle took a party in, to listen to the nightingales, and an elite of that party on Midsummer Night, for the dawn chorus in what he called 'a cathedral of beeches'. Others went in solitary, for good or ill. There was a black pond that no one could look you in the eye and mention. So that evening of his revelation the Reverend Peter Simple went in late and very stealthily at a point nearest the last trodden breach in the potato rows. After that, of course, he was clueless. In the big wood his naked angel, beggar, outcast or witness might have been anywhere. There was a new track through the justly famous bluebells but, for all Peter could tell, it had been made by muntjac, badgers or a girl leading a boy to a place she desired to show him. But really Peter did not care whether he found his naked man or not; and after a while of wandering in a way that would have baffled God's spies, and wishing to make less noise, he sat down against a tree nowhere in particular and fell asleep. When he awoke, some minutes or hours later, he could not for the life of him think who or where he was. He felt the damp, the chill, he smelled the earth and its mould, there was a crawling on his cheek, his lashes were wet. He had toppled sideways, curled like a grub, and in the very faint light saw everything slant and odd. Then particular self with a rush came back into him and he felt gladness, gratitude and pride. His naked savage was somewhere among these peculiarly living and breathing night-time trees and he, the Vicar of Penton Mewsey, Duxford and the three Slaughters, was in among them with him.

Riots in Burnley, said the Devil. Another stabbing in Brixton. Peter shrugged. Not that I don't care, he said, but as you yourself have often pointed out to me, there's work to be done here, even here. Happier lately, aren't we? said the Devil. If I didn't know you better, I'd say you had found a good woman at last. Instead it's an unlovely nudist with no manners. Sneer all you like, said Peter, you won't spoil this for me.

Peter's faith was high. Twice more at Early Communion, after gaps that caused him suffering, he had seen the eyes, and alone after the Blessing he had spoken to them, down the slit. No language had answered, or nothing that sounded like language, but some grunts, and the gaze became fiercer, more urgent. To pursue the wild man as on the first occasion now seemed a tactlessness. Instead, each in his own voice, they conversed through the ancient wall. No more than that, but decisive for Peter. He felt called.

Others besides the Devil had noticed a change in Peter. You seem better in yourself, Vicar, said Mrs Wychwood, fixing a Ramblers notice to her front door. I believe I am, Mrs Wychwood, Peter replied. The ladies had been watching him since his desertion for signs of his getting over it and perking up. And now he was indeed, as the Devil had observed, like a man in love who has energy and goodwill in abundance because of it. He became extraordinarily amenable. Already nobbled by Dr Lyons, he agreed at a public meeting that if the Government went ahead with its damnable policy and extinguished Penton Mewsey's Post Office he would give Mrs Begbroke a home in St Mary's vestry. Furthermore, Lyons announced, the service would become peripatetic, rather as the Vicar's was, and would visit Duxford and the three Slaughters at least once a week in a Securicor van kindly offered by Colonel Akeman who still had what he called a foothold on their board. Thank you, Colonel. Thank you, Vicar. On ragwort and hogweed days the Reverend

Simple was outstanding. In the fields being cleansed for Aunty Betty's new horses his pile of forked and golden corpses exceeded everyone else's. Merry village work, and their vicar was tireless. And Yes, he said at once, when the mummers asked could they gather as they always had in the vicarage on Boxing Day, half a dozen ladies springing forward to help him with the catering, Mrs Simple now being gone. And even on the day's most difficult issue, the future of the old USAF base at Frideswide's, at last he made up his mind and swung against the County Council, who wanted it for social housing, to the ramblers, the birders, the painters, the environmentalists, who wanted it for a nature reserve. There was much rejoicing in that camp when he spoke his mind. Many were old campaigners from the Cruise days, who had tracked and harried the giant weapons down the flowery lanes like hunt saboteurs. We'll plant a tree there, said Joanna, hugging him, and set a stone below it saying The Triumph of Peace. Shan't we, Bob? Bob smiled. Poor Bob, said Joanna, but I know he's thrilled. Good for you, Pete, said the Devil, catching up with him after the meeting. I'm glad to see you popular. And a very good thing, after yesterday's bombings, that you add your voice to the call for the Triumph of Peace. To be honest, said Peter, I was thinking of my savage. Where will he go if they keep on building?

A day or two later, not entirely easy about his vote on the Frideswide Base and in a deep thought and concentration arriving at Purgatory, Peter saw himself preceded at the spring. The naked man was kneeling over the water and for the first time Peter saw him close: his tight grizzled hair; his scratched, scarred, encrusted, swart skin; the large fleshy shoulders. Then the heavy head lifted and showed, beneath a flattened nose, a dripping green beard of cress and weed, abundant, frothing and hard to say was he swallowing it or spewing it forth. Silence; the thrush of the place resumed. The naked man sat back on his heels and glared at Peter over the muddy greenery of his mouth. Peter raised his hands, in the gesture of harmlessness and surrender, and when the man made no move to flee, Peter opened the satchel he always had with him on his walks, a good leather bag, like a pilgrim's scrip, so he often told himself, took out a hunk of bread and offered it. The savage glared, then snatched; and crammed the bread fiercely through the cress and weed into his mouth. Peter nodded and smiled. There see, no harm, he said. And he took a step forward, offering his empty hand. But this was too much. The savage stood up, revealing his filthy paunch and a fat sexual organ retracted into a matted nest of hair, backed away, turned and fled. Peter watched him go, through a field of beans, through another of mangolds, shambling at his fastest towards the distant wood. The man's exposure under the sky on the open fields quickened his heart with wonder and pity.

A couple of days after this breakthrough (as he would call it) in Peter's relationship with the innocent savage, the Devil intercepted him on his way into the wood and suggested they climb the hill together, for a change. Not much of a hill, five hundred feet or so, but high for thereabouts and offering clear perspectives in all directions. It was slow summer nightfall. See, said the Devil, the last train, such a brave sight, two small lighted carriages bearing away west to the beginnings of some real hills. And over there, east, the deflected motorway, its lights so close in both directions they make two shivering cords, one white, one red, of the stuff of modern life. And down there, north, barely a mile away, under the arc lights, our chicken battery, and down there, south, what's that, old chap, that bigger battery, that even harder lighting? Yes, yes, said Peter. And yes there was a vacancy for a C of E chaplain, part-time, and yes I might have applied and didn't and yes Dr Lyons said what on earth would be the point, they're all Muslims in there or Catholics, Greek Orthodox, Hindu, Voodoo, that sort of thing, and no I would not have made a difference, better off where I was, doing no harm at least. South, beyond the Detention Centre, the town threw up its orange stain on the eternal sky aching to darken. Look at the moor, said Peter, filling with darkness, and the few lights of the villages slung on a necklace around it. And the wood, such a substantial darkness, not a light showing, a black-out. And west, on the softly quietening sunset, the brave train heading towards the big hills, the borderland, the beginnings of something like a homeland for the pilgrim soul. Would that be fire? asked the Devil, pointing south. Would that be the red smoke of yet another fire in the Runnymede Detention Centre? Peter watched. Soon the sight established itself incontrovertibly as smoke and fire. Sweet Christ, not again, said the Reverend Peter Simple. There'll be a break-out, won't there? I suppose so, said the Devil. They heard the sirens, faintly but gathering. Helicopters over Purgatory? Very likely, said the Devil. Private and public uniforms with their guns and dogs? That's usually the way, said the Devil. But try to admire it as a spectacle while you can. The red smoke, the lights. Reminds me of the wallpaintings at Middle Slaughter, the ones you don't much care for. I often wonder what you'd find under the whitewash of St Mary's, if you looked. Ah, the good old days... But Peter was thinking of his Green Man. I'll hide him, he said. I'll have him in the vicarage, if he'll come. By the way, said the Devil, still viewing the distant but impressive fire, I've been meaning to ask you. Are you sure he's green? Are you sure he's black? Might it not be dirt? Where do you suppose he came from? Is he a moon calf? Did he fall out of the sky the way frogs do after a tornado? Has there been a tornado in these parts lately? Why won't he speak? Why is he naked? Has he got a conscience? Is there anything on it if he has? Peter shook his head. For I was an hungred, said the Devil, and ye gave me meat: I was thirsty and ye gave me drink: I was a stranger and ye took me in: Naked, and ye clothed me... That sort of thing. What a pretty fire. Looks like the east wing this time. What a waste of private public money. And by the way, have you called on Mr Hampton yet? You visited his wife when she believed him dead. But what about him? He's back, is he not? Another thing I can't stand about you, said Peter, is that you're forever asking me questions to which you know the answers. You're very like my wife in that respect.

2

Even before the July bombings there was something heroic about the daily commuting to London from Penton Mewsey and the other rescued stations along that surviving line. The heroism of effort; every day the summoning up of the necessary resolve, patience and resourcefulness into the will to get there and back. So much went wrong, when things went right it made an extra anxiety for surely something worse must soon happen, to restore disorder, the natural state. The standing pressed their middle parts into the faces of the sitting. At one station or another, for some ferociously determined customer in a wheelchair the guard would lower the ramp and drive a dozen able-bodied out of the coop reserved for the one. Daily he told the sitting, standing, leaning, crouching in the aisles, seats, doorways and toilets that if they were animals transporting them thus to the slaughter would be illegal. People read, it might be a newspaper or *War and Peace* or the top-secret documents for a meeting in the Home Office, and tickled one another's faces turning the pages. They roared into their phones, they shared their emails. Some slept, held upright or suddenly slumping sideways into unasked-for intimacy; others strove – you could see the effort of it crizzling their faces – to expand the confines of the head into boundlessness. And train after train arriving in Paddington, and down all the other radii into all the other stations, disbursed anxiety down the tube lines and the bus lanes, the fear of halting, the continuous reassessing of the options for escape and arrival should a failure or a fatality block the way. Setting forth and returning in the more or less light, the worse or better weather of the earth's seasons, the sensations of it entered every hurrying soul ineradicably. Why do it? For the relief when it was done, the meadowsweet branch-line, the coming home to the orchards, moths and scented gardens, the golden-retriever stone, the drinks, the lawns, the river terraces, the log fires, the high walls, the chimes, the hot shower, the eats, the more drinks, their perhaps not yet sleeping, perhaps not yet left-home children, their spouses.

The Devil was right when he charged the Reverend Simple with being reluctant to visit the returned Mr Hampton. He, Peter, had done well enough with Mrs Hampton on his visit to her in the missing days. Don't give up hope, he said. And lo and behold, on the Monday after the bombs the lost man came home. But even before his front door had opened and closed on him most of Penton Mewsey and much of Duxford and the three Slaughters knew that the blessing was mixed and that straightforward congratulations were not in order.

Mr Hampton's arrival was unforgettable. The three Johns, his first witnesses, recounted it till the end of their time on earth. They were at work in the station garden, the jewel of Penton Mewsey, winner every year among the Rescued Stations in Bloom, when John W., taking a leak into the compost heap, saw through the screening delphiniums a figure, Mr Hampton, limping in a heat haze towards him down the track. He alerted the others, Johnny P. and John Mac, and together amidst their flowers they watched the man they had known pretty well come nearer as a stranger. His suit was torn and horribly stained, his decent shoes were battered; face, hair, and the bare hands gripping a newspaper to his chest, were filthy. Reaching the wooden crossing where the platform ended in a slope, he halted. The three gardeners hurried out to help. He ignored them. When they called to him − Stan was his Christian name − he started again into painful motion, climbed the slope and passed close by them without a sign of common life. On the platform they watched him exit through the Tuscan-coloured station, the back of his suit was grey and mottled, like a shroud. Again they shouted, Stan! But he went on his way, crippled and mechanically, down the cherry road into Penton Mewsey, past the cricket pitch, over the stone bridge, to his home.

As everyone points out, said the Devil, approaching the Old School House with the Reverend Simple, our Stanley had no business being anywhere near the bombs. For twenty years he went west on the District and Circle to St James's Park and so to Petty France. Then why? Peter began, but the Hamptons' door opened, Dr Lyons appeared on the step, and the Devil quitted Peter without farewells. One for you, old boy, said Dr Lyons. Beyond me anyway. Will he see me? Peter asked. I'm not sure he *sees* anybody, said Lyons. Not among the living at least. Mrs Hampton, averting her eyes, let Peter in. Back room, she said. Be careful. It's dark.

Peter stood on the threshold. The heavy curtains were drawn but he could make out Mr Hampton sitting oddly on a high-backed chair in the quite large and grossly over-furnished room. The clutter, and the sitter's arbitrary place in the midst of it, made the loss of any holding centre palpable. My dear Stanley, said Peter. Stanley was dressed as he had been when he appeared to the three Johns, still pressing the soiled newspaper against his chest. He looked at the Vicar, his visitor, as though his eyes had had their seeing parts removed and continued in existence only vacantly. Peter went closer, stood over him – the eyes lifted blankly – then kneeled before him, and the eyes were lowered. Mr Hampton stank, he was still clad in the filth of his long march from a place underground. The newspaper was folded open on a page, an extensive gallery, of photographs. At Peter's closeness the fingers tightened on it. They were perhaps more conscious than the voided eyes. Can we speak? Peter asked. No answer. Can you give me any sign that you understand? None. Then as Peter looked he began to feel himself appraised, but as though by an insect, a crustacean, a stone, something that lives and feels in a way a human can't begin to fathom, and he backed away, appraised and failing. In the living room, against a gallery of photographs of her children and grandchildren, Mrs Hampton stood vaguely waiting for him. He saw his own depths of failure in her look. She shrugged. He began to try to speak but became aware of a growing noise in the sky above the Old School House. The helicopter, searching. He let himself out. The helicopter, as though summoned, tugged away abruptly and headed for the moor.

There were armed police in the vicarage garden. One officer said, Excuse us, Vicar. Just looking. You've seen nobody? Peter shook his head. How many might there be? A dozen or more. They never rightly know. In the kitchen Peter heated up some soup and took two glasses of wine with it. My nerves, he said aloud. Between Mr Hampton and the naked savage he turned in perplexity and fear. Hampton frightened him; and for the savage, in the wood, in the fields, on the moor somewhere, he felt an even greater fear. In this paralysis of body and soul he sobbed with relief when his familiar, the Devil, spoke. Odd thing about these occasions, the Devil said: more go missing than will ever be accounted for. Some, like our friend Stanley, set off walking, they walk and walk and, unlike Stanley, they never end up anywhere. Others see the chance they've been waiting for and quite deliberately they vanish. What will happen to him? Peter asked. Stan? No, my savage. The Devil shrugged, I don't pretend to know what will be. But with all the force and hardware around his chances don't look good. I should help him, shouldn't I? said Peter. You should indeed, old chap, and soon. Instead of the Devil, Peter saw Stanley Hampton, his eyes, their light put out, his ripped and bloodstained clothes, the photographs clutched against his heart. The word I hear, said the Devil, is that he had a plan. And if he'd got past Liverpool Street and if the other half of his plan had got through too, they'd be away, among the missing, absent for good and mourned. Peter scarcely entertained this attractive possibility. Instead the gorgon fact of Mr and Mrs Hampton stared him in the face. He saw them jailed in the Old School House for ever more. And he saw himself, their priest, avoiding them like lepers.

Peter corked his wine, thrust it into his satchel; added bread, sausage and fruit from Saturday's Farmers' Market; put on the long loose jacket and the wide hat he affected for his longer walks; strode to the door; but returned for the roll of notes his wife had always kept hidden, for emergencies, in the old teapot above the range. At this last forethought the Devil smiled. Nice of her to leave it, Peter said.

The police had gone but two officers from Runnymede stood at the vicarage gates with dogs. Good evening, Father, said the burlier of the two. Peter nodded. Please don't call me 'Father'. Found anyone yet? Not yet, not yet. Peter was moving off, but the officer detained him, saying, And to be honest, Father, we're not quite getting the co-operation we should be getting. Peter shrugged. Then the second officer began to speak, but in a language so rapid, vehement and barbarous that Peter only understood its tone. He turned to the first officer, who said, Yes, Father, my colleague here thinks there's misguided people in this place think it's clever to hide the runaways under their beds and smuggle them on from house to house under cover of darkness and what these people don't seem to realise, my colleague Vlad here thinks, is that in Africa or wherever else they've come from these escaping persons have done the most horrible things – chopped off kiddies' hands, for example, thrown their neighbours' grannies into burning churches, fed their wives to the crocodiles etc – and it's no wonder, Vlad here says, they lose their passports and lose their tongues and run around naked so we shan't know where they belong and send them back there on an aeroplane to get their just deserts, my colleague says. I see, said Peter. Enjoy your walk, father. I will, said Peter.

Avoiding the Old School House, Peter came circuitously

to the main road from the station which was busy with pedestrians, cyclists and drivers of 4x4s arriving home after another day in the anxious city. Their faces showed an imminent relief. Drinks on the patio. Water the tomatoes and the runner beans. Ten hours at least before they need go back. All saluted their vicar and he saluted them. Along came the three Johns in a convoy, cycling with little trailers that contained their tools, waterproofs and lunch-boxes. Each in turn waved very cheerily. They had grown in stature since the homecoming of Mr Hampton. They would for ever be the witnesses. They had seem him appear out of the heat haze down the miles of inexorable track. They had seen that he had stopped seeing the world they saw. He saw another world they could not see. They spread this news through the paradisal villages. Whose blood was on his clothes? Only his own?

Peter crossed the road and set off walking rapidly on his own paths towards Purgatory. Yes, said the Devil, no time to lose. Peter told him what the Runnymede officers had said about a village network that aided and abetted the runaways. Joanna, I suppose, and poor Bob? I know they visit. Indeed, said the Devil. And Alan and Betty from among the painters, Ted in the Ramblers, Johnny P.'s wife, the old campaigners... What I can't stand about you, said Peter, is that I can never tell you anything. My wife was just the same. Always knew everything I ever told her, not once did she ever say, Well, goodness me, I didn't know that. Very sorry, said the Devil. But unlike Some I could mention I don't pretend to be omniscient. Really I only know what you know or should know or won't admit you know. Then Peter was ashamed of his bad temper. He cleared his mind for the innocent savage. How to save him?

Nearing Purgatory, Peter trod as quietly as he could. He had ceased to expect his visitant at the leper slit and since the break-out had begged him in prayers not to risk showing himself there. Purgatory was a solitude. In all the years Peter had met no one in it but the Devil in conversation and the wild man in the flesh. He came through the willows and the buttercups, saw the place before him, and halted. His naked savage was seated in the clover, leaning back against the remains of the ancient wall, entirely exposed. His face, draggled green from eating and drinking at the spring and lit by the declining sun, showed such terror, such helpless dread, that Peter clutched at his own heart in the shock of pity.

The savage sensed him, turned, but made no move to flee. Fear seemed to paralyse him. Peter came close, but shyly, and ashamed to have a wild thing at his mercy. Come, he said, let me help you. Let me find you sanctuary. The naked man began to whimper; his hands, lifting towards the sky, shook. I know, said Peter, the noise. But they won't find you, I promise. Then, very faintly, came another noise: dogs. At that the wild man yelped, leapt to his feet and after turning and turning in terrified bewilderment, set off at a clumsy run across the big fields. Peter followed. How could he make his pursuit appear benevolent? At first he called out, but soon desisted, fearful of his own voice and the real pursuers. But the wild man halted, looked back, waited, and only when Peter came within twenty yards or so did he resume his shambling run. And in this fashion, halting, waiting, fleeing, the two men, naked and clothed, crossed three or four fields and stood at last face to face, only ten yards between them, at the border of the wood. You're about my age, said Peter. Let me help you. I've got food and wine in here – patting his satchel – let me share them with you. The wild man glared, his fingers scratched unceasingly at his blotched thighs and paunch. Grunts came from him, but nothing remotely like a language. Then both men heard the dogs, closer, and behind Peter's back, still at some distance, the savage seemed to spy them. The timbre of his utterances changed, rising again into little yelps and squeals. Then he turned and entered the wood, Peter following more clumsily, with more noise, far louder and closer on the wild man than the dogs. They stamped through the bluebells, long finished, on the track that might have been made by beasts or lovers. They tangled with honeysuckle and old man's beard. They ran through the long high cathedral of beeches. Stop! cried Peter. Do stop! Don't run away from me any more! But his savage would not stop. Peter got close enough to hear his grunts and snuffles, to smell his fear, and almost, once, to touch his soiled and lacerated flesh, but stumbled, fell, and a hazel branch swept off his pilgrim's hat. The savage broke through into the hole in the heart of the wood and there, as Peter and the howling of dogs came after him, he ran full tilt into the pool, its heart of hearts, and vanished. The dogs, like the rattle of the helicopter over the Old School House, suddenly swerved and careered off elsewhere, to the moor perhaps, fainter and fainter, to the dire moor that had swallowed up so much before Domesday and after. Peter stood on the edge of the pool that no one can mention and look you in the eye. Its liquid is so thick and black with rotted leaves as hardly to permit any rising bubbles through.

The Devil came and stood by him. Your hat, he said. Peter put it on. He was not surprised to see the Devil entirely visible in the flesh. Nothing about him was unfamiliar. Time I went to see Dr Lyons again, said Peter. Time we had another think. You're way beyond him, said the Devil. More your own sort of territory, I should say. Right as usual, said Peter, staring into the pool. The wood was darkening, the pool, blacker and blacker, sucked and heaved on its own foul substance. He thought of bubbles in it unable to reach the air. I'm leaving, he said. Salford? said the Devil. They torched a primary school there yesterday. Burnley? They trashed the Asian Community Centre. No, said Peter. I'm going missing. I'm going to walk and walk and be among the missing. West, I'm going, and now, before it gets quite dark. Well, I'll be damned, said the Devil. You do surprise me.

# The Blind Home

Then between the wars the new houses – decent semis with bay windows and generous gardens – occupied the fields in which the halls and villas had enjoyed fresh air and privacy for fifty or a hundred years or more. Old and new, the rich were overwhelmed. The first war took their sons, coachmen and gardeners till they could hardly manage among the deteriorating fields. They sold and moved, the markets sliced their dwellings into flats or left them over decades to the trespassers, the ghosts and demolition. One became a hotel for commercial travellers. But Fair Hope, on the old road west, almost opposite the Union and the infirmary, passed to the Corporation for its blinded men.

I found all this out not very long ago in the little public library, visiting; all this and more, all public knowledge, in the course of one short winter afternoon. Dear me, I thought, that house we smashed the mirrors in was Jacobean. I stayed two nights in the hotel for commercial travellers (a vanished breed) and poked around. I thought the past was a foreign country and I'd be all right in it for a day or two, as a traveller, not stopping; but it isn't and I wasn't and I'll not go back there again, not this side of the grave.

Smithy and me. Laburnum Avenue ended at the Fair Hope Blind Home wall and that's where we were, in our pair of semis, right up under the black high wall, Smithy closest to it. Owls at night, and such a singing at first light as the year began, you'd have thought you were in the country.

One thing we had in common, the Smiths and us, we

were both bombed out from where we did belong, in our case Myrtle Grove, off Tootal Road, in theirs Cow Lane, between Oldfield Road and Liverpool Street. But that, so my mother often said, was as far as any similarity went. Our semi we got properly but next door's, left vacant when the owner fled the Blitz, was requisitioned for them and in they moved and there they intended staying. Also, my mother said, we knew how to live in a nice new house in a nice area and next door did not. Still my mother never stopped me playing there. She feared I was growing up lonely. Smithy had Enid, Angie, Brian, Shirley, Reggie and Kevin around him in the family whereas I had no one, two brothers and two sisters having tried and failed to live before and after I succeeded.

Because of the war my father was away, and even after it for long periods also, near London, I believe, on courses training for a better job so that we'd be able to seize the opportunities, when they came. Smithy's dad was soon back on the scene, large as life, and took up his old trade at the abattoir. Which reminds me that just beyond the Blind Home in those first years after the war there was still a farm and I saw cattle now and then slopping along in the traffic and herded right at Stott Lane over the railway line and through to Liverpool Street and the slaughterhouse. Smithy said his dad said he'd take us in there any day we liked, to watch the business. He showed me trophies his dad had brought him home, a snout, a pair of ears, a bull-pizzle. See these, he said. There's a photo of me at our front door, Whit Sunday, in the new clothes I always got for walking with the scholars. I can't bear to look at it, and not just because of the brothers and sisters who might have been there either side of me. So no wonder I never did ask Smithy when are we going to the abattoir with your dad?

You can't see Smithy's semi in that photograph but, take my word, it was a wreck compared with ours. My first time in there, they had the front room floorboards up and only single planks laid across the joists, for bridges. Smithy's mam gave us both a sugar butty and we sat side by side on a plank and ate it, dangling our bare legs down over the hole. Crunching sugar through the bread and marge, the sweet harshness through that softness, and the damp of the earth coming up from under us, I never felt such a reckless happiness before or since. Same with his garden. In all the photos of me in ours what you never even catch a glimpse of is next door's and the junk chucked out in it. But Smithy had the trees, black poplars, along the Blind Home wall, three in his garden but another, the best, stood in the home itself and reached across, in the far corner, over Smithy's air-raid shelter, and that was our way in, by a ladder on the shelter roof, out along a level branch and down by a knotted rope. Fun and games. In the shelter were a few old things, a couple of gasmasks, for example, which we put on and stared at one another goggle-eyed. Smithy's older brothers were away at sea and brought back curiosities whenever they came home: a monkey once, a blue hare, a cockatoo. These creatures lived in a draughty shed until they died. The brothers home on leave would remember their gypsy origins and go off with a gun to what was left of Swinton Fields. In they came, down Laburnum Avenue, swinging a rabbit and chortling. Their mam was proud of them. Or they sat on the Blind Home wall and shot crows with an air rifle. Once when Smithy and me were in there crawling through the undergrowth indian-fashion, they fired and a jay fell down in front of us. I rested my hand on it until it died. There's no blue in the world like that in the feathers of a jay.

For me the Blind Home was the best but there were other places I liked going to with Smithy and sometimes his kid sister Enid tagging on. The ponds in Swinton Fields where we made a raft of drums and planks and shoved out heavily over the idling pike. And the Camp, that was the army's during the war, where we lit fires in the smashed-up prefabs and took the trenches on Bonfire Night with fistfuls of Little Demons. And the Hall, the one I learned was

Jacobean, some fun we had in there till the Corporation arrived to demolish it, trespassing on our ground. Smithy told me going to school that a lorry had backed over a workman's head and the massive stain of it was on the gravel, would I like to come and see?

My father, when he was home for good, worked a couple of evenings as club collector and in a little factory for electro-plating. That was extra, so we should get on. His main work, for which he wore a suit, was behind the counter in the Labour Exchange, close by the Docks. A lot of effing and blinding and some actual thumping and kicking went on down there, which must have upset him, since he was a gentle person. There was none of that in our house, needless to say, but next door many Fridays and most Saturdays, especially when the brothers were home, there would be fights. It woke me and I listened. Once or twice Mrs Smith slammed out of the house and yelled she was going to her mother's and would never come back, but mostly it kept indoors. It was the father mainly, the slaughterman, hitting out and smashing things. Then he'd go down bump, shaking our semi as much as theirs, and Kevin or Reggie or Brian would shout to tie the bugger up. After that we had some peace. And next day, Sunday, we might see the whole happy family in the garden cooking dinner over a campfire just for a lark. Once it was hedgehogs baked in clay, gipsy-fashion, the skin and prickles coming off together when you cracked the earthen shell, and the strong meat laid bare. Smithy's dad said try a bit when he saw me spying through the fence.

Most Sundays, weather permitting, my father spent up a ladder. Six days shalt thou labour, he liked to say, and the seventh do odd jobs. So he would be up a ladder, as high as the meeting of the roofs if necessary, painting the woodwork, pointing the brickwork, fixing gutters, sills, windows, downspouts. His upkeep halted exactly where the Smiths' semi joined, making comparison unavoidable. Mr Smith stood in the wasteland of his garden genially calling up praise which my father acknowledged with thanks in a very civil way.

What excited me about the Fair Hope Blind Home was that by its inmates, its proper denizens, I could not be seen. Neither the ponds nor the Camp nor the ruined hall did I ever go to on my own, but by a secret route I had discovered for myself (through the old coach house, off the adjoining road) I did get into the Blind Home all alone, crept through the fringe of trees, located an inmate sitting exposed on the well-kept lawn, stood up and walked towards him, quiet as a ghost, invisible. It felt, between my legs, like the thrill of being naked in a place where discovery would have ended my life in shame. It felt like trespass on the innocence of their eyes. But mostly I was with Smithy, sometimes also with Enid, each crossing the lawn from his or her own direction, the loser being the one the blind man turned his seeking face to first. The lawns were vast, well-kept, and in many places, because of incoming trees, quite out of sight of the big house that had been the private hall. This favoured our stalking. The blind were brought out by the keepers and left in a strange isolation on benches or in their wheelchairs, at our mercy.

Fun and games. Once Smithy did a thing that will surely have haunted him for the rest of his life. He threw a firework towards a blind old gentleman sitting in a greatcoat with his hands on his knees and his face lit by the winter sun. Not a big firework and not very near the old man, but the bang caused a scream, such a scream, and the face of the scream, staring blindly, was stretched and exposed in terror till the owner covered it with hands as white as tripe and rolled on the grass, screaming and seeking to make himself very small, small as a foetus, small as a grub, to get in under the bench out of harm's way. We ran, fearing the keepers, and left him to his fit. We called that one the Shaker because we never saw him sitting still again.

You never knew where you were with Smithy. At thirty

151

paces the blind, their noses compensating for their extinguished
eyes, could smell him, he smelled of piss and unwashed
clothes and sometimes of carbolic or a strong stuff for his hair.
They might hear him too, he sniffed a good deal and wiped
away the snot on his jersey sleeve. Sunny Jim, they'd say, we
know you're there. Come nearer, son, and sing us one of your
songs. For Smithy had the voice of an angel, the clearest,
sweetest voice I've ever heard. Blackbird, thrush and
nightingale, but human. He had that perfection in him till his
voice broke, I suppose.

I first heard Smithy sing when I was sent with a message
from my teacher, Mr Chapman, in 3A, to his, Miss Benson, in
3B – from a quiet class of 30 to a bedlam of 50. School
decided pretty quickly, A or B, what would become of you
when it had done with you, and me and Smithy, although
most days we went together and even came back together,
often to his air-raid shelter, from the start we had been
moving along parting lines. But that day, handing Miss
Benson, who was in tears, her note from Mr Chapman I saw
Smithy in the midst of the riot and he saw me, the messenger
from 3A. Something happened in him, I couldn't say what
exactly, and he walked unbidden to the front of the class, up
on to Miss Benson's daïs and said, Please, Miss, I'll sing a song
if that's all right with you. And not waiting for her yes or no
he blew his nose in his hand, wiped his hand on the bum of
his pants, and in a sudden total hush, looking only at me, he
began to sing. It was 'Over the Sea to Skye' in the classroom
then, everybody hushed, but on the lawn in the Blind Home,
singing to the General, say, or Pegleg, Dracula, or the one
called Freddy, it was 'Danny Boy', 'Barbara Allen' and 'Silent
Night', if my memory serves. It did something to Freddy,
hard to say what exactly, and whenever we stalked him after
that and got anywhere near he turned his white face Smithy's
way and said, Is that you, son? Is that the singing boy?

Two horse-drawn vehicles visited Laburnum Avenue, at their times. One was Vincent, the ice-cream man. He pulled up and shouted, Ice Cream, yes! The old firm! and my mother sent me out to queue with a bowl for a family helping and a dash of crimson raspberry on top. And the other was the rag and bone man. Rag Bone! Sam Bone! he shouted, and a few women came out who had moved into Laburnum Avenue from elsewhere when they had their chance, because of the war perhaps. What stuff they gave him he gave them a donkey stone in return, for doing the step with, though for that there was no call in Laburnum Avenue and most, I daresay, did what we did and took it to any of the family still living in parts that had a step to donkeystone.

My mother felt more and more sorry for my friend Smithy, and for Enid and Angie too, but mostly for Smithy, and she would sometimes give the rag and bone man clothes of mine and show him with a nod next door where he should pass them on. And Mrs Smith, after a decent interval, would come out to the cart with perhaps a bit of lead that Mister had nicked and Sam Bone would give her the package instead of a stone. Then Smithy went to school in my cast-offs and nobody mentioned it.

In due course I began to see less of Smithy because most afternoons I stayed behind for extra teaching to get into the grammar school and at the weekend too I had more homework. But whenever I could I was climbing on his air-raid shelter and up and over with him into the Blind Home grounds. One day we were in there lying on our bellies just where the lawns began, waiting for a blinded man to be walked or wheeled to a seat exposed in the sun. Smithy had brought his dad's old bayonet with him and was stabbing it again and again into the ground. He asked me what my dad did in the war and I told him I didn't rightly know, only that he had bad eyes and couldn't use a gun so they sent him to London clearing houses in the Blitz and after that he was in India doing I don't know what. So you reckon he never killed anyone? Smithy asked. Pretty sure not, I said. My dad killed lots, he said. And he explained that when you stabbed with a bayonet and it was in, you had to twist it hard before you pulled it out. Maybe I'll join the army when you're not my friend any more, he said. Then he went back to stabbing the bayonet into the ground. Next thing he said was, Our Enid says you can see her twat if you like, she'll show it you in the shelter, if you like. But I didn't say yes or no because at that moment we saw the one we called Dracula being wheeled into his usual place and when the keeper had gone we split to begin our silent approach down different angles. And the next time I saw Enid she didn't look at me as though she'd ever said any such thing and I might have been able to put it out of my mind except that a day or so later when I was in there on my own, spying on the one we called the Dribbler with Smithy's dad's old fieldglasses, I saw her and Smithy walk up together bold as brass and heard Smithy begin to sing – 'Bread of Heaven', it was – and saw Enid lift up her white frock and show the Dribbler, if he'd had eyes to see, the thing that Smithy had said I could see in the air-raid shelter, if I liked. The song affected the Dribbler powerfully, I could see his droopy mouth working, the white spit slavered down and his little paws shook out of all control.

Smithy's dad had very big hands. They were red with black hairs on. I met him once by the entrance into the coach house, which was my private way into the Blind Home grounds. He was just getting off the bus with his overalls under his arm brought home for washing. Afternoon, son, he said. And where are you off? I said I was running an errand for my mother and he nodded as though he knew that was a lie. I like you, son, he said. I think you're a good influence on my lad. As always I thought of his offer to take me and Smithy to the slaughterhouse, to watch him and his mates there at the business. I wondered had he really made that offer or whether Smithy had invented it. But I dreaded ever meeting him in case he suddenly did say it for real.

Next time it wasn't Enid Smithy offered. He was there waiting for me when I came out late after my extra teaching and together we walked home. Of the two Smith girls before Enid, the eldest, Shirley, was done with education and had a job in town, in Woolworth's, I believe. She wore a tight white jumper and high heels. Her mam was proud of her. Nearer to Enid was Angie, she was one year on in the secondary mod. Smithy said, Our Angie says you can see her twat if you like. She says to tell you it's got hair on and her tits are quite big now. She says she'll show you in the air-raid shelter and also you can touch her, if you like. Truth? I asked. He crossed his heart.

I thought about it for a week or so. I was thinking after my exam I'll maybe not see Smithy much and I might never get the chance again. So in the end I agreed – the price was my best silver dobber and six of my best blue glass – and that Saturday I got through our fence and crossed Smithy's grass and dockweed to the air-raid shelter. He was standing on the roof as he usually did when we were going over to stalk the blind, but he looked snottier than normal, abject really, as I might say now, and when I reached the steps down into the shelter and looked up at him on the concrete roof, I saw that he was trembling and I could smell him worse than normal. He shook his head but I went down anyway because by that time I had thought about it all too much.

The iron door was shut. I stood on the step and looked in through the spyhole. I wish I hadn't. Smithy's dad was in there and Angie with him. I believe it was Angie, I thought I recognised her purple socks. But I couldn't swear it in a court of law. She was facing away and bending over a chair with her knickers down and her frock up over her head and he had the bull-thing in his big red hand and was ever so gently swatting and tickling her bum with it and in his left hand, between finger and thumb, as though holding it ready, delicately he held an object I couldn't identify at first but I stared and stared until I saw it was an eye. Then before I could get away he turned to the peephole in the door and smiled.

When I came up the steps Smithy was gone. So I went over the wall and found him face down in the leaves snuffling like a hedgehog. Next day, on the way to school, he gave me a little package, from his dad, he said, and in it was an eye from the abattoir.

And talking of hedgehogs, by that time my father had made a little concrete paddling pool, just beyond the rustic of red roses, and a whole family of hedghogs had taken to drinking at it. There are so many photos of me in the garden, on a trike or with a cricket bat or smartly dressed for visiting. All black and white but you can see how colourful the beds of lupins, peonies, snap-dragons and wallflowers must have been, and the scent of roses, stocks and honeysuckle is easy to imagine. My mother in the photographs looks shadowed by the sadness of her losses but she smiles at my father's camera bravely enough.

The Sunday after that Saturday Smithy and his mam and sisters upped and left. Out on Laburnum Avenue Mrs Smith shouted for all to hear, You'll cop it this time! Oh won't you cop it when my three lads get home! Then off they went, with their belongings on a hand cart, Mrs and Shirley dragging it, Smithy, Angie and Enid trailing after, observed by me from our front bedroom window.

Later, while my mother and father were gardening, I took my chance and soon got into the Blind Home through the coach house. I followed the wall in cover, looking out, and at last saw Freddy on his seat, facing the trees. I walked over the grass and his face soon registered my coming. When I was near enough, he said, Good afternoon, sunshine. Just you, is it? I can't smell your pal. He's gone, I said. Flitted. Shame, said Freddy. Though I'm not surprised. And I don't suppose you can sing, can you? Not like him at least. I don't suppose there's many in the world can sing like your pal Smithy. No, I said, there's none. And me, I can't sing at all. So how will you entertain me when you come visiting, son?

You'll be my only visitor now Smithy's upped and left. I'll tell you things, I said. Like what? Tell me a thing. So I told him that when the rag and bone man had been or Vincent the ice cream man my mother would send me out with a bucket and the coal shovel to look if the horses had left anything behind and to scoop it up for our roses and the rhubarb if they had. Good, said Freddy. That's the sort of thing I mean. I hear them calling, of course, old Vincent and Sam Bone. The cries come over the wall. And now when I hear them I'll see you going out after with your bucket and shovel. That sort of picture will do very well, if you can't sing. Freddy wore a decent dark blue suit and a shirt without a collar open at the neck. His shoes were so polished he could have seen his face in them. His face was ghastly, his straining eyes were the mildest blue I ever saw. Just that sort of thing, he said. The other sort of thing I've seen enough of, thank you very much. But I'll be glad of a bit more rhubarb and roses to contemplate on the backs of my eyes. I've got to go, I said.

I should have gone home through the coach house. Instead, I went to our wall. Smithy's dad was there waiting – he'll wait for ever now. First, at eye-level, so that I could not understand what I was seeing, I saw his boots. Then the rest: his stained white overalls, his red fists gripping at our rope, his purple tongue sticking out, his eyes. He wasn't quite dead, he saw me, I left him clawing all for nothing at our rope around his throat.

By the coach house I sicked up all I could of it into the leaves. I was in my bed, shivering, when my mother came up to say I'd done enough for the day and to come down in the garden with her and my father. But seeing how ill I was, upset over Smithy, she supposed, she let me be. It was days before they found the dad. The one we called the Shaker, being pushed that lovely May evening across the lawn, smelled him at an astonishing distance, so I heard.

After a while, after I'd passed my exam and my course away from Smithy was as fixed as a railway line, I did go into the Fair Hope Blind Home, through the coach house, and looked for Freddy on his seat, to tell him a few things I thought he'd like to hear. That my father had bought my mother a floral dress, for example, got the size right and everything, all on his own, for a nice surprise. That the new next door had already dug a vegetable patch and planted things over the air-raid shelter so that you'd hardly see it next summer for greenery and flowers. I never mentioned Smithy. I had no word of him. I said I'd got a new bike for passing the exam and my father and me had cycled into the country and seen the big ships passing through the fields along the canal. Good, said Freddy, keep telling me things like that. What make of bike? What colour? Drop handle bars? How many gears? I want to see this bike of yours, Sunny Jim.

# Living On

This is a story about a man and three women. The man's name is Francis (nobody ever calls him Frank). The women are Anne, dead, whom he loves; Judith, his wife, whom he also loves but not as he loves Anne; and Marie, Anne's oldest and closest friend, whom he is very fond of because when they meet, which is not often, he can talk to her about Anne. In addition he has two grown-up daughters, whom he adores and could not bear to lose. They won't figure much in this story, but they might. We might shift aside into their intersecting circle, have them at the centre, and wonder what the whole *histoire* has done to them. And Sophia, Anne's only child, what about her?

Francis is a big man, not at all corpulent, but very tall, very strongly and handsomely made. When Marie meets him – it is the first anniversary of Anne's death – he has to bow and she has to lift on tiptoe to embrace. How he stands out in a crowd! What a hopeless spy or suicide-bomber he would make! The police, going through their miles of footage, would easily identify him. Assignations in the big city are an anxious business. It is hard to believe that the only person you desire to see will indeed appear among the thousands hurrying through the barriers or forcing up shoulder to shoulder from underground. Any small lateness and the faith lapses out of you like blood from a stuck pig. But meeting Francis does not make you anxious in that way. He is there first. And so prominent! Head and shoulders above the crowd.

He wears a black overcoat and a black woollen hat. In the little restaurant – he has reconnoitred a quiet place – Marie is shocked to see how white his hair is now.

Francis has an open face. He looks like the honourable hero of a boys' adventure story, he might be called Sir Henry, out in Africa in the 1890s, obeying a simple code of honesty and decency among foreigners who live slyly. He looks so at risk. His bigness and candour must expose him to all manner of harms. That is the appearance he presents across the little table on 7 January, a year after the death of Anne, his lover, to Marie, her dearest friend. Candidly he tells her what she knows already – knows from Anne, from many conversations – that he can't stop lying. In that respect at least death has made no difference. Did you think it would?

That's what Judith says. Did I really think it would? She says I need my head seeing to if I ever thought for a minute it would make any difference, that woman being dead.

Judith is a psychotherapist. Her particular concern is children and what their parents do to them. She knows, says Francis. The problem is she doesn't know, says Marie. I mean she knows how the mind works or the soul, says Francis. But it does not do her any good.

Marie knows that Francis will have lied to see her. Her rare meetings with him are so clandestine, so hard to arrange – she may not write, email, phone him at home or on his mobile but must wait for the call – that she has felt, in those circumstances at least, like the continuation of Anne in his life, as though she, in the place of the dead woman, were now his lover. And sometimes she has wondered could she fall in love with him. He is in many ways lovable. Even in his lying he is more pitiable than detestable. She is sure he cannot be good at lying. Still she is not inclined to love him. And he has never looked at her as though he might love her. Anne is the one. She is their beloved subject. And how rich Marie is in that respect! She had decades of the life of Anne. She pities Francis who had so little. Sometimes she feels him to be trying to increase his portion by asking her about the years before his time. Strange that we ever say the dead are at rest. Truly, death seems to goad them into more and more life, in us, who are left.

Marie was right to say that *not* knowing was Judith's problem. Which is not to say that knowing would have brought her peace. Francis began lying about Anne even before he suspected he was falling in love with her. For that he blamed Judith. I can't speak easily about any woman, he said, without her becoming suspicious. So even before he loved Anne he was watching Judith's face for the signs of suspicion. What exactly are you afraid of? Marie asked him. That she will kill herself, he answered. I see, said Marie. But having mentioned Anne a few times, as casually as possible, when he knew he loved her and she vanished from his speech, Judith wondered why, and asked. Then he began lying thoroughly and in earnest and she knew at once, by his bearing, that he was unfaithful, she knew the fact of his infidelity but none of the body of it, none of the details; and after that substance she hungered, and Anne's being dead made no difference to her hunger, if anything she got hungrier, she starved, because the fact of his faithless love was now unalterable, he would never fall out of love with the other woman and come home to her, faithful again and chastened and dutiful, he would always love someone else, who was now untouchable. She knows the fact but not the body and blood of it, not the living details, because he has always kept them to himself and lied, because, try as she will, she has never found them out, never enough of them. And what she hungers after is the full enormity, the fullness of its terrible power to hurt her. That, at least, is Francis's present understanding of his wife's tormented state.

Francis speaks most, Marie listens. Listens and thinks her own thoughts. Francis is just the sort of man a woman will think her own thoughts about as he talks, entirely involved in what he is saying, and she sits listening, sympathetic but at a slight remove. She knows a good deal about him, intimate things, from having been the confidante of the woman he loves. She knows of his passion and gentleness, and that his wife is frigid. Is Judith really frigid? He told Anne she was and Anne told Marie. Anne, almost to the end, believed that gave her an advantage in the struggle. When Francis compared the two women, the love he felt for them and the love they felt for him, relative warmth was a measure. Another was trust. One woman trusted him, one absolutely does not.

Marie is thinking everyone in this restaurant will suppose we are having an affair. And perhaps that we are at a critical stage in it. They will observe the helpless trouble in his face and his indifference to what we are eating and drinking. And how Judith hates you! Francis says. Really, Marie thinks, I might as well be the other woman. She suspects that you aided and abetted us. Allowed us to stay in your house. That sort of thing. So I did, says Marie. So I would again if Anne were alive. She was my dearest friend. I was glad for her. I saw that you made her happy. She had less happiness in her life than she deserved. Oh far less! Of course I aided and abetted you.

Still it is strange to be hated by a woman she has never met but whom, through confidences, she knows intimately. And she knows me hardly at all. Only as agent and accomplice in her suffering. She has seen your photograph, says Francis. She went through my books the other day and found that photograph of you and Anne embracing and laughing in the sunshine with the big waves at your backs. It was on the table, on my plate, when I came down for supper. I could not think of anything to say. No wonder she hates me, says Marie.

Marie has tried to placate this malevolent spirit with pity and understanding, but in vain. Do you have a photograph of Judith? she asks. Judith has asked him the same question. Of course I do, he answers. And takes it out of his wallet hurriedly. Judith is standing outside the home, in the front porch, between her two daughters, holding them in against her. She is smiling, the girls are also smiling; but in Judith's look – she has a transparent beauty – Marie at least, knowing what she does, discerns fear and provocation in equal measure. I see, she says. And hands the photograph back to Francis.

*Would* Judith kill herself? Even now, with the rival already dead? Anne always doubted she would kill herself. Anne believed it to be the wife's gambit, in desperate self-defence. And she also believed – does Francis truly know this, does he carry it around in him, unsleeping, as betrayal? – that in the end he, Francis, would call his wife's bluff, risk it, move out of house and home and live with her, Anne. Many times she told Marie she was sure that would happen. By his assurances she was persuaded that he loved her more and more, that he was only waiting for the necessary courage to grow in him and spread till he was full of it. Then he would act. But she got ill and began to die. And Francis has not lost his wife, his beloved daughters and his home. Might he still? If he goes on grieving and secretly meeting the friend, the confidante, the accomplice, might Judith still not do it, feeling herself to have been defeated, knowing even without the body and blood of evidence that he lived with her, had children with her, but loved another woman with a romantic and ineradicable passion?

Marie wearies of Francis and Judith, stops eating, stops listening, and grieves over her dead friend. Francis runs on a while, he is possessed, but at length he notices that Marie has absented herself, and he halts. Forgive me, he says. I have nobody to talk to. It is all in hiding still. I daren't show anything that will betray me. Marie wonders at this. Would he not be better even now, even too late, in a room of his own? There he could have some mementoes of Anne on view around him and show an honest face to a mirror at least and sit and think about her and write about her whenever he wished. Would not that be a place where she, Anne, could visit? For she cannot visit him in his married home. Marie is about to say, Tell me, Francis, tell me truthfully (it troubles me) would you in fact in the end have left Judith and your children and gone to live with Anne, as she believed you would, had she not fallen ill and died? The sentence is formed, she is about to utter it, when he pre-empts her by asking, Did you bring the photograph with you? Marie takes what he wishes to see out of her bag. It is a picture of Anne in a forest quite close to the beach where she, Marie, had stood with her to be photographed by Francis on a background of the rising incoming waves. It might be a forest in Celtic legend. Indeed, they christened it Brocéliande. The trees are hazels, willows, small oaks, all draped in a sunny hoar frost. And the woman in this enchanted place is radiantly happy. When Anne smiles with happiness, as she did very often during her couple of years in love with Francis, it is whole and pure, without forethought, question or regret, it is entire and on the verge of laughter, the body and soul of this woman in love are lit up in the luminously shrouded Celtic wood with merriment, she is showing her lover what it feels like to be loved and what it feels like and looks like loving him in return. Yes, Francis, says Marie, kind to him again, that is what you made her feel like. It is undeniable. Can you not be comforted by that? Now take this photograph and hide it somewhere, if you must, and look at it very occasionally and be comforted. But Francis shakes his head. How white he has become. But not like an old man, he looks quite youthful still, like the hero of an adventure whose hair blanched overnight because of some horror he had to pass through. I can't, he says. You keep it for me.

The waiter clears away their plates. Will they have coffee? Francis looks at his watch. Yes, says Marie. Two espressos, please. Funny thing about lying, says Francis. I lie all the time now whether there's any need or not. Judith asks me did I see a certain colleague. No, I say, he was off sick. But in truth I stood and chatted with him in the staffroom about the war. She asks did I come straight home. Yes, I say, though I got off two stops early and walked the rest for some fresh air. And so on. I live in fear that she will sit me down and unravel me.

Suddenly at the table or while they are sitting quietly together in the evening, she will ask him what he is thinking. He must guard his face so that it never looks absent. Lying side by side in the dark, neither sleeping, he fears she will begin to question him. There is a particular tone of voice, that of possession, of being ridden, of being entirely at the mercy, she shifts into another key, monotonous, the way the deaf speak, merciless to herself and to him. When he hears that tone of voice in the darkness he feels cold around the heart, all the courage goes out of him, he is mere bulk, waiting abjectly for torment. These passages are cumulative, each new one comes compounded with its predecessors. There seems to be no past tense, only present. It is now that she suffers and inflicts. I don't mind you fucking her, the voice says – but she does, oh she does, and besides the woman is dead – you're a man and that is what men do. But if you hold her hand in public or she takes your arm or you call her 'my love' or any such thing or if you ever talk about me and tell her of my difficulties and pity me, the pair of you, and I find out for sure, I'll kill you or I'll kill myself and it won't matter which. No, he says, none of those things. Swear it. He swears it, the liar. You're lying, the voice says, foreign, refracted away from both of them through the icy medium of her loathing, fear and shame. He has turned on the light, they have sat up in bed together, he has seen that the features of her face are like the voice, they have slanted away, they are a slant and helpless version of her beautiful face, ugly as a devil's, like the insult of a stroke. He takes her in his arms, he enfolds her in his greater strength, though she struggles, she wants none of him, so that his force is only another violation. He begs her to have pity on herself and on him. And sometimes she does, she will, the strength needed to torment them both goes out of her, and she weeps and begs him to be kind to her, to do as he must or as he likes, but be kind to her, love her, never leave

THE SHIELING

her. So in love and pity he renews his promises.

Marie and Francis have finished their coffees. They get the bill. Marie sees that he is nervous about the time. Again her pity for him is wearing thin. What manner of memorial is this for her dead friend? At least I nursed her, he says, when it was already too late, I was resolute then, I called every evening after school, sat with her, held her hand, read to her, saw she was comfortable, carried her through from the sitting room to the bed, she was nothing in my arms, she was as light as the wing of a swan that has been severed and the wind and the sun have wasted it, my strength was out of all proportion. I gave her the morphine. I settled her to sleep. I waited till her daughter came or the night nurse. Judith knew. I said nothing, I answered nothing, she knew and I let her suffer it. I know that, says Marie. I do know that. She takes his big hand between hers. His face looks like that of a large beast, bewildered by its captivity and torment.

The street is heaving, the people are all in a hurry. Francis covers his white hair, bows down to Marie who lifts on tiptoe into his embrace. *Bon courage*, she says. Then he turns and leaves her, forcing through the crowd, head and shoulders above them. And long before he goes out of sight – has he no shame, is he so helpless? – he claps his left hand to his ear and Marie knows he is answering a call from Judith who is asking why for an hour and seventeen minutes his phone has been switched off. Marie remembers the funeral service, in the church with which Anne had no living connection. Anne's husband stayed away on principle. He is an atheist Marxist materialist and will have no truck with foolery. But their sixteen-year-old daughter Sophia was present, on the front row with Marie, looking quite lost, as though she had years of catching-up to do. Until the service began Marie turned round continually to see had Francis come. Then she desisted, let him and his problems go, took Sophia by the hand, and concentrated wholly on the coffin. Only when it was over did she look round for Francis again.

And there he was, standing at the door, bare-headed in his black overcoat, almost gigantic over the mourners sitting or kneeling. Seeing her he hid his eyes, then all of his face, like a child, behind his hands. Then he fled. Marie, leaving Sophia, hurried down the aisle and out. But all she saw of him on the street was his flight, and his left hand clapping the phone to his ear.

Marie stands aside from the crowd, against the window of the restaurant. They are thousands, pushing through and on and on, and beyond them the traffic, the noise. And a feeling she knows and fears begins to take hold of her: that it doesn't matter, that nothing and nobody matters, all mere complexities, all mire and blood, the more or less of misery, the more or less of happiness, such meagre portions, it does not matter. All the trouble, for what? All the hours of talk and brooding over it. Nothing but noise, confusion and pointless hastening. So many people, rising, passing, descending. Marie's friend is dead and now she must fag to a railway station and catch a train to the other end of the country.

2

In early March, on a morning that feels like spring, Marie receives two letters, one from Sophia, the other from Francis. She opens Francis's first, because she has not heard from him since their anniversary meeting; also because she has a hope in Sophia's letter which, if it is disappointed (as it has been before), might make the letter from Francis harder to bear.

Inside his letter Francis has enclosed a sheet of paper with a poem on. The paper, torn from an exercise book, has been screwed up into a ball and then smoothed out again. It has been inside a fist and wears a thousand creases. The poem, in Francis's handwriting, is this:

> You fetched me up by force of the will
> Of magic out of the grave.

167

# THE SHIELING

You heated me with your lust and can't
Quench it now I'm alive.

Fasten your mouth on mine, human
Breath is heavenly stuff.
I'll drink your soul up, every drop.
The dead can't get enough.

Marie sets the poem aside and reads Francis's letter. In haste,
he writes. I copied the poem out of an anthology that Anne
used to like. I don't say she especially liked this poem. But I
do. It says it all, don't you think? (PLEASE DON'T WRITE
BACK.) But I was careless again and Judith found it in my
pocket. She scrumpled it up and threw it in my face. She says
she can't win. She says for the rest of her life she will be eaten
up by that woman – Anne – who can't get enough. Tell her
she got more than I got, Judith says. She got your love. How
do you think I feel about that? I could live to be a hundred
with you, which God forbid, and all those years and all the
years before still wouldn't weigh a pennyworth against any
one of your afternoons in bed with her. So Judith says. Howls
really. Marie, she actually howls. And any minute the girls
were arriving for our wedding anniversary. She says the
cancer that ate Anne is eating her now. Only it's not a cancer
it's the woman herself, Anne, eating away at her, Judith, the
wife, for vengeance. I tell her she's ill. She says indeed she is
but who's making her ill? You and her have made me ill, the
pair of you. And then she says a cancer is one thing, everybody
sympathises if you get a cancer, because there it is, you can
prove you've got it, your pain is reasonable. But what I've got
won't show up on a screen. You're like everybody else, she
says, you don't count sickness in the soul, you don't think it's
real. Well I've got a sickness in my soul and it's real enough,
whether it shows up on a screen or not. Your woman is eating
me.

There is more of this. Francis writes as though he were Judith's medium. He opens his mouth and she howls through him. Marie skips some. Finally Francis leaves the subject of Judith and recounts what he calls 'the fiasco of the ashes'. Anne's husband, the materialist Marxist atheist, had agreed to let him have a half of Anne's ashes. Weighing the lover's brief passion against the husband's long affection, he thought that fair. So it was agreed, the rest was practicalities. Francis had decided that he would take his half all the way to the luminous hoar-frost forest and scatter them there, among the Celtic trees. But after months and months of rearrangements and prevarications – imagine what it cost him in lies and effort! – when Francis, without an appointment, finally called on the husband in his very comfortable flat, he was told, cheerfully and with not a word of apology, that he, the husband, had disposed of the ashes, all of them, himself. He would not say where. He said it was wrong to be sentimental about such things. The dead are dead, he said. And that is that. So now he, Francis, doesn't know where Anne's ashes are. Which means she is nowhere. Which is to say everywhere. So Judith and the poem are right, Anne is a wraith of starvation, she is in the winds and the waters and hungry everywhere.

Marie shakes her head. But she finishes Francis's letter. He has been re-reading 'The Dead'. He is haunted by the spectre of Michael Furey at the bottom of Gretta's garden in the rain. He has an idea to adapt it for his drama group. There will be three characters: Gretta, Michael Furey and the generous Gabriel. Also a chorus of perhaps half a dozen voices. They will recount and comment on the tragic action. Perhaps they will seek to make it less unbearable. Francis has a hope – far-fetched no doubt – that in time, if he is patient and gentle, he may induce Judith into the generosity of Gabriel. The dead are not implacable, he says. If Anne appears vengefully that is because she, Judith, will not permit her to be at peace in the little bit of life she shared with me.

Marie is angered by the letter. She has tears of sorrow

and pain in her eyes for her dead friend. She has a mind to scrumple up the letter and the enclosure and hurl it at the pair of them, for what they are doing to Anne. So now she is a female Michael Furey, starving to death at the bottom of the garden. She is a vampire, a visitation like cancer in another woman's life. I won't have it, says Marie aloud. That is not how she was and is. True, she didn't get her due of happiness. True, in her last weeks she grieved that she was stinted. (And Marie grieved with her, held her, cradled her, lamented with her over the cruel fact of it.) But this was a beautiful, brave and intelligent woman. How chic she was, even to near the end. How funny and scurrilous, lively and careless. Such a talker, such a cheering arrival in any company. Did anyone ever laugh with such free merriment? In a trice, no magic, no evildoing, Marie can conjure up her dead friend's gaiety: arm in arm on the street with her, men stopping in their tracks, men turning their heads, amused and glad; or in the restaurant, always in the window if possible, so that in the midst of conversation, she would have the street to watch, its myriad lives, to recount and further enliven. Of course she was hungry for life, she died wanting more of it. But hear this, says Marie, indignant, even when she was dying, when the game was up, when she knew she would never get her proper share, in any interlude without pain, in the kindness of morphine, she asked after my life, after its fullness, blessed it without envy, always glad for me, never once did she begrudge it me, never once turn it to wormwood in self-pity.

Marie opens Sophia's letter, hoping for the best. She is not disappointed. In childish big handwriting, with strange formality, Sophia thanks Marie (who held her the day she was born) for her kind invitation and says that she will be glad to spend Easter with her and her family. Good, says Marie, there at least something can be done.

# The Cause

What shall I read to you? What shall it be today?

Whatever you like, child. I'll always be glad to listen to your voice.

I've been reading *The Prelude*. Shall I read you a passage from that? I've been reading Book IX. I'm in love with Michel Beaupuy.

There wasn't much room in the bay window. Sylvia sat looking out. Her chair rather blocked the bookshelves and Myfanwy had to go on all fours to tug out Wordsworth from his alphabetical slot, bottom shelf, far right, almost the last. Here he is, she said, and took her own seat in the window, to read. The two women, seventy years between them, were knee to knee. Myfanwy opened the volume. Goodness, she said. The very place is marked. There's a postcard in it. Ah, said Sylvia. That postcard in that place.

Shall I read now?

Yes, do.

Myfanwy read. She forgot herself. Knee to knee with the old woman who, though blind, was listening with open eyes, blue eyes, so blue against her white hair, Myfanwy read in a voice

171

of the closest conversation. Letters in words, words in lines, lines of sense in rhythm, black signs on a page, they had been waiting for this, to be wakened, the life in them, always waiting, quickened again in the girl's soft accent. She read:

By birth he ranked
With the most noble, but unto the poor
Among mankind he was in service bound,
As by some tie invisible, oaths professed
To a religious order. Man he loved
As man; and, to the mean and the obscure,
And all the homely in their homely works,
Transferred a courtesy which had no air
Of condescension; but did rather seem
A passion and a gallantry...

And when we chanced
One day to meet a hunger-bitten girl,
Who crept along fitting her languid self
Unto a heifer's motion, by a cord
Tied to her arm, and picking thus from the lane
Its sustenance, while the girl with her two hands
Was busy knitting in a heartless mood
Of solitude, and at that sight my friend
In agitation said, "Tis against *that*
Which we are fighting', I with him believed
Devoutly that a spirit was abroad
Which could not be withstood, that poverty
At least like this would in a little time
Be found no more, that we should see the earth
Unthwarted in her wish to recompense
The industrious, and the lowly child of toil,
All institutes forever blotted out
That legalized exclusion, empty pomp
Abolished, sensual state and cruel power,
Whether by edict of the one or few;

And finally, as sum and crown of all,
Should see the people having a strong hand
In making their own laws; whence better days
To all mankind.

Myfanwy paused. Sylvia said: I was to catch the 8.12 bus from
St Asaph, the Bangor bus, coming from Chester. He would
catch the 7.50 from Bangor (the Chester bus) and would be
there waiting for me at Glan Conway Corner, when I
alighted at five past nine. We would walk from there to
Caerhun, crossing the river at Tal-y-Cafn, to see the
excavations. Would I bring half of the picnic? From Caerhun
we would walk to Llanrwst, for tea. Catch the bus from there
at 5, travelling together as far as Glan Conway. He would see
me on to the St Asaph bus at 5.47 and catch his back to
Bangor at five past six. You may look at the card if you wish.
He was a great one for planning. Myfanwy read the card,
dated 1 March 1935, addressed to Miss Sylvia Richmond,
Cathedral Walk, Llanelwy. The arrangements were as Sylvia
had remembered them. He calls you Miss Richmond, said
Myfanwy. He did then, said Sylvia. And I do wish they would
in here. I hate their being so familiar. I only want people like
you to call me Sylvia. You and the dead. A few among the
dead.

And he signs himself M.

Michael.

There's a coincidence!

I wouldn't call it that.

Then Sylvia said: I *was* listening. You will think I was dreaming not
listening. But I listened very closely. It was like my own voice. And
yet yours and nobody else's. My voice was never like yours. I think
Michael might have preferred your voice to mine.

# THE SHIELING

The picture is of Happy Valley.

Yes, Happy Valley. We went there sometimes, though Michael said he despised the place. But it was about half way, so we went there, by our separate buses or trains, on days when we did not have much time. We could have a walk on the Orme at least and a cup of tea. Later we found a little place to stay, in the valley itself. Then he stopped despising it. How strange that I should end up here, so close to Happy Valley. But at least from this window you can see the mountains and the estuary, and going into the estuary, if you know where they lie, you will soon find Caerhun and the grey church at Llanrwst. Are the mountains snowy? They were that day. How strange life is. I never thought I'd end up here. Never in a place like this. I should be dead and buried somewhere nobody knows. Is it very bad downstairs?

Quite bad.

Tell me.

They are mostly women, they sit around dozing with the television on. Often it is a wild-life programme, when I pass through. Today it was a film about a war. It is very hot. Why must it be so hot? The people fall asleep. I think if they knew, they would not want to be seen like that. I mean the look on them and the shapes they fall into when the heat overpowers them.

I live here among the lost.

No, no. All your books. I will always come in and read to you.

It is like the underworld. You come and go as if you had the password among the shades.

174

# THE CAUSE

*4 March*

Now I know that Spring will come again,
Perhaps tomorrow: however late I've patience
After this night following on such a day.

While still my temples ached from the cold burning
Of hail and wind, and still the primroses
Torn by the hail were covered up in it,
The sun filled earth and heaven with a great light
And a tenderness, almost warmth, where the hail dripped,
As if the mighty sun wept tears of joy.
But 'twas too late for warmth. The sunset piled
Mountains on mountains of snow and ice in the west:
Somewhere among their folds the wind was lost,
And yet 'twas cold, and though I knew that Spring
Would come again, I knew it had not come,
That it was lost, too, in those mountains cold.

What did the thrushes know? Rain, snow, sleet, hail,
Had kept them quiet as the primroses.
They had but an hour to sing. On boughs they sang,
On gates, on ground; they sang while they changed perches
And while they fought, if they remembered to fight:
So earnest were they to pack into that hour
Their unwilling hoard of song before the moon
Grew brighter than the clouds. Then 'twas no time
For singing merely. So they could keep off silence
And night, they cared not what they sang or screamed,
Whether 'twas hoarse or sweet or fierce or soft,
And to me all was sweet: they could do no wrong.
Something they knew — I also, while they sang
And after. Not till night had half its stars
And never a cloud, was I aware of silence
Rich with all that riot of songs, a silence
Saying that Spring returns, perhaps tomorrow.

Myfanwy paused.

Thank you, child. That is how it was and is. I remember more precisely when you read.

I did your walk.

My walk?

Yours and Michael's. From Glan Conwy Corner to Caerhun. From Caerhun to Llanrwst. There were no buses, of course. I cycled to Glan Conwy and left my bike there.

And home? How did you get home? It was dark by then.

I was happy.

But how did you get home?

There were no buses. I was wondering about the train when a lady stopped and offered me a lift. She was going to visit her mother not far from here.

And the picnic?

My half was enough.

Tell.

The Carneddau looked very close, because of the snow, and the sky behind them very blue. The tide was out. The mud of the estuary was shining silver. Those were the large things. But mostly everything was closer. For a while I followed a sunken lane, some left-over berries of holly and hawthorn, dark, nearly black-green ivy, white boles of ash, their dead keys, the white and purple birches. Everywhere a speckle of buds. The blackthorn, twisted and as hard as iron, softening at the tips, the blossom nearly starting. The sun flickered through, but the body of it, the main thrust of the light, came in a low slant from behind and down this illumination the birds went ahead, fieldfares, blackbirds, many undulating finches. Then the hazels. Oh Sylvia, the hazels! This lane, almost a tunnel, was hung either side and from its delicately vaulted roof with hazels, loose golden tassels, imagine that, like water hanging but for longer than any strung droplets of water could possibly hang unless they were ice, but these were not ice, they had loosened, they were relaxed, each with its dot of red fire, like garnet on soft gold, such beautiful pendants, in thousands.

Myfanwy's voice became rapid, whispering, Sylvia was watching her intently, as though she could listen and hear through her eyes that could not see. Myfanwy stared and whispered into her listening face.

It's the moisture, isn't it? The soft earth under your feet, the celandines, the black mosses, the light ferns that need the damp. The softness. The catkins like trickles of sunny water. The ice is a thousand feet up, the blue sky is cold, we know how cold it is, but in that sweet tunnel of a sunken lane you may be shivery but you can feel the warming, you can hear it, the necessary water so that things will live and flower in the sun. Stand still, there's always the welling up and running of real water. Nowhere can you walk round there and not hear water if you stand and listen. And the birdsong, bubbling and fluting. How could you bear it?

I was Miss Richmond to him then. For most of that day. He was an archaeologist. He wrote articles for the *Archaeologia Cambrensis*. So when we reached Canovium, on the river, by the mouth, he could tell me all about it. He had uncovered some of it himself. He showed me on the map how the Roman road ran from there to Segontium, near Carnarvon, through the Pass of the Two Stones. Should I like to walk that road with him one day? The lines of subjugation, he said. He was a great one for making things connect. The Roman forts, the English castles, that sort of thing. And underneath it the Welsh people and their language and their song. Caerhun is the old name, of course. There was a camp at Caerhun before the Romans came and after they had gone. He hated the English. All except me. He made an exception of me. But he would not let me call my town St Asaph. Always Llanelwy. He was teaching me Welsh. I was doing pretty well in my very English voice. But now if you read me one of your poets, child, I should hardly understand a word. So sad, not to have got further in my learning.

I will teach you, if you like.

There will not be time. But thank you. Michael's father had been hurt by the police in the General Strike. So Michael always knew where he stood on things like that. He was in the protests against the reservoirs, for example. He wanted everything to connect. His archaeology was a part of it. He wanted to know what had been and might be again. Good and ill, had been, might be again.

Sylvia paused. Myfanwy said: Last year I hitchhiked through France.

On your own?

On my own.

Silly. Very silly.

I had been reading Laurie Lee. My last lift was with a lady

who was taking her grandfather back to a certain place in Spain that he wanted to see again before he died. The bends were making me sick. And besides, I wanted to walk across, as I had imagined it. So I asked them to set me down. When I got out the old gentleman got out too. He was very ceremonious. He kissed me on both cheeks and said: Bon courage, mademoiselle. Si le fascisme revient, ce n'est pas la peine d'avoir des enfants ou de planter des arbres. Then his grandaughter helped him back into the car and they left me there on the cold mountainside.

Myfanwy paused. Sylvia said: When you reached Llanrwst, did you look in the Gwydir chapel?

It was locked.

Next time you must get them to open it for you. There are marvellous things in there. Marvellous and beautiful. And one very terrible thing.

*11 March*

My house was called
The house of flowers, because from every cranny
Geraniums sprang forth, it was
A beautiful house
With its dogs and children.
Federico, from under the ground
Do you remember my balconies
Flowers in your mouth swimming in the light of June?
My brother, oh my brother!
Everything
Loud with big voices, salty with buying and selling,
Mounds of quickening bread

# THE SHIELING

The stalls of my local streets of Argüelles, the statue
Like a pallid inkwell in the shoals of hake:
Oil flowed on spoons,
Feet and hands
Amplified in the streets,
Metres, litres, the sharp
Essentials of life,
                    the stacked fish,
The texture of roofs with a cold sun in which
The weather vane wearies,
The fine, frenzied ivory of potatoes,
Unending tomatoes piling down to the sea.

And one morning all that was burning,
One morning the fires
Leapt out of the earth
And ate human beings –
And from then on fire,
Gunpowder from then on,
And from then on blood.
Bandits with Moors and aeroplanes
Bandits with rings and duchesses
Bandits with black friars blessing
Came through the sky to kill children
And through the streets ran the blood of children
Quite simply, like the blood of children...

Myfanwy paused. Sylvia asked: What was on the television
when you passed through?

Dolphins, said Myfanwy. Then she said: I was let into the
chapel.

So now you know.

The dead baby?

Sylvia said: It was spring in all but name. The river was high, so close by the grey church. And it was as you said, the greening, the moisture, the birdsong, the constant hurrying of water, they raise your demands on life, do they not? You want more and more. We were looking around inside the church, the grey-silver light streaming through. Then Michael said that we must view the chapel. There was an old woman cleaning and tidying along the south aisle and he asked her in Welsh would she open the chapel for us. She looked at me and him and at me again. I felt she was weighing up did we go well together. Then she nodded and hobbled away, beckoning us, out of the church to the chapel and opened its door with a big iron key from her apron.

Inside, Michael began explaining things as he had done at Caerhun. But then he left off and stood at that big empty sarcophagus, Llewellyn's, looking very absent and resting his fingers on the rim. So I turned away and behind his back came upon the effigy of the dead baby. And the next I knew I was bending down with my two hands on it, truly as if I might lift it up and warm it against my breast. And though of course I could not lift it, I *knew* the weight of it, the solid cold marble weight of it, oh the absolute heavy and terrible fact of it, and between my two hands I felt the cold ascending through my arms into my breasts and heart. And the silver light in the chapel swam in my tears, as though the river had risen and I were deep under its waters. Then Michael came over, embraced me, held me against him, and for the first time called me by my Christian name, again and again said it into my hair in a whisper, all the while stroking me.

We had a year and a half. Then he went to Spain. Do not think he deserted me. He struggled, and I agreed. When he had gone I was glad to find that I was pregnant. He wrote to me often. Soon he was bitterly disappointed. He said they were spoiling the cause even as they fought for it. But that they must fight for it. So they had to spoil it and be disappointed. He said I was the only thing in the world that would never disappoint him. He rejoiced in the baby, and when he was dead I too continued to rejoice in that at least, for a while. But he died in me. He became as heavy and dead as marble under my heart. I felt it happen, the turning to stone. Everybody said that really there could be no connection, medically there could not, it was a bad coincidence. I had to go through with the birth. I had to give birth to a child as still and silent as the lump of marble in that chapel. I called him after his father and buried him.

Myfanwy stood up and said very quickly: He shouldn't have gone. He should have stayed and looked after you. It might not have happened like that if he hadn't gone. Did you not blame him?

I never blamed him.

I should have blamed him then and for evermore.

But you are in love with Michel Beaupuy! Most certainly *he* would have left you, for the cause. Remember it was a cause 'Good, and which no one could stand up against,/ Who was not lost, abandoned, selfish, proud,/ Mean, miserable, wilfully depraved,/ Hater perverse of equity and truth.'

Myfanwy stood pressing her forehead against the cold window.

Sylvia said: Till then, till he died, everything had been kind to me. I was not spoiled exactly, but everyone had always been kind. And even over the baby, even so long ago, my mother and father, so very English, were kind. So it was hard, truly as hard as stone. But I did not mope. He had said I would never disappoint him, so I determined to prove him right. In the war, the bigger war that followed, I went to London, I was a nurse, I drove ambulances, I worked.

Myfanwy said: I have to go.

You come and go. You pass through that gathering of twilight souls to visit me. And now I feel your shadow. You are standing in the window against the light. You have been looking at the white mountains, the blue sky, the way in through the rivermouth to the beautiful watery places. After the war I went to Spain. I travelled alone, I had learned a little Spanish. I found the village, east of Huesca, from where he had written me his last letter. He died of pneumonia, in the terrible cold. He always had that weakness in him. I asked where the fighting had been and where the dead were buried. They showed me the places but I could not find his grave. Many were nameless, they said. But that was the place, very high up, sunny and cold, a hard place to make a living. I went early in the year, about now. It gave me no solace. Why should it? I wanted none. Afterwards I stayed away from here, I worked, I had other men, even lived with one or another for a while. But never a baby, there was something wrong and I could not.

Myfanwy stooped and kissed her on the forehead. Sylvia said: This time before you go will you let me feel your face?

Myfanwy knelt and allowed the old woman's cold hands to learn her face.

And your hair? May I touch your hair?

She allowed it.

And tell me what colour your eyes are.

Grey-blue, not blue like yours.

And your hands, you have long fingers. Tonight I shall think of you on the cold mountainside where the ceremonious old gentleman and his grandaughter left you. I will think of you climbing over as you had imagined it, unharmed and not at all disappointed.

# Words To Say It

1

Ben Benson took solitary holidays. His friends – none close – wondered why he did not join a party of one sort or another. That way he might have met somebody. But he was shy; or he liked his own company; at work he had to talk to, or at least listen to, people all day and every day, so perhaps he wanted a rest from people.

That year he left it late. But in the first week of September he took a plane to Athens, stayed the night in Piraeus, and next morning, very early, scouted along the waterfront for a destination and a boat. He liked the sound of Skleros – though the name means 'harsh'; the boat left at eight. So there he was in no time, alone and under way. He fell at once into the contentment of having to say very little, and that in a difficult foreign language which he had studied hard and was competent at, in a formal style. Speaking foreign languages was always a release for Ben. He measured his words, carefully composed his syntax, the organs of speech almost never let him down. And after these exertions, which gave him great satisfaction, he indulged himself in hours of silence. He watched the blue-black sea for dolphins, longing like a child.

Ben disembarked at the first port, the south, and found a room from which, across the low valley, he could see the ancient acropolis. Slept that night thinking: I shall climb there tomorrow. And duly did. Gathered provisions, made the arduous climb, meeting nobody. But the pleasure of it, the pleasingness of the track that so cleverly and patiently solved all the problems of ascent over hard terrain, the feel under foot, the ever more widely delighted eyes! The day developed in him a steady joy. The old city was a wonder, so evident still its management of the steep hillside, such tact, the feel for contours, the settling of levels, to plant or build. Shards everywhere, of marble and earthenware, slithering in millions year after year down the slopes towards the distant sea. With his eyes and fingers he sifted through them, in a manner both idle and intense, and was pleased to pick up a couple of pieces of obsidian, which must have come from elsewhere, from Melos very likely. Two ravens overhead, but for earthly fellow creatures only goats, yellow-eyed and unperturbed. The guidebook said the earliest settlement was the highest, just under the summit, and he found it, the worshipping place at least, a crack and den of surprising dampness in all the dry slither of shards and terracing and the bared bulk of the grey-white rock. He ate there with relish, sharp tastes, tearing at his bread. And again the happiness, as though some yeast was working it, rose on tears into his eyes and contracted his throat.

That evening he was restless. He ate in a tranquil place, as slowly as he could, observing people. No one else was alone. In the darkness a ship arrived, too large for the port it seemed, an apparition of bright lights. Racket of anchor chains, a sudden busyness, a pellmell, almost a head to head, of the embarkers and the disembarkers. Then it was over, the ship vanished, seemed an illusion, and the little port continued *sotto voce*.

Ben wanted to settle, be more collected, more entirely self-possessed for a few days. Perhaps the northern port would be the place? He caught the bus next morning. Up and up it climbed, from sea-level, laboriously, the same view swinging round smaller and smaller on the repeating bends. At the top there was a halt outside a bar on a level square. The village lay over the flank of the mountain like a blanket full of holes. The driver went into the bar. Nobody else got on or off. It was about midday. Ben stood up. He would stay here. He lugged his pack off the seat and climbed down into the hot sun. The driver was coming back. Not yet, he said. Not here. Ben said fluently, Thank you. I have changed my mind. He meant: I've made up my mind. The driver shrugged.

The bar was all old men, a young woman serving. Ben asked her about rooms. Nobody stays up here, she said. But she directed him to her grandmother. She had a room. She went ahead of him into it, pushed open the shutters and stood there small and black against the inrush of light, grinning. The ground fell away, he was on the edge of nothing, over a vast bowl in the stony hills. The toothless granny chuckled at her room. It seemed to fill her with a mischievous glee. And see here, she said, and tugged him away along a corridor to a corkscrew iron staircase ascending out of a bougainvillea and lemon-blossom yard. Sleep up there, if you wish. Thank you, said Ben, I might. The old woman liked him, he bowed down to her so courteously. Where is your wife? she asked. Why aren't you married? Such a pleasant English gentleman. But how he and her room and her rooftop made her laugh!

Now Ben had what he wanted, the simplicities: table and chair, the neat single bed, a small stove to brew his own coffee. There was an icon of the Virgin on the bare white wall above his bed. Through his window, or from the roof, he could see the full compass of all the walking he would have the time and the strength to do. The paths! The paths! The village gave out at a line of derelict windmills, their stumps and broken sails, along the crest. Behind them the sky seemed to be leaning over an immense descent.

The nights were quiet, nothing passed through after the same bus returning. Ben took a blanket and lay on the roof, under a sky stripped bare and showing its millions of pulsing stars. The life below him, the small stirrings and voices of the village, became less, far less, than the white noise of the milky river of stars. All his own life, all the lives it was his job to listen to, became remote to him, he viewed them with kindly detachment. He could even think of his father without much pain. He felt the possibility of pity, he was tempted almost towards forgiveness. And for his mother he vowed a more effective love – more solace, help, cheerfulness. Then mother and dead father lapsed away, their son lay alone on a rooftop hearkening to nothing but the constant arrival of the throbbing light of stars.

The paths were a wonder. Their makers, so it seemed, had thought walking as noble as it was necessary and had expended all possible art on ways fit for the feet and pleasing to the eye. Through the valleys, climbing up, long stretches were flagged with marble beautifully veined in an almost watery play of white and green and rose. Smooth underfoot and quite ungiving. Set in the embrace of a hillside, after a long climb, there might be a well, itself of marble, notched on the lip to let fall a battered copper bucket on a thin iron chain to haul up the cold with, the water of the deep earth, brimming and slopping. And marble threshing-floors, entire clear discs, could be seen from above to have survived the collapsing terraces. For the villages themselves were largely abandoned, at most there might be a filthy sty, or a few chickens scratching, or a donkey picketed in the sun, and Ben passed through with his courtesies unsaid. The flowers up there had burned out months ago and if he quitted the path, to make for a vantage point, his boots rasped through dryness and thorns. Still there were asphodels, come up slenderly out of nothing, out of the rock itself, out of a visible bulb that had sustained enough moisture of life to put forth with complete economy, a slender tall pink stem and the ghostly cone of flowers. Stonefields of asphodels, like a smouldering mist around his legs.

He came back to his room, his cell and its roof, burning and in body and soul at the limit of fatigue and elation. Everything tasted, savoured, whetted and gladdened him keenly. He lay on the roof under the cold sheet of stars; descended like a watcher after a vigil, passed through the scent of lemon, and slept warm; woke early hearing the strange noises of dawn in the vast stone hollow of the hill below: cockcrow, the barking of dogs, amplified and echoing; the braying of donkeys, that sounded – or felt – like a mortal retching for utterance or breath; and once came a howling or singing, that he couldn't place, couldn't locate it anywhere close or far, couldn't say for sure was it man or beast, but it rode or was racked on the unsteady endings of night and the beginnings of day, lived for an eerie while on the borders between the two, died when the daylight decided.

And so for some days and their nights Ben lived as he wished and the scant provisions and company of the village sufficed him. He was courteous, for the few necessary sentences the organs of speech never failed him. The old woman asked him frankly how he liked the solitary life. Very much indeed, he replied. She chortled, and began to tease him, almost to flirt with him, wanting to know how he lived in England. He went a little way towards her curiosity, the foreign language leading him on; but only so far, he halted, he smiled and bowed. After any conversation, with her or at the one shop or in the bar, the pull of silence and remoteness was all the stronger and his return to them a deep pleasure. He felt himself to be almost in love with the beauties of marble paths and fields of nothing but stone and ghostly asphodel. He laid the bits of obsidian on the table, next to the few olives, the bread, an orange, the moist white cheese, the black black coffee, laid all on the table and turned up his hands either side of them, objects on a bare board. When he thought of his work, of the people whose troubles were his work, of his dead and unquiet father, of all their irresolvable complexities, he wished he might bide for ever in a white-washed room among objects simplified to the point of pitilessness and as uninterested in personal complexity as the stars.

Friday. His chosen path began at the Monastery of the Virgin of Palestine. Began there. But to reach that beginning he must first pass through the line of broken windmills, descend several hundred marble steps to a shelf not far above the sea, and ascend again by a second stairway to the monastery stuck on the sheer cliff at a great height like a swallow's nest. He was not intending to visit the place, but as he climbed he overtook several, all women and girls, who were. The available flat space jutted out only a little from the sheer rock, against which the edifice itself was flattened. And there was a well, a capillary of icy water, a shoot of it, reaching so high. The females Ben had overtaken were examined through a Judas hole and allowed in to view the holy icon of Mary and her child – which had floated across from Palestine – only if they could cover themselves. Those who couldn't swilled their faces and their bare arms and shoulders at the well and looked down to the small scallop of turquoise sea very far below. Ben's path exited along the contour at the far end of the monastery's strip of garden through a gate. He rounded the hill, and the house of the miraculous icon and the women let in or not let in continued in his consciousness only as dreams do.

He walked for hours. The path, notched into a contour, contented him. He had a bare exposure of hillside on his left above, and a steep falling away towards the sea on his right below. He must be watchful, his footing was his responsibility, his alone. The sea itself looked hard, a deep hard blue almost black; resistant, it looked, to any use or working. The dried-out clumps and bushes had a savoury smell but nothing else about the terrain was at all sustaining. No one would survive who did not watch out for himself. He thought of his father occasionally, whose self-assertion had been murderous. His own was as fierce, but solitary. I hurt nobody, so he said to himself.

Mid-afternoon, rounding a headland, Ben saw the path descending and – rather to his surprise – quite a broad track coming in and down from the left, to meet it, above a small bay. His own path climbed away barrenly on the other side. Sure of that, relishing the prospect of it, he allowed himself to idle. He thought of the girls at the monastery of the Virgin; and their climbing and descending the hundreds of steps closed in his mind with the long capillary of cold water drawn up as through a taproot to the marble bowl of the monkish well. Soon he was at the meeting place with the broad track, his path crossed and continued but another set off steeply down to the beach tucked out of sight below. Thinking of it afterwards – again and again – he conceded that he had not hesitated, had not altered his pace, but had turned off and down as if through all the previous miles and days, almost through all the previous years, that had always been his intention.

The beach was nothing much. There was little room between the sea and the cliff, a curve of it, barely more than a new moon sickle of it, from point to point. He saw nothing else, and nobody. Without pause, without hesitation, he slung down his pack and undressed. The sea was ten yards distant. He crossed the gap quickly, the sand burning his soles; waded in and swam. The pleasure shocked him by its thoroughness. Never in his life before had he entered into anything, been taken into anything, so entirely. Coolness, sliding all over him, silkily close. He dipped his head, and felt himself to be one vein of feeling, one channel of it, entirely flowed through. And every movement of his limbs refreshed the sensation. He swam till the arc of cliff and sand was distant, lay back on the buoyant water, idling, alone under the sun, vaguely drifting.

But he must resume his trek. The pleasure of the water seemed to have entered him so thoroughly it felt like a virtue he could bear away in his body and soul. He swam in, scarcely aware, and realised too late that he was some way off course for his pile of clothes. He saw a young woman, standing with her back to him. She was tall, her skin very clear and white. She had a child on the sand below her, under a white sunshade, and bent down now to attend to it. Ben came nearer. He was in shallow water. He stood up. Her back was arced over and down, her head gone out of sight. He stood in the waves staring at her buttocks and the tuft of black hair in the opening below them. Stared, the waves breaking in quite a rapid rhythm around his ankles. Then the woman stood up, looked over her shoulder, saw him staring. Slate-blue eyes, a wide mouth, a cool and open gaze. She turned to face him fully. He was aware of her breasts but, held by her eyes, dared not look. Her expression, first of affront, shifted as she outfaced him into curiosity, a cool appraisal, a desire to discountenance him. She looked him up and down. All his usual gaucheness came over him. He blushed, and crossed his two hands together below his waist. At that she smiled, her eyes hardened, she raised her head in a slow upward nod. Then turned, parted her legs, and bowed again over the child. Through the black hair now the lips of her sex were clearly displayed. He stared and stared. His eyes felt the soft bulging of the place, its foldedness, its moistness, how it would open. Then he turned, went in deep again, swam fast to his clothes, dressed rapidly, and fled.

2

That winter, one dreary late afternoon, Ben's supervisor asked him would he see a last client before the office closed, and handed him the file. Rehousing, she said, higher-rate allowances, the usual. But really she needs a husband, one with a UK passport, quick. Ben ignored her look and took the file. Ask her why on earth she wants to stay in this benighted land, the supervisor said. Ben read the file. The client was a Marina Milova, born in the Ukraine, single, with a daughter rising five, variously employed, her work permit and residence permit extended for a further three months, with no prospect of any extension beyond that. When Ben had read it – he had read scores like it – he pressed the button to summon Ms Milova, by her number, to booth number 9, for an interview. He was tired. Especially in winter the office felt close and unhealthy with the anxieties, false hopes and resentments of the countless people wanting help. It oppressed him, latterly more and more. But he hurried, he hated to keep a client waiting, he liked to be there first, to welcome the petitioner in. On this occasion, however, he was held up by a colleague with a facetious question, a man who always, on principle, made the client wait; and when Ben got to his desk in the slightly sordid privacy of the booth the woman was already in place, sitting on the grey plastic chair and within her right arm enfolding her child, who stood beside her on the pocked and spattered floor. Their eyes met. It was the woman on the beach. Her fair skin paled, then blushed. Ben sat down, because there was no strength, energy or will in him except to stare. He felt the blood leave him, felt its tumultuous return, as on a coast in a seismic shock, the sea. Her file trembled in his hands. He set it down. The child regarded him disinterestedly, and the mother soon composed herself, her paleness assumed an aura of ice. She waited in silence. But Ben had to speak, he was the officer and he parted his lips to speak, knowing himself lost, lost all over again, the stammer had come home into his mouth again, the hammering at utterance, the blurting, the straining hee-haw-hee-haw, all the beast sounds and nothing else, only effort. As he struggled, he bulged his eyes at the woman's pale face and they did note an alteration there, from ice towards something akin to curiosity, human interest, not pity quite, but not quite without pity either. Not pitiless, he said to himself in his head in silence where he could articulate all he liked, not entirely pitiless. But then he stood up, showed her his hands in a gesture of helplessness, seized her file, and fled.

Late that night Ben wrote a letter to his supervisor saying that his old trouble had come over him again and he would be obliged to stay away from work for a while, until it passed. Then, in foul weather, he cycled to the office and posted his letter through the steel door.

Early next morning Ben's supervisor rang. He let her speak into his answerphone, knowing that he would not be able to make any reply. She said she had no idea what his old trouble was but she was sorry to hear it had come over him again. Of course, he must take a few days off. But would he mind letting her have Ms Milova's file? She gathered he had left in a hurry. Perhaps the interview had been unusually difficult?

Ben read the file again. He judged from past experience that Ms Milova would certainly be deported. He copied out her name, address and telephone number; put the file into a suitable envelope, for the attention of the supervisor, cycled to the office and left it at the lodge, pointing at his mouth when the porter, in a friendly fashion, asked him how he was. A couple of hours later, lying on the sofa, he listened to a message from his supervisor. They had contacted Ms Milova. She had decided not to pursue her claims. So that was that. Perhaps she thought the Black Sea a better option after all.

Ben lay on his bed thinking, as he had incessantly for three months, of the encounter on the beach. It had simplified and clarified in his memory. The path, the descent, the sickle of hot sand. His careless certainty of purpose. The water, his wellbeing. Then the woman and her sleeping child. Sometimes he could imagine that he had swum in from elsewhere, from an adjoining bay perhaps, and had arrived by an innocent chance at that small scallop of sand, where she was. And again he experienced the sudden, unmediated deep intimacy. And then her face, turning to him over her left shoulder, her pale skin, her candid, at first shocked and affronted, then scornful, then vengefully mocking face. And then – as it seemed to him – the knowing and deliberate self-exposure, which he understood now one way now another, again and again, but never in any way except discomforting. And he dreamed or wilfully added or truly remembered a further detail: that with

194

her right hand, as she bowed over the sleeping child, with two of the long white fingers of that right hand, reaching back, she opened and held open the outer lips of the vulva, so that the entrance into it was through a divining fork or wishbone. Then followed his flight, in ignominy, shot through by the shafts of the sight of her. He had thought never to see her again, the image would fade in time, his life, troubled enough by his mother and dead father, would continue bearably. Now this.

Late that night, in a mixture of feelings, chief among them being, so he told himself, professional shame, he wrote Ms Milova a letter and having first located her address exactly on the city map and worked out the safest route, he cycled there at once. It was a tower block on a poor estate. The foyer, which should have been locked, was open and very defaced. But he found her name on one of the scores of postboxes, inserted his letter, and left, more in horror than in fear. He knew of the estate from many files, but this was his first visit to its reality.

Ben had written: Dear Ms Milova, I was very distressed to hear from my supervisor this morning that you have decided not to seek rehousing and an increase in your allowances. I feel myself to blame for this change of plan and am writing to you now in the hope that you will let me make you some amends. I should be very glad if you and your child would come and live in my house. I have plenty of room and you could live quite separately from me. You could contribute to the costs of heating and lighting, if you wished, but I should not want any rent. Please say yes. It makes me unhappy to think that I may have worsened your circumstances when it is my job to improve them, if at all possible. Yours sincerely, Ben Benson.

He couldn't sleep. He knew that mulling things over in the small hours does no good. But this was different: it was riding him, sitting on his chest and riding him. He tried speaking aloud, but even alone, his bulging eyes on nobody,

195

all his mouth could make was the braying noise. He had recourse to an old strategy, the adoption of a strange voice, and that did work. Impersonating a very old man, he could enunciate clearly a few opening courtesies. But it was laughable. Must he speak to her beauty through the mask of a satyr? He tried his foreign languages. All worked, more or less well – Greek, the hardest, by far the best. The thing squatting on his ribs chortled merrily. Could he look her in the eyes and address her in Greek? He saw his father's face, the eyes bulging like a squid's, the lips munching savagely on the iron of consonants, a white spittle working up. And then, in desperation, the fist. He saw his mother, twisting the strap of her handbag in her lap, twisting and twisting, her eyes on the man in terror. I was doing all right, said Ben aloud in his old man's voice. I was doing all right. And now this.

At four, daylight still miles away, he got out of bed and wrote a PS to his letter: Please do not think I was forgetting or ignoring your greater problem. Only I did not dare suggest the obvious solution. Forgive me my want of courage. I am a single man and should, of course, be glad to marry you, in a formal way, and we could live separately in my house until you obtained British citizenship and the arrangement became unnecessary. Shall we meet (he suggested a time and place), and you will tell me what you think of this idea? I'm afraid my speech then may be very bad. Will you be patient with me? I have various strategies, all ridiculous. Be patient with me. Yours sincerely, Ben Benson.

He dressed up again in his cycling gear and pedalled through the dark and the wet to her notorious tower block. The drunks, the homeless, the dealers looked at him in wonderment. Perhaps he seemed to them an angel. Certainly he felt unlikely to be harmed. Back home, as people rose to go to work and school, he washed, shaved, lay down and waited.

Her voice, when it came, affected him profoundly. He played the message half a dozen times. What moved him most was her careful enunciation of his mother tongue – his tongue and the aura of her utter foreignness, that mixing. She thanked him for his two letters. She was sorry, but she could not meet him at ten-thirty, as he suggested. She had to see a teacher at the little school. Tanya was having a few problems. Would eleven-thirty suit him? She would hope so. Goodbye for now.

Ben never sat in cafés, certainly not during the working week. For a meeting place he had suggested the crypt of St Mary the Virgin, because his supervisor had once remarked that they did a very good lemon-drizzle cake there. He arrived early, to reconnoitre, then waited outside. The rain was turning to sleet. Soon Ms Milova appeared, walking quickly. She wore a long coat buttoned up to a scarf around her throat, gloves, a red woollen hat. Her shoes were not good enough for the weather. And she seemed less tall than he remembered, her face looked troubled. The thought that she might be vulnerable shocked him. It was something he felt he could not have foreseen. Neither spoke. Inside he was relieved to see that the table he had hoped for – back against the wall – was still unoccupied.

Ben took out a ten-pound note, gave it to Ms Milova, pointing at his mouth and grimacing. He motioned her towards the distant counter. Café, he said, pronouncing the word as though it were French or German. When she came back and had set out the two cups, laid aside the tray, given him his change, he handed her a sheet of paper on which he had typed: I may be able to talk well enough in a foreign language. Please point to the one you would best understand me in. French, German, Italian, Serbo-Croat… He had left off Greek. The thought of speaking to her in Greek appalled him, like an indecency. She pointed to French. Je parle assez bien le français, she said. J'ai suivi des cours, il y a quelques ans, au lycée français à Kiev. Then she took off her gloves. Seeing her white hands, the long fine fingers, he thought that even via a foreign language he would be unable to speak; but then, haltingly, the words came. He watched her watching his lips, in mirrors he had watched them himself, practising, they were repellent to him, they reminded him of his father's, and he watched the young woman's face now, that was so open, for signs of helpless disgust, but saw none, only a curiosity that was not unkind.

Ben's persona in French was elderly, far older than his years, but not nearly so old as the person he must become in English to have a hope of circumventing the stammers. He spoke a meticulous and ancient French with some of the mannerisms of a scholar of independent means. When she replied in French he held up a hand and begged her to speak to him in English. French was a strategy that only he needed to employ. He said nothing of the secret pleasure her English gave him, his tongue, her foreign voice. In English then she told him of Tanya's difficulties at her school. It is her language, she said. My Tanya speaks a good deal but it is in a foreign language. Mais elle apprendra l'anglais, said Ben. Une petite fille si vive et si intelligente, assurément elle parlera l'anglais aussi bien que sa mère. Ms Milova shook her head. No, she said, my Tanya speaks a language nobody understands. She has made one up. Though I know what she means, I do not understand any of the words. Ben was halted, he listened very closely, beginning to forget himself. She cannot join in, she sits in a corner and covers her face with her hands. It was like at work, hearing the problems, the myriad ways of being unhappy. Soon, without thinking, he could say a few little things in English: I see. I'm very sorry. Poor child. But then for his greater statement he reverted to French and a pedantic gravity. Madame, he said, là aussi je crois pouvoir vous être utile... He felt sure of being able to place Tanya in his own neighbourhood, a better area, where she would thrive. Raison de plus, he said, que vous acceptiez de venir loger chez moi. Her face assumed a wondering look, not in the least fearful, but curious and wondering. Alors, he said, rising to his feet, 'no time like the present'. He used the expression as a

Frenchman might who had learned it at school and was delighted to place it in speech at last.

The bus was crowded with women and small children going back to the estates. Ben and Ms Milova were separated. She found a seat, he stood watching and listening. The women were familiar to him, their kind at least, the women, their children, their men. The family, best system yet devised for inflicting damage down the generations on and on. The bus was full of women far younger than he was, with bitter faces, one in particular in foul language continually scolding and threatening her fat and malevolent child. The weight, a bus-load, all the difficulty, the clutter, the struggle to manage, worsened to screaming-point by the hostile weather. He saw that Ms Milova was watching too, he saw in an almost violent access of sympathy that being on the bus among the ravened women dispirited her, her face was clouding over with disgust and fear. But then she caught his eye, she looked affronted, as though he had surprised her unfairly in a weakness. And he bowed his head in a memory of insult, of slate-blue eyes, the clear skin, a gaze turned on him as implacable as white marble and black obsidian. Approaching their stop, he signalled to her with extreme formality, and as the bus drew away and they walked the short distance to his house, neither spoke.

Arrive with a foreigner, home looks very strange. Ben thought the wide street, its trees, its semis and gardens, quite inane and his life there a cowardice. In the porch, which had the shape of a large keyhole, he was mortally ashamed. She will see my life, he said to himself, and think it risible. He showed her round with very few words and those few French: kitchen, sitting room, dining room... Upstairs, blushing, averting his eyes, mumbling like a dotard, he pushed open the door to his bedroom, that would be hers. She appraised it. Then a small bedroom adjacent, where Tanya might like to sleep. C'est la maison de ma mère, he said. The little sentence sounded like a first lesson. I live in it. And where will you sleep? Ms Milova asked. Ben pointed upwards. There is an attic room, he said, in which I shall be very comfortable. Ms Milova nodded, eyed him curiously. He began a long sentence in French, grammatically and syntactically complex, but manageable, he thought. He foresaw its difficulties and trusted his memory and inventiveness to solve them. He wanted to say that if she felt able to accept this offer of accommodation, as he sincerely hoped she would, they might perhaps defer for a few days – but not for much longer, given her circumstances that would surely be unwise – their discussion of his offer to marry her; but he hit a bad stammer at once and could utter nothing but a helpless and insistent braying. So he stood before her, eyes bulging, beastly, showing her in despair his empty hands. She watched him for a little while. Perhaps she thought he might break through into the sweetness of human discourse. But then she raised her left hand, open and gloved, in a sign that he felt to be benevolent. He felt that it meant he should stop, there was no need, he could be kinder on himself. I have to fetch Tanya, she said. Don't trouble to accompany me. I can find my way.

Ben lay on his bed, that had been his mother and father's bed. When the phone rang he did not go down to listen. He had decided he must begin again, by any strategy recover some power of conventional speech, return to work, go back to where he was before September, begin again from there. Then he dozed and dreamed. He suffered ugly metamorphoses, he passed through foul incarnations, and the worst of it was that however hard he tried, however cleverly he applied the intelligence still housing undiminished inside his head, all he could make was a braying noise that excited only laughter in his tormentors. But the message when he listened to it late that night was simple and clear: Tanya and I should like to come and live in your house. Would a week on Friday be too soon? Goodbye for now. You are very kind. Ben replied at once: Dear Ms Milova, That is very good news. Thank you. No, a week on Friday is not too soon. I will come for you both in a taxi at 6 pm. In the meantime I will see what I can do for your little girl in my neighbourhood. Yours sincerely, Ben Benson. He dressed, cycled through the bleak streets and delivered the letter.

Ben took one more day off work, to compose himself and begin the reorganization of his living space. Then he resumed his public duties. Better? his supervisor asked. He nodded. He would keep his speech to the minimum.

3

Ben liked his new bedroom and wondered why he had not moved in there years before. With very little hesitation he cleared it of all signs and memories of his mother and father, brought into it only the simplest necessities of his own, and soon had a room that was almost as sparsely appointed as the one he had occupied in the high mountain village on Skleros. Its only ornament, presented to him on the first evening and stuck with blutack to the white wall, was a picture of a house whose door and windows seemed the mouth and eyes of a smiling face. The picture had an inscription, added by Ms Milova: Thank You Ben. With Love From Tanya.

Tanya's language was a wondrous affair. Ms Milova had said she understood it – the will and the import of it – whilst understanding none of the words, and Ben believed her. She and the child were of course very close, most nights sleeping at least a part of the night together. And though the words of the language were all of Tanya's own invention, its tone, rhythms, character were, Ms Milova had said, those of Russian, the mother tongue. So woman and child were helped by love and familiarity and got the sense of one another very well. Indeed, Ms Milova said, she had picked up many of Tanya's words – that is, she could say them aloud almost in Tanya's accent and might have used them herself in their conversations – but she sensed that Tanya did not want her to and would drop a word altogether or change its meaning to prevent the language she had invented being grasped and used by anyone else. And this was the cause or a symptom of her problems with the outside world.

To Ben, when he overhead it or when, little by little, she began to address him in it, Tanya's language was doubly strange since he understood neither her peculiar vocabulary nor even, knowing no Russian, her rhythms and her tone. Yet he was powerfully drawn to her and after only a few days sharing his house he sensed that she liked and trusted him. So he bought a Russian course and spent some part of every evening copying out sentences far beyond his small understanding – to get the script through his eyes into his fingers – and repeating aloud, after a voice on a tape, the very first simple courtesies. Around a centre of unrest, even of downright fear, step by step he paced himself into some assurance. Russian, he soon believed, might serve him even better than his forbidden Greek, the tongue in his mouth, the teeth, the lips, acted for him faithfully, he could make the sounds, he could utter the words, make a simple sentence with no more let, hindrance and impediment than any healthy linguist might encounter beginning again.

They really did lead separate lives. The house had only one kitchen and only one bathroom and Ben, having promised separateness, was at first very anxious on that count and went to extraordinary lengths not to see or be seen. Then little by little he relaxed. Ms Milova was marvellously discreet, and though he never forgot that she lived with him – his every second thought was of her, coming home he had to steady himself before opening the door – actual signs of her being in his house were few and on some days none. Curious, the fact without proof; the certainty with nothing to go on; the life of the certain fact sustained on less than a hint of scent.

The child, with her lovely talk, was a more tangible presence, though still very flitting and elusive. Every evening she climbed up to his room to say goodnight: stood in the doorway, clasped her hands and made a little singing speech whose purpose was surely to wish him and her a safe passage through the night. If he came home late, he felt she had been there, his attic door was open, it seemed she had uttered the blessing in his absence and he might apprehend it, the singing sentences, still lingering, waiting for him, on the empty air. Then one evening – how glad he was to be already home! – she knocked and entered with a saucer and on it a slice of cake, over which she delivered a speech of greater length and vivacity, curtsied, handed him the gift, and vanished. And once, early on, he did not hear her enter, he was absorbed, listening, and repeating his lessons, and perhaps she had stood behind him for some while before he knew and turned. The expression on her face – a face as open as her mother's – was of helpless fascination. When he turned, it increased, she looked shocked by the sight of the mouth of a man who had been making some words of the mother tongue she declined to speak. Very decidedly then she composed herself, clasped her hands and made her singing goodnight speech.

The following Sunday, early evening, Ben came home from visiting his mother, and through the kitchen window, as he pushed his bicycle into the yard, he saw Tanya and her mother at the little table conversing happily. Tanya, facing away from him, was in her red dressing-gown and held a cup of milk clasped tightly on the table top; Ms Milova, facing him, wore a green long-sleeved dress buttoned up to the throat. Despondent anyway, fatigued by the journey, dispirited by the hours with his mother, at the sight of the young woman through the glass he felt, like a leadening around the heart, a consolidation of his hopelessness. Her looks were on the child, wholly encouraging. Did they still speak two languages, the child's and the world's? Or had Tanya allowed the adult into hers? That was how it looked. The language of such contentment, of being so contentedly at home, was surely a child's, unlearnable by him however hard he tried.

Ben entered, because he must, and the woman and child looked his way without fear or annoyance or any embarrassment but benignly, as though still under the enchantment of their dream, as though waking out of it quite happy to deal with the world if they must and fortified to do so by the virtue of where they had been. Ben apologised, feeling oafish in his wet and bulky clothes, and passed through to get out of them and climb to his own room where he would wait a decent time before coming down to make himself a supper. Meanwhile, so as not to dwell on his mother in her nursing home, he would copy out some Russian verses and repeat a few basic sentences aloud. But before he had well begun Tanya knocked at his door and came in carrying the saucer on which was an envelope and over it she delivered her lilting goodnight words, curtsied, offered him her message, and waited. He read: Won't you come down and eat with me at 8? I will cook something for both of us. M. The child watched him anxiously. He wrote in Russian with childish care: Yes. Thank you very much. Folded the note back into its envelope. She curtsied already turning and hastened away down the stairs.

On the dot of eight Ben presented himself as though in a stranger's room. The small kitchen table was set. Plates, cutlery, glasses, familiar since his childhood, had become very strange. The young woman smiled, motioned him to sit down, poured out the wine, cut the bread and fetched from his mother's stove the meal she had made, served him, sat facing him and smiled. I hope you will like it, she said. He bowed. They ate in silence. He emptied his glass, she replenished it. They ate, she sided away the plates, fetched the cheese and two apples, again replenished his glass. We saw that you were troubled when you came in, she said. Tell me why. Tell me in English, if you can. In one of your voices. Or in French if you must. Say it slowly. Don't be worried.

Ben began. It was a good performance. He used his voices, even the ancient's. He foresaw the hamperings of his utterance and shifted among the languages adroitly. Once, in desperation, driven by a terrible necessity, he thrust his words out into Greek. He saw the puzzlement on her face, then a dawning. She shook her head, looked down. He shifted back into English, stumbling, begging her forgiveness through the gaps in his words that of themselves were saying something else. But it was several sentences before Ms Milova would look him in the eyes again. Then his faith picked up, she forgave him, she sympathised, what tumbled out of the zoo and babel of his mouth she understood, so he believed, she could translate, she made it clear.

Today was worse than ever. They think she will not live much longer and her death will be a blessing, I am sure. Again she mistook me for my brother.

You have a brother?

An elder brother, there is a big gap in years between him and me. She never sees him, I never see him, he lives away.

Is it so bad that she mistakes you for your brother?

My brother fought with my father, wrestled with him, they were like two demons, on the landing outside your room, they fought. The father did his best to fling the son downstairs but he was not strong enough, my brother hit him hard in the mouth, my brother's knuckles were cut by my father's teeth, they had blood on them, my mother and I were witnesses, we saw the blood of the father's mouth on the knuckles of his eldest son's right hand. She has not forgiven him, though, as always, it was my father who had begun the quarrel. My brother left the house, they did not see him again, he did not come to my father's funeral, for which she will never forgive him. I visit her every Sunday in her nursing home and though neither his name nor mine comes to her tongue I see from the fear and hatred in her face that she mistakes me for him.

Why was there fighting in your family?

My father, you must know, was a stammerer, worse than me. I have my strategies, I devised them after watching his. He had only one, it failed him always but he would not, or did not have the wit to, seek another. His one resource was rage. He roared, he brayed like an ass. And he would take us, *en famille*, into places where his torment would be public, so martyring us also. We stood or sat around in a public place – it might be a restaurant, the foyer of a theatre or a gathering of his colleagues and their families – and he made us witness what he looked like when the stammer stopped his speech and all he could do was flail with his arms and bray. My poor mother. I believe he lay awake inventing ordeals for himself. He schemed how he could put himself into situations in which he would be lost if his language failed. Nightmares – a recitation, a lecture, the presentation of an important and complicated policy: he woke, and in the real world sought a venue for his own calamity. And if he possibly could he made us watch. At home he blamed us, he asserted that our behaviour – any little noise or mischief, the very meekness of my abject mother – brought his affliction on, aggravated his agony, left him incurable. And so at home in privacy he punished us.

The worst – was it the worst? – came one Sunday morning at breakfast. I had spilled a little milk over the cloth. He began to tell me off. He soon hit the impediment, battered with the ram of his rage at his own teeth and tongue and lips, then ripped the cloth from the table, filthying the carpet. My brother ran from the house, my mother dragged me out of my father's way to what she thought would be safety in the bathroom if she locked the door. He shook at the knob. He brayed and sounded to be heaving up the bile out of his belly, to assail us. Then came his fist. Notice, next time you are in the bathroom, that the middle panel of the door has been replaced. The wood is slightly different, even under the paint you can detect it if you look. That is where he smashed his fist through. I was in my mother's embrace, backing away, we heard his final roar and then the smash, and his fist came through a splintering hole in the centre of the door and rested there in a sudden total silence, rested at the wrist on the thorns of his own making, and from the broken knuckles began to bleed. I can see my father's fist whenever I like, and often I see it whether I like to or not: in a crown of splinters very slowly beginning to bleed, and then the black drops pit-patting on the lino.

The home is a terrible place. I suppose all such homes are. They slump and doze in an unbearable heat around the walls and at least two television sets are always on. The woman in charge has bought a very large tank of tropical fish and positioned it so that the residents may watch its vivid inmates idling to and fro. She bought twenty-three of them but there must be something wrong with the climate or the feeding and when I visited this afternoon only three were left. Not that my mother thinks about the fish. She thinks about the tyranny she endured. But 'thinks' is the wrong word, I don't believe she thinks. I believe she sits and dozes and is visited by images. It was an abundant tyranny, she could never exhaust its well of images. And when I arrive, if the day is unlucky, she mistakes me for the young man who hit his father in the mouth and all my love for her and all my years of striving to put something good in the place of harm, they are in vain, they do not work, I arrive like the devil himself, so like my brother she mistakes me for him or perhaps by now so like my father in my crippled speech she believes I'm him as well and all in one I am the very worst she has endured of pain. She becomes distressed, she clings to a girl from Estonia or the Philippines and holds her flat hand out at me to ward me off.

Are there no lucky days?

There were. Then she knew me and seemed to remember how she loved me when I was born. She told me once that she had believed she might start again with me, after the gap of years in which only hatred grew between my brother and my father. Those were the lucky days, when I visited her in the home and she recognised me and remembered. But there have not been many of them lately.

How did your father die?

Of apoplexy, I believe they used to call it that. He brought it on by rage one evening when he couldn't get his curses out. I had to watch him die. I believe he disliked me even more than my brother who hit him in the mouth. No doubt my mother chose my name but my father was very glad of it because Benjamin Benson is hard for a stammerer to say. He used to make me say it, to get me over it, he said.

Ms Milova went to check that Tanya was safe asleep. Ben washed up. After a while, supposing she had gone to bed, he locked the doors, put out the lights and, still agitated by so much talking, climbed the stairs. She was standing on the landing where the father and his eldest boy had fought. I was coming to say goodnight, she said. Goodnight, he said. And thank you for supper. He turned; then halted, facing her again. Forgive me, I have to ask you whether you have decided to marry me or not. They won't deport you if you do. But it occurred to me that I ought to tell you that aside from that one benefit there is little else about me that would do you any good. For a start, they tell me that my mother will die soon and when she does we shall have to sell this house to meet the accumulated bill at the nursing home. And when my brother learns that she is dead he will claim his half of what is left, which will be very little since there is still a substantial mortgage to pay off. She watched him curiously. He suspected, as often before, that she had criteria he did not know about, and this unnerved him in his formal declaration and brought him to a stammering halt. He tried hard, but could make no sensible sound. He became distressed. Then she lifted her left hand open towards him and laid her bare fingers on his struggling lips. Enough, she said. I was only coming to say goodnight.

Next morning Ben's supervisor said, in passing, I see our friend Ms Milova has changed her post office. She would, said Ben. She has, said the supervisor. One quite near you, I see. And the school is quite near here. And her address… Indeed, said Ben. She is living with me. By which I mean she and her daughter occupy two rooms in my house. I see, said the supervisor. And has she found a UK husband yet? Not that I know of, Ben replied. I see very little of her, you understand.

During the lunch hour, if he possibly could, Ben took a walk, to clear his head. Waiting to cross the street, he saw Ms Milova on the other side, on the corner near Tesco's. She had her hands thrust deep into her pockets. Had she been waiting for him? Fierce as lightning, he felt the want she had opened in his life. He crossed and stood before her without a greeting. I'm glad to have met you, she said. I wanted to ask you something. They walked together towards Tanya's school, but halted at a little distance from it and stood still in the cold. Last night, she said, you told me that when you have to sell your mother's house very little money will come to you from the sale. That's correct, said Ben. And do you have any other capital? Did your father leave you anything, for example? Ben's mouth rebelled. With his hand he motioned her to look away. Then he assumed the voice and the mannerisms of an old man and said, fluently enough, My father ruined himself and us. It was a part of his brutal self-assertion that he must, again and again until nothing was left, gamble his own and my mother's money on business ventures. They were all as hazardous as the occasions he set up to test his stammer. Money and speech were equally unlikely to spring forth. The debacles were public, humiliating, laughable. And almost his last act was to take out a second mortgage on the house, which I am still paying off, needless to say. Between my mother – her debts – and my brother – his vengeful greed – I have very little room to move. No savings of your own? Ms Milova asked, looking up now into Ben's very youthful face. Scarcely any, he replied. Ms Milova looked pleased. Thank you for answering my questions, she said. Je vous en prie, he replied.

He was turning to go back to work when she touched his arm and added, Tanya is very happy where you placed her. She can speak her special language and nobody minds. The lady has told me it is a lovely tongue, like a mountain stream, she said. And there are so many languages in that house. It is like paradise. They all have the gift of tongues. Ben bowed his head. He saw again that her shoes were inadequate. Are you warm enough? he asked. Not quite, she answered. No, not quite. But warmer than I'd be where I come from.

The afternoon was arduous, but Ben's sympathies were quickened and he did his job well. He saw through people's truculence and mendacity into their fear, and tried to help. He saw young women, aged around the mouth, their children burdening them. He saw that they feared they were entering into disappointment and could not turn back. They were beginning to panic. This is it, this is what life will be like: disappointing. Briefly they had believed it would be a joyous affair. Ben listened, he knew ways and means at least for some material alleviation. And he knew it needed more than that, it needed change – not just help and good fortune but the energy to seize them if they came. But the lower you get the less energy you have. That is the law: the lower, the harder to get out. The more it saps you, the more you need. Ben knew all that. Some days it disheartened him utterly. His clients were fathomless in their need, not all the social services in the kingdom could begin to fill them up. Love might begin, but where should they turn for that? Ben's job was clear: to make a space, to set up and reinforce more favourable circumstances for hope of love to come into and settle in and for the winds of faith and energy to blow through. So he listened, attended carefully, and did not need to say very much, which suited him.

Back home, as so often, he could not tell whether his lodgers were in the house or not. What if they had vanished? Then he would have to wake out of the dream of her and live his life in her absence. More and more he doubted whether he could manage that. Then he was shocked to find that she had left a message on the answerphone; the fact itself shocked him, it seemed a sign of her imminent disembodiment. The message began confidently enough – thanking him again for his willingness to answer her questions; but then it faltered and abruptly came to a stop. He supposed he would never have the resources to understand such things.

He made himself a pot of tea, took it up to his room, and resumed his Russian. He tried not to think of the line of her back, of her green dress, of her hand raised like a blessing to his struggling mouth, of the likely coldness of her feet. He was doing well, he was congratulating himself, when Tanya knocked and came in to say goodnight. Again she was carrying an envelope on a saucer; she curtsied and he took it. Her eyes were round, she was biting her lip in her eagerness and importance. Opening the envelope, seeing that it contained more than a note, Ben indicated to Tanya that she should come and sit on his neat bed while he read and thought about what her mother had written. So there she sat, barefooted in her red dressing gown, staring at him almost savagely and murmuring to herself in her own language.

Ms Milova had written in French. Cher M. Benson, Je vous remercie encore de votre franchise envers moi. Sur des détails importants vous m'avez tout à fait rassurée. Maintenant c'est à moi de vous dire des choses – quoique je sache que vous, de vous-même, ne me poseriez jamais de questions indiscrètes. And she went on to say that Tanya was not her daughter, but her twin sister's; the sister, together with the sister's lover, the father of the child, had been shot; she herself had no children; indeed, she was a virgin. And she concluded: If, after learning these things (which Tanya does not know) your offer of marriage still stands, I should be very happy to accept it. And she thanked him for his patience and for his kindness to her and the child.

Tanya, watching keenly, now addressed her babbling to him. She was asking him a question, that much he could be sure of, and repeating it, again and again, the same lilt, the same hurried rising rhythm. Yes, it did sound like Russian, but wasn't. That at least he knew by now. He crossed the small space between them and stood over the child. She looked up at him, still with her question. But noticing her feet he bent down and took them into his hands. They were cold in his frugal room, he chafed them warm. You need slippers, he said, or some warm socks. But she shook her head and pointed at the letter on his desk, jumped off the bed and tugged him back to his seat. She was at his elbow, watching closely, as he turned over the letter and wrote: Dear Ms Milova, Of course the offer still stands and I am very glad that you accept it. The sooner we act, the better. I will make the arrangements tomorrow, if you agree. Yours sincerely, Ben Benson. He folded the paper, put it into the envelope, and at once Tanya seized it and without a curtsey hurried from the room and down the stairs – leaving him the empty saucer which, he now noticed, was a pretty one that he had given his mother on a birthday and whose matching cup his father had hurled at the dining-room wall.

4

Ms Milova, temping, knew nobody well enough. Ben did have friends but asked his sardonic supervisor and the colleague who always kept clients waiting, to be the necessary witnesses. Tanya, shining like a full moon in wonderment, held a bouquet of blood-red anemones. For the kiss Ms Milova presented her left cheek. Ben, entering her aura, into the scent of her hair, close to her earlobe and its jade adornment, felt it to be a licence he was bound to take but ought not to. And yet when they left the town hall Ms Milova took his arm and they might have walked like that on the sunny street for quite some distance had not Tanya come between them to be hand in hand with both. Ben carried her anemones.

Back home – No time like the present, he said – he sat down at the kitchen table with Ms Milova and the necessary documents and helped her complete the application for UK citizenship and a UK passport, as his wife. Then he said he would walk to the post office with it, and that would be that. Thank you, Ben, Ms Milova said. And you will call me Marina now, won't you? Yes, of course, he replied. Of course I will, if you want me to. But testing this liberty on his lips he could not, at the first time, go through with it; and left the house rather than stare into her eyes above the stumbling on her name.

Habituation – only in the sense that he grew used to being in the ways of love and desire, but in those ways he could never settle, never move in and feel at home, he was always restless, always keenly alert to events, new aspects and perspectives he could not possibly have prepared himself against. Their marriage made all the difference – and none. It was like the kiss in the presence of those few spectators, a formal licence; except that the kiss, a small thing and a great, he had felt bound to take, whereas into the space at home, the

213

rooms of the form of marriage, he dared not step, a power like taboo kept him out. Yet he lived there in a terrible proximity, in the shape of a life crying out for fullness. And still he held back. He had offered her the form, for her material benefit, that was the deal; and if he had himself already filled out that form with the spirit of love and desire, she wasn't required to do likewise. So he kept to the letter of the deal, anxiously in character. At work his supervisor asked him at least once a week how he was enjoying married life. Very well, thank you, he replied, avoiding her sardonic eyes.

Marina seemed easier. She was more often in the kitchen – the friendliest room in the house – when he came home. They ate together and not just on Sundays when, as she had seen, he wanted her company after visiting his mother. Three or four times a week, without any planning, so it seemed, they might sit down together, with Tanya or not, in the evening for their meal. And he talked more easily, and if he began to stammer, his strategies for circumventing it had become accustomed between them and scarcely embarrassed him now. And if no voice or language helped and he stopped dead, mouthing and staring, then she would lift her fingers in the gesture of peace and blessing and healing, to touch his lips, and the silence ensuing then was very sweet. One afternoon at work, reading a file, he suddenly saw those moments not just as her touching his lips but also, with a shock, as his kissing her offered fingers.

Still Ben never presumed. He kept punctiliously to his side of the bargain. He felt in all honour that he must. And at heart he was afraid. Too often he saw the coolness come over her, like shadow. Then she withdrew, she was a mystery to him. He never forgot the intimacy they had begun with, but never her scorn either, her vengefulness, as it had looked to him. Then above all she was strange to him, a stranger in his house, from somewhere very foreign and remote, with a life he knew little about that had touched, he assumed, on passions and violences beyond his own limits. Once she told him, à propos of nothing, that before leaving the Ukraine she had almost completed a doctorate in forestry, that she had worked in forests, lived in them for months at a time. They are all different, she said, and the parts of the same forest are all different too. The languages of the trees vary not only from kind to kind but also, being richer than ours, according to age, location and, above all, weather, and these differences are more than dialects, so that to understand and converse you must listen, in a studying fashion, more closely even than humans must who want to communicate with foreigners in their species.

Perhaps because of learning from Marina about the languages of trees, Ben listened ever more closely to Tanya's private speech. Soon he could always follow her drift; and little by little, as she allowed him, he even began to talk with her. Most days he dropped her off at the school on his way to work, and walking to and from the bus the child would take his hand and babble as melodiously as a hurrying water in her tongue. When he judged from her tone that she was asking him a question, he answered – at first in words, or sounds, of his own devising, but later, as he grew more adept and she more permissive, in a foreigner's version of hers. Then she smiled, corrected his pronunciation, commended him; and on especially gracious days she would give him the names of things as they passed them on the street: *sloken, lakia, esp*; and their qualities: *flisty, kappitty, swee*; and what they did or might do: *flisty lakia oolin*. What she first uttered, he solemnly said after her, two or three times, until she nodded her head. Ben never stammered in this childish speech.

At the school, dropping her off and sometimes also fetching her, he soon had a recognised status, and it was to him one morning that Tanya's teacher said that, having settled in and now having acquired an English stepfather, really she must begin trying to speak English, as all the other foreign children did, or she would fall behind in her development, be more and more excluded, and suffer. Ben saw the truth of this and promised to see to it; but he felt sorrowful also, thinking of the loss he and the child must undergo.

The year was moving, the air softened, they had more daylight. It worsened his trouble. Every morning he woke to a sort of whispering, of conscience or temptation: Soon, very soon now. And what will you do? Things will decide. Will you let them? Will you merely suffer them? Will you not act? Birdsong at first light fell like dewfall or a light rain that will insist without mercy that germination in the soil and in the soul begin again. He said yes; but in fear, without much hope. It was a helpless opening, and for what?

One early Sunday morning, as he tried to fortify himself by reading and learning against the visit to the home where the tropical fish had been replenished and had begun to die again – that morning, in a silver-grey light, he looked down from his hermit's room and saw Marina in the garden facing away. She was still wearing her long winter coat and her hands, he could tell, were thrust deep into its pockets. As always when she was suddenly there and he had not been able to prepare himself, she threw him into a stranger's perception of the place, and he felt ashamed, humiliated. The garden, he saw, was merely held in, not entirely neglected, but held down to be least trouble, held off. Marina walked as far as the rockery, the rest could be seen from there: the shed, the wrecked swing, the remnants of an orchard that four gardens shared. He saw that a child might be entranced by that far end where the gardens came together and at nights there were owls and foxes. Saw, felt keenly – and resisted. Marina stood still, her back to him. Then turned, hands in pockets, came slowly down the length of the draggled and dewy lawn and about half way halted, looked up, and again saw herself observed. Through the glass, up and down the diagonal of sight, neither smiled, only looked for longer than a decent while until she ended it with that deliberate upward nodding of the head, the appraising and somehow decisive movement with which she had terminated his looking at her naked on the beach. He felt himself appraised, now in the context of his house and garden, and inscrutably decided upon.

Later, when she and Tanya had gone to the park, he went to her room, stood in the doorway, and looked. Strictly, he had not done that before, and now he knew why. Her tenancy had scarcely marked the place. It was still the room of his mother and father, the room of their enduring unhappiness, the room he had slept in when they vacated it. A very few of Marina's things lay on the dressing-table – he noticed the green earrings – there was a book by the bed and her dressing-gown hung on the door he had pushed open, but everything else she had tidied away into the ugly drawers and the even uglier large wardrobe he had cleared for her. So little evidence. He felt she might vanish in a moment, like a snowflake on a window, there beautifully for a moment, visibly beautiful, then gone. She would never repeat the walk into the garden. She had looked the place over and decided. Her footsteps had long since gone from the grass.

Then came a letter from the Home Office, inviting them to an interview in a room in Petty France. Ben passed it to Marina, she read it, asked him with her eyes, What for? They want to see are we real, he said. Slowly she uplifted her head in the gesture whose sense he was never sure he had understood.

They made arrangements for Tanya, and at work. Ben's supervisor asked him straight was it 'the interview'? Don't worry, she said. You look the part all right.

On the journey Ben and Marina scarcely spoke. They sat side by side at an empty table, not face to face. As they ran into London Marina took his hand in her lap.

First they were seen together. The woman looked from their papers to their faces, courteously enough. We have to do this, she said. You understand. Then she asked Ben would he mind waiting outside while she and Mrs Benson – the name

217

shook him – had a little talk. He stood at a window at the far end of the corridor, looking down on the traffic. Against the glass, touching it with his moving lips, he enunciated very clearly: My speech will fail me. Said it three times. How long did he stand there? He could not have said. He thought of the island, the heat, the cool water, her coldly appraising eyes. Then of the wedding, their public kiss. He woke when the woman touched his sleeve. Marina was nowhere to be seen. Mrs Benson is in reception, the woman said. It seemed to Ben he had never heard anything stranger than that name and the phrase 'in reception'.

Back in the room, Ben's speech did indeed desert him. Invited to say how he and Mrs Benson had met, he blushed and the translation of his head, especially the mouth, into something not human, occurred at once. He tried all his languages, he adopted the persona of a very old man, in vain. The woman sat calmly watching Chaos and Babel. Then Ben abandoned his mouth. He shrugged, showed the woman his empty palms, reached across the desk for her paper and pen and in best copperplate, fluently, wrote: Marina came into my life like the hounds and arrows of Artemis, first when I saw her naked on a Greek island, then, after a period of darkness, when I had to interview her – I work for the DSS – about a claim for housing benefit. The second occasion was as much an epiphany as the first, though she was, needless to say, fully clothed. I married her because I love her and do not want to live apart from her. If she is not allowed to stay in the United Kingdom I will go wherever she has to go. But it would be better for her child, whom I love and will always care for as my own, if Marina and I could live here as what we are, man and wife, without any more upheaval for a while at least. So that is how it is.

Ben handed the paper to the woman. She read it. I see, she said. Thank you, Mr Benson. You and Mrs Benson will hear from us or the Passport Office shortly. Again Ben showed her the empty palms of his hands.

Marina was not in reception but on the cold street outside. She took Ben's arm. Walking quickly to the station he became convinced that he had lost his case. They will think I am a fool, he muttered, and that she has abused me. On the train, sitting side by side, watching London fall away, Marina asked him how he had got on. I couldn't speak, he said. I had to write it down. They will think me very foolish. His voice came easily, the stammer had left him. And you? How did you get on? I told her the truth, said Marina simply. Then she blushed. Only once before had Ben seen Marina blush. Her pale clear skin suffusing, she looked away. He felt it around his heart like a spreading out of cold.

Ben had told Marina what they had said at the school about Tanya's speech; they had discussed it, almost like parents; and he agreed he would induct the child into English for a necessary second language, Russian continuing between her and Marina, and the babytalk, the subtle swift running of her private tongue, would little by little be induced to lapse away. He had agreed and he had promised, but his heart wasn't in it. Tanya scowled and refused. She wanted her own talk for ever and the Englishman bowing down to her conversing, the two of them, for ever. Marina frowned.

He knocked, he heard her say, Come in, he opened the door. She was on the far side of the bed, leaning over Tanya in the bed asleep. He saw her breasts in the opening of her green silk dressing-gown. I'm sorry, he said, staring and his speech faltering. I have to go to work. Marina stood up. Tanya didn't sleep, she said. She will stay home today. Then they were facing each other across the bed over the sleeping child with nothing else to say. The dressing-gown wrapped around and was to be held to with a silk belt but that had come loose. As Marina stood upright the silk softly of its own accord parted and a line of her nakedness appeared from throat to between her feet. But she held his gaze by hers into hers. Ben, she said,

my poor Ben. Look now. Loosing the belt completely, she slid
the gown off her shoulders, it slipped to the floor like a
sudden chute of water. Now do you like me or not? He
nodded, his mouth was dry. See here, she said – the inside of
her left thigh – is a birthmark which I very much dislike. And
here – above the right knee – is a scar I got from sledging
when I was a child. Then she turned to the dressing table, so
that he saw her and her reflection bending; took out her
underclothes from one of the heavy brass-handled drawers;
crossed back to the bed and laid them out there ready. Next
she opened the righthand door of the wardrobe and behind
it stood choosing a dress for the day. That done, she stood
before him again and he watched her slowly put on her
clothes. Her eyes were on him watching. And as she clothed
herself, she seemed to be leaving him; or at least to be
showing him step by step that she would whenever she
pleased. She buttoned her dress up to the throat, sat on the
chair and laced up her shoes. Then faced him again. There
now, she said. He backed away in his formal office clothes,
shutting the door.

They were sitting at the kitchen table face to face, he and
Tanya, conversing. He was master of her tongue by now, she
commended him and inspired him to ever more variety,
depth and fluency. He let himself go, he put his promise to
the back of his mind and gave himself up to the delight of
speaking irresponsibly. It was joyous, so unlike work where he
must attend to complexities of need and resentment and
answer only as the regulations allowed. Easier also than
conversations with Marina, for then too often his speech was
flung from side to side, into other voices, to keep going and
say what he felt and meant and too much desire, fear and
unuttered love clogging it and bringing it to a halt. With the
child he hit no impediments, he could run on and on, as she
did, with a dreamer's miraculous facility. Tanya chortled at his
sounds and his fitting of them into intricate and ebullient

sentences, he could see how well he was doing in her wide eyes and when she clapped her hand to her mouth in excitement, as though it were perilous. Then he would pause, or she would not wait for a pause but would interrupt and seize the tongue from him, outdo him in it easily and present him with more that in his turn he could run through a dozen variations.

Then from sideways on – they were face to face, absorbed in each other's eyes and rapid lips – came Marina's voice, harshly. How long had she stood there in the open door? Long enough to listen in on them and witness. To Tanya she said, in Russian: Mummy doesn't want you to talk in that language any more. You must talk in proper languages. Do you understand? The child set her face hard and shook her head. Marina shrugged. You will have to, she said. Then she addressed Ben, in English. Grow up, Ben, she said. Even if you will not help yourself, you are a gentleman and you will help this little girl. Please only speak to her in English from now on, until she is very good at it and can manage at school. Or in Russian sometimes, if you will, to help her over difficulties. But not in her babytalk any more. Marina's face was as set as she could make it, but he saw what the effort cost her, and though he did not understand her pallor, the tears in her slate-blue eyes, the twisting of her white hands, he bowed to all those signs, stood up and nodded, feeling the child's shock and anger, like a slap, at his betrayal, on his averted cheek.

Quite late that evening – he was getting some Russian verses by heart, laboriously interrupting a recitation and saying the lines back, again and again, improving – he felt her presence behind him. Perhaps he felt a chill through the open door, an apprehension of more or a different coldness than that of his unheated room, and he turned and saw her standing behind him barefooted in her winter coat below which showed the hem of her dressing gown. I came to say goodnight, she said, gently backing the door to. Ben stood up to offer her the one chair, but she went and sat on the bed and in a huddled way, her hands between her knees, sat looking at him, rather at a loss, he felt, unsure of herself, anxious. I distressed you, he said in Russian. Please forgive me. I am very sorry. But she shook her head quite definitely. No, no, she said, nothing to forgive, nothing to be sorry for. Even in her winter coat she was shivering a little. My room, he said, I'm sorry. I've got used to it but it must be cold for you. Not so very cold, I don't think, she replied. But *I* am cold. I'll make some tea, he said decisively. We'll have tea. Let me make us some tea. She looked up at him in surprise and uncertainty. I only came to say goodnight, she said. Sit there, he answered. I'll be quick.

When he returned with the two mugs of tea he felt sure that in the meantime she had not moved at all. Still her hands were thrust between her knees, under the coat her shoulders trembled slightly, she looked unsure, almost fearful. This will warm you up, he said. She took the mug in both hands, bowed her head into the steam, and sipped. When I came home from visiting my mother, that Sunday evening a long time ago, he said, you saw that I was troubled and you asked me to tell you why. And you helped me. Can I not help you now? It is harder for me to speak, she answered. You stammer sometimes and I don't stammer. Still it is harder. I am very cold when I even think about it. She was murmuring into the mug of tea, into the steam, which gave her an odd appearance, as though she were in a place apart, in horror and fear, and the past was forcing itself through her, forcing her to speak it – which was not at all what Ben had wished for. He had wanted to hand her some warmth and homeliness. But she raised her eyes to him, her hands at least holding the warmth, so that there, if nowhere else, there was a little heart of warmth and courage that she could sip at while she spoke.

I went with her through the forests and the mountains, almost to the border, with her and her lover and their baby

Tanya.

What was her name?

Lydia was her name. His name was Grisha. He came from over there, he went to and fro although it was so dangerous, and Lydia said she would go back with him, for one trip, for a little while, because he wanted her to and she could help. And I would look after Tanya until she came back. She gave me her passport with Tanya on it. She and Grisha had their own, which were forged. And because we were twins, it seemed not very risky for me, and indeed it never was. Or at least I haven't been caught out yet. But for her and Grisha it seemed terribly risky, and indeed it was, and both were caught before long. As soon as they had left me I went south again with Tanya, all the way back to the sea, and there I waited, continuing my studies in forestry the best I could. I waited and waited. It was almost a year before I heard.

How did you hear?

A man came to my door late at night. I opened only a little, on the chain. He said he could tell me what had happened to Grisha and my sister, Lydia. I did not recognise his accent, but still he was plausible, so I let him in. At first he seemed very considerate. He said it was bad news that he brought and I would have to be brave, to bear it. Then he told me, as kindly as any person could tell such a thing, that they had been shot, both of them, quite soon after crossing the border.

Could he be sure? Did you have to believe him?

Marina's hands began to shake so much that she could not hold the mug of tea. Ben took it from her, brought close his chair, took her hands in his.

When he had told me that one fact and he could see that I was the right person because he saw how it undid me and put me at his mercy, then he began to go into such details and to describe my sister's ways so exactly that I knew it was true and that he must have seen her and have been a witness. And his accent which I had not been able to place, I placed then with certainty over there.

And why had he come? To warn you?

Perhaps to warn me off. Perhaps just to terrorise me. He said what had happened to my sister should be a lesson to me and to any like me who thought to interfere. Then he told me in detail what they had done to her – what they had made Grisha watch them doing to her – before they shot them both and left them lying. I see it as though I saw with my own eyes. And I see him too, the face of the very devil, his fluent never-faltering lips, his smiling eyes. Then he left. He wished me goodnight. And he added, over his shoulder, that they knew about the child.

Marina was shaking so badly now, with the said and the unsaid, truly like a priestess who can only speak through the riddling cold, that Ben was at a loss how to comfort and warm her. He sat by her on the bed, held her shoulders within his left arm, fetched the tea to her lips with his right hand as he had to his mother's lips more than once on days when she took him to be the son he was. But still Marina shook with cold. Oh dear, she said, through chattering teeth, I only came to say goodnight. But please, Ben, now will you let me stay? Of course, he replied, if it will warm you. Of course you must stay. She stood up, faced away from him, and he lifted the winter coat off her shoulders and drew it down off her arms. Then he turned back the covers of his narrow bed for her to get in still wearing her dressing gown. He put her coat round his own shoulders, switched off the desk light, sat on the floor by the bed, took her hand. Hush now, he said. Go to sleep. Soon she stopped shivering. He listened. Her breathing quietened into sleeping. He listened and listened.

After a while, still sleeping, Marina began to speak. She spoke in the tongue she had forbidden Tanya and Ben. Then some of the fear and horror he suffered listening came from the realization that she was straining that language into saying things it did not have the words for, that it was never meant for, that abused and tormented it, telling. Poor childish tongue, suffering desecration. But there was no other way, he conceded that. Foul and unforgiveable and a horror for ever, taboo and *nefas*, what she had to say and could only say asleep in the sleepy language with a man who loved her listening and letting her fasten her hand on his, as he listened and understood through her sleep darkly, enough, more than enough. So in its quiet way, inexhaustible as the waters of the maltreated earth, Marina's langue howled and cursed, it tore its hair, dug up its cheeks with bloody nails, she shrieked and sobbed and lost her breath in horror, slowed and stumbled and went on like unstoppable bleeding, all in a tongue not old enough to say it, forced into inventiveness, forced to devise the means out of its own small body to begin to utter what the adult world is like, what people do to other people, knowingly, deliberately, what they dream up and do and can bear to watch and turn away and resume their daily lives and eat and drink and converse with friends and make love and go on living, having done it. Listening, he knew there was more and worse, beyond the limit of her telling, it was worse and worse, her farthest reach of language could only point to the more and worse beyond its power to say. She babbled as the priestess did at Delphi, wracked and raddled by the speaking water's cold, conducting them, the things that can't be buried under however many mounds and mountains but here or there will always surface, as the waters surface that the woman drinks and that turn her blood sub-zero and on and on she utters it through chattering teeth. Ben hushed and soothed and answered the best he could. For often it was a question, it was a desperate questioning, and though he was only at Tanya's level in the tongue, he understood enough, more than enough, and strove there and then in the very act to improve his language for the grown woman's sake, to answer back, say no to her, agree yes it had been, say no it would not always be so, concede where he must, but with might and main answer back, contradict her with body and soul, to rescue her, say her no, no, no, as in her sleepy tongue deep below the surface, far far below any healthful sleeping she spoke and railed against and grieved over what the devil had told her they did to her twin sister. He knelt close, pushed the hair off her face, held her cheek in the poor protection of his palm, kissed her brows, kissed her shut eyes behind which as clear as noon she saw those things and had deduced from them that it must be so and always only so and begged him, if he could, to tell her otherwise. And in the end she slept, the devil tired of riding her, she surfaced a little into humane waters, slept there quietly, and Ben with her winter coat around his shoulders dozed against his narrow bed till first light and the birdsong, the merciful, the soft small rain of singing which she woke to hear, he heard her breathing modulate into the waking, he knew she was lying still in his hospitality, listening with him to the early summer singing.

When the singing subsided and an ordinary daylight was established in the outside world she asked him matter-of-factly had she talked very much. Yes, you did, he answered. And you listened? Yes, I did. And you understood? You answered when I asked? The best I could, he said. She was silent for a while. Then she said, in quite a different voice, I slept with you. Oh, Ben I slept with you.

5

Events hastened. Around midsummer, in the middle of the night, they phoned from the nursing home to tell Ben that his mother was dying. They added that she was raving. He must hurry. He did – upstairs and down again – thinking to leave a message for Marina, when she appeared on the landing as he passed her door. She wished him courage; hesitated; then kissed him quickly, very quickly, on the lips.

Ben's mother was in her own room, still among a few belongings of her married life. The doctor had called and would call again, when summoned, to issue the certificate. Ben – regarded curiously by the night staff – went to sit by her; but as he approached, bowing, smiling gently, saying who he was, she thrust out a hand like a talon, to ward him off. The two rings that had bound her to his father slid down the finger shaft. Her eyes stared out blackly through rings of manifest bone; the mouth, toothless, drivelling a black saliva, worked like a stammerer's on imprecations. By all the means of tenderness he owned, by soothing, hushing, stroking, childish pleading, Ben tried to force himself upon her consciousness as himself, and failed. Wherever the mother had withdrawn to, in whatever oubliette of hell she was dwelling in, there she mistook him, and stared out through her sockets in fear and hatred. So all his caresses were a violence to her and all his lovetalk lies. When she could speak, she uttered words whose tone in all the slurring and the muddle, was a malediction. He withdrew his chair to the foot of her bed, sat there, covered his face and wept. And by this spectacle, in a grisly spasm, she was lent a final energy: she sat up, pointing at him derisively, he heard in amazement the distinctive squealing and gasping of a demonic pleasure, of triumph and glee over his defeat. Then she fell back and began her rattle. A sister came in, shook her head over the pair of them and left. Ben stayed. When his mother was certainly unconscious he sat by her again, but now he felt held off from attending

227

to her by the terrible prohibition she had exerted against him till she lapsed. Would it not be a violation of her helplessness? He debated and havered, but decided in the end that he must act in truth and not bring his life into line with her mistake. So he wiped her mouth and her forehead and stroked her married hand until she was dead. Then he closed her eyes and keeping himself to himself, declining all sympathy, he asked the staff to inform the doctor and the undertaker and said he would be back later to clear her room.

Marina was home. Did you stay home for me? he asked. Of course I did, she replied. She mistook you still? Yes, said Ben. And he told her how he had anguished over what to do at the end. Oh, said Marina, I'm so glad you did as you did. That was the truth whether she knew it or not. And who knows what she knew so deep down where she had gone and deeper where she was going?

They went to collect Tanya together. The school seemed a horn of plenty, children of many nations pouring forth. Tanya, hand in hand between Ben and Marina, babbled gaily in three languages. Later Ben took a taxi to the nursing home and collected his mother's belongings which had already been removed from her room and were awaiting him in three black plastic bags.

Next morning he arranged the cremation and wrote to inform his brother. But, as he expected, he had nobody with him on the day except Marina. The ceremony was brief and entirely nominal, but had a certain decency, which was all he wanted. He asked that his mother's ashes be scattered in the general rose garden where his father's were. No, he did not want a stone tablet in the surrounding wall.

Next he must sell the house, to pay the local authority what his mother owed them for the nursing home. Do so, said Marina, do so quickly. Shall I not wait until you have your passports? She shook her head. Have you begun to think of your own future? She nodded. Roughly he worked out his liabilities, and instructed an estate agent to put the house on the market at a price that would be sufficient and sell it quickly.

He was clenching his heart against the world. He thought more and more about Skleros, about himself on the stony island before he ever saw Marina. He thought of dry shards slithering down the terraces into the sea, blades of obsidian, thorns and dead flowers, the marble paths, the abandoned marble threshing floors. Marina was the spring of living water, the shapely well, the slaking and solace in all that, but he fought against the thought of her, in a sort of pre-emptive hopelessness but also in bitterness hardening his heart. He wished to harden the idea of himself, he would possess himself in simplicity and be as he was in the bare room in the mountain village or lying on the roof there under the rush of beautiful and uninterested stars. He would quit his job, he was sick of people and their complex miseries. His stammer was bad again. He wished to be somewhere where he need not speak, or remotely abroad where nobody knew him and he might speak or not speak just as he pleased in their difficult tongue. He saw that Marina was watching him, he saw that her look was both curious and fearful. That she should be fearful in her waking life moved him and frightened him in almost equal measure. Sometimes she stood with the child, an arm around her, and both were watching him with the same expression, more fearful than curious. When Tanya came up to say goodnight – still in the old tongue, a lovely archaic survival, tacitly agreed between them – she hesitated in his room, once or twice went and sat on the bed, and watched him.

But what could he do? He had his father's braying and violence in his head and his mother's ecstatic derision. He must deal with agents and his malevolent brother. He must harden himself, be like marble. So he thought he would abide by the letter of his agreement with Marina, keep his side of the bargain strictly, as part of his trial with the world.

Very soon he got an offer for the house and accepted it.

The buyer had ready money. The whole thing could be done by September. Events were hurrying. He wrote to ask his brother was there anything in the house he wanted. Back came the one word: no.

Then on 1 September, a Saturday, by special delivery, Ben signing for it, Tanya's and Marina's passports arrived, British, E.U. Ben laid them on the kitchen table and went to his room. He had two weeks. He would ask Marina if she wanted any items in his mother's house; ask a charity could they use the cooker, any furniture, the beds; carry the smaller things to Oxfam; get a house-clearance man to finish. It could all be done very quickly. He would hire a van for his own few possessions and Marina's, to transport wherever. He worked out the money – what his mother owed for her nursing home, what he still owed the building society, his brother's share of what was left – and calculated that the little remaining, if he did not quit his job, might get him a mortage on a very small flat.

Marina and Tanya came into the garden. Tanya was wearing the little rucksack she put her few things in for the school. But on Saturdays there was no school. The oddity shocked him. That is how she will look when she leaves, he thought. But Marina settled her at the garden table he had fetched from the shed, adjusted the sunshade over her, helped her begin a picture on white paper with coloured crayons. Ben stood watching. Somewhere else, he thought. They will be somewhere else. He saw before him barrenness, a life without touch, shards and sterility, hardness, harshness and the only flowers the asphodels, the ghost flowers, the troops of the dead. It pulled him and excited him, but it was the pull of giving in, of turning the way of least struggle, of drifting and accelerating into death. He saw his mother's sunken and triumphant eyes, the blood on his father's mouth, the fist in its crown of thorns. And of Marina he saw not her beauty, not her softness nor her grief and need, but only her cool appraisal of him and the upward nodding of her head by which he felt dismissed. So it was without hope, it was in a setting of his heart against love and hope, that he saw her leave Tanya on the unkempt lawn and stride, head down, back into the house, heard her climb the stairs, push open the door and felt her there behind him.

When he turned he saw that she was looking at the crude arithmetic on the desk. Will you be poor? she asked. He shrugged. Not destitute. I wanted us to be poor. Us? You and me and Tanya, us. I wanted us to start out poor, start again. I was going to say, Ben began, but he hit a bad stammer and she sealed his mouth with her hand. You were going to say, she said, that now we have our passports and nobody will deport us we are free to do as we like and after the proper interval, whatever that is, I will divorce you and go my own way, wherever I like, as free as a bird, with my sister's child. Yes, that is exactly what I was going to say, said Ben in Russian. Well now you needn't, Marina said in English. I have said it for you.

She stood by him at the window, leaning her forehead against the cool glass. Softer, so that he had to stand close to hear it, her voice continued, saying,

I was thinking I must come and say to you that now your mother is dead and you have sold the house and thanks to you we have our passports and are free to leave, you do perhaps want rid of us so that you can start again with nobody, in another town or even another country, just as you please, free as a bird, and that of course I should understand that, though Tanya wouldn't, and we'll make our own way, she and I, it wouldn't much matter where. But I shan't say that, I won't, it makes no sense, I'll say the truth instead, which is this, that I want you to marry me properly, Ben, in a simple place that would have a little room for Tanya on her own and a bigger room with a nice bed in it for you and me. First it could be a holiday place, for a few days perhaps, where we can lie awake if we want to and listen to the sea. Passionately

I want to do with you the things I know you want to do with me. Marry me properly, as I will you, so that the word fills up with what it means in truth.

Still she looked away, pressing her forehead against the glass. Her voice was quietening into the sleepy tongue, becoming a murmur, water at a distance, so that he had to attend very closely, if he would hear. On and on it ran, saying,

I am cold still, there is ice in my heart still for what they did to my twin sister and when you sleep with me I'm afraid I shall talk in my sleep and you will have to listen, it will be terrible for you, night after night for however many nights it takes for my ice to melt, you must listen and warm me the best you can. But when we have married one another properly and I have held you and felt you inside me perhaps it won't be long then, not very many nights, and we shall sleep and if you wake you will hear me smiling in my sleep, you will hear me babbling the way Tanya did and still can, if we let her, because she knows nothing yet that is too hard to bear.

Good, said Ben, as though he was waking up. Soon as you like. What is she drawing down there so very seriously? Islands, said Marina. Lately she draws nothing but islands. Always more than one, often three or four, and a ship with flags going between them.

# About the Author

**David Constantine** is an award-winning poet and translator. His collections of poetry include *Madder, Watching for Dolphins, Caspar Hauser, The Pelt of Wasps, Something for the Ghosts* (shortlisted for the Whitbread Poetry Prize), *Collected Poems* and most recently *Nine Fathom Deep* (all Bloodaxe). He is a translator of Hölderlin, Brecht, Goethe, Kleist, Michaux and Jaccottet. In 2003 his translation of Hans Magnus Enzensberger's *Lighter than Air* (Bloodaxe) won the Corneliu M Popescu Prize for European Poetry Translation. He is also author of one novel, *Davies* (Bloodaxe) and *Fields of Fire: A Life of Sir William Hamilton* (Weidenfeld). This is his third collection of short stories, following *Back at the Spike* (Ryburn), and the highly acclaimed *Under the Dam* (Comma). He lives in Oxford, where he edits *Modern Poetry in Translation* with his wife Helen.

# Under the Dam

## David Constantine

ISBN 0954828011
RRP: £7.95

In the middle of a speech a businessman realises his soul has just left his body.

In an Athens marketplace, a jealous lover finds himself staggering through a vision of hell.

High in the Alps, a young woman's body re-appears in the glacier, perfectly preserved, where she fell 50 years before.

Entering Constantine's stories is like stepping out into a wind of words, a swarm of language. His prose is as fluid as the water that surges and swells through all his landscapes. Yet, against this fluidity, his stories are able to stop time, to freeze-frame each protagonist's life just at the moment when the past breaks the surface, or when the present - like the dam of the title - collapses under its own weight.

*'Flawless but unsettling'*
- Boyd Tonkin, Christmas Books of the Year, The Independent

*'I started reading these stories quietly, and then became obsessed, read them all fast, and started reading them again and again.... The description of the estuary is one of the best descriptions of the surface of the Earth I have ever read.'*
- AS Byatt, Book of the Year, The Guardian